The Innocent Witch

BELINDA CARLI

Belinda Carli is an Industry leading Cosmetic Chemist and Founder of the Institute of Personal Care Science. She started her career as a Degree trained Naturopath specialising in herbal medicine in a clinic setting. She then moved into a Research & Development role, formulating a wide range of cosmetic products and herbal supplements for a multitude of national and international companies.

She has presented hundreds of videos on YouTube, where subscribers can watch a variety of topics covering formulation, regulatory affairs and brand management specific to the cosmetics and personal care industry. She was the Official Technical Advisor to the in-cosmetics Group for 5 years and judge on International Beauty Awards Panels. She has written six non-fiction books on Beginners and Advanced Cosmetic Formulation, Organic and Colour Cosmetic Formulation, and Cosmetic Brand Management available through personalcarescience.com. She has also written dozens of articles for various industry magazines and is a decorated speaker at Cosmetic Conferences and events globally.

She is a member of the Australian Society of Cosmetic Chemists (ASCC) and International Federation of Societies of Cosmetic Chemists (IFSCC). She was the winner of the Annual Industry Award from CHC Australia for her contribution to Research and Training, and was a finalist in the Australian Telstra Business Women's Awards in 3 categories.

Belinda lives on the Sunshine Coast in Australia with her husband, three children, two stepdaughters and pet dog.

First published in 2022

Copyright © Belinda Carli 2022

Cover design by Hanna Moon.

ISBN: 978-0-6454573-0-8

belindacarli.com

https://www.youtube.com/c/TheInstituteofPersonalCareScience

@belindacarli.author

@belindacarli.author

For my husband, Richard

Prologue

You are not only responsible for what you say,
but also for what you do not say. - Martin Luther

Tauber Bridge, Germany
May, 1588

It was an unseasonably cold grey day for spring. Masses of dark clouds were being swept along by a surprisingly chilly wind that whipped at the heels of the locals. It was almost as if the weather disapproved of the events about to occur, making it even more sombre.

The pastors smirk grew, and his black robes fluttered hauntingly, as he watched the accused wheeled in on the crude wooden cart. Her hair hung messy and matted, her face barely recognisable beneath. Her hands were secured by rough knots to a high bar at the front, holding her upright, as the cart rocked over the uneven path. It drew to a halt next to the mayor, dressed resplendently in his finest velvet cloak and stiff ruffled collar. He screwed up his nose and snarled as he cast his face away, obviously revolted.

"The sooner we can rid the town of these wretched witches the better," the pastor whispered to the mayor.

"Not to worry, a guilty verdict will be ours soon," the mayor muttered back.

Behind them stood Ernest Baumann, his lips pressed firmly together, his eyes colder than the day. He heard the conversation between the officials; egotistical, foolish old men. He glared at their backs, his hatred brewing.

The guards removed the frail woman from the cart, half-leading, half-dragging her to stand her final trial. The townsfolk wrapped their capes tightly around their chests, waiting silently to see what would happen. The occasional gust of wind was the only other stir of movement.

Ernest kept his eyes on his daughter as she was led to the edge of the bridge. She was poorly dressed in her linen undergarments with a thick braided rope secured firmly around her waist. A guard standing behind her held the loose end, but it was not to stop her from escaping, anyone could see she was far too weak for that. It would instead be used for retrieval, should she fail to resurface from the dunking. She was gaunt, bloodied and bruised, a shadow of the daughter he knew and loved. His heart ached at the thought of the torture and starvation she would have been made to endure over the past week. As she was led along, he could see her face was covered in dirt and muck from her squalid living conditions, spare two clean streaks where tears had run. Her fingernails were jagged, her thumbs black and broken. Dried blood and dirt stained her feet. He clenched his fists, hiding them beneath his folded arms. His paternal urge was to run to her, save her, yell out for them to stop; but he knew he could not. He had to use every ounce of his will not to move or speak.

She swayed unsteadily at the edge of the bridge, emotionless, while the guards tied her hands together and then reached down to bind her ankles. Ernest had been at the court a few days earlier, where she had refused to confess despite the interrogations, accusations, and apparent torture. The council residing over her case were unable to agree on a verdict, so the penalty of dunking was chosen to make the decision for them.

"Leyna Baumann, you have been accused of crimes of magic and making a pact with the devil. It has been claimed He has given you special powers to heal or harm under his direction, using treatments not recognised

8

by the council." The elderly mayor addressed the crowd authoritatively, ignoring the fragile woman as he spoke. "You have been labelled as a sorcerer and seducer, enticing lewd acts of misconduct, causing the rain to cry for your soul and flood our land." The townsfolk murmured quietly to each other. He nodded as if pleased with their reaction. "You have proclaimed your innocence yet hold the mark of the devil on your flesh; and offer no other explanation for the devastation to our crops and cattle. For this, we must put you in the water you have been charged with summoning, and see what truth be told."

Ernest's lips trembled as he battled to stifle his emotions. His granddaughter Ella, barely two years old, sat at his feet using a stick to clear dirt from between the cobblestones, showing no sign of understanding what was happening. The wreck of a woman who had just been led past was such a ghost of her former self, even her own daughter failed to recognise her. Leyna had acted recklessly, Ernest knew this, but he also knew she was no witch. To speak up would have meant a death sentence for him too, leaving young Ella an orphan without even a grandparent to care for her. So he waited, resolutely still, for the water to prove her innocent; even though by doing so, he knew it would be too late.

The mayor tipped his hat at the guards standing either side of Leyna. They placed their hands on her back and pushed her from the bridge. A gasp rose from the crowd as they watched her fall silently, like a sack of flour, into the swirling river below, then flocked to the edge to see what would happen next. Ernest heard the ripple of mumblings spread through the crowd: would the water prove her innocent, or would the devil give her power to float? Rain misted down then became droplets, dampening the mood and the townspeople who waited.

The rope jerked in the guards' hand, indicating a brief struggle occurring below. The flood that had impacted the town's farming, vital to their survival, meant the water flowed uncommonly fast and deep beneath the bridge.

Within moments the rope fell slack, but the surface of the water did not break. The rain continued to fall, getting heavier, as if to let the gathering of people know it was not Leyna causing the weather after all, but some darker evil that remained lurking.

Ernest had not moved to watch. He was rooted to his spot, his eyes closed in silent prayer for this insanity to end, hoping it would be swift for his daughter. Several seconds passed before he turned his attention to the child at his feet; she was the only thing enabling him to get through this horrible ordeal. Ella huddled closer as it got colder, then reached out to be picked up. He lifted her and held her close, feeling the warmth of her precious living body against his. She was breathing deeply as she cuddled into his shoulder, her arms wrapped tightly around his neck.

The townspeople stepped back from the bridge, one or two at a time, turning to the mayor for an explanation or verdict. He exchanged glances with the pastor. The surprise she did not float, which would have proven her guilt, was etched upon both their faces. This went against everything they had made claim to, everything they had tried so hard to accuse her of.

Eventually, the pastor addressed the crowd. "It has been long enough. We shall see if she still lives." He snapped his fingers at the guards. "Pull her up so that we may verify her innocence."

It did not take much effort for the burly men to haul the lifeless body out of the water. Her dress clung to her blue skin, her hair partly covered her empty eyes and purple lips. There were gasps from the crowd as many recoiled in horror. She died confirming that she was, in fact, not a witch after all.

The mayor remained obstinately still, not uttering a word.

The pastor eventually spoke. "Let the record show that Leyna Baumann has been proven innocent of the accused acts of witchcraft or cavorting with the devil." His performance was no doubt to appease the crowd. "By the grace of God, she will enter an eternity in heaven, and her memories may live warm in your hearts. She will be granted a proper burial in two days from now. Go home and pray for this woman's soul, but remain vigilant, for the devil still walks among us." He raised his right arm and made the symbol of the cross, marking the end of the trial. He bowed his head then flicked his hands, directing the mob to disperse.

The townsfolk left quietly as the weather worsened. A few glanced toward Ernest with sympathy but did not dare to offer their condolences. He held Ella in his arms, his hand holding her tightly to his shoulder to stop her from turning to see her mother, now pale, cold, gone from this world. That image would haunt him forever, there was no need to expose her to that sort of pain so young. The guards carried Leyna's lifeless body, respectfully now, to the cart that had brought her to the bridge. One of the guards adjusted her skirt to cover her legs. Previously, they had handled her with soulless aggression, but now their tender acts of kindness seemed like pitiful attempts to absolve their sins.

A line of blood trickled down the side of Leyna's face from an open gash, small and dark red, at her temple. *A rock below the surface.* His eyes filled with tears. *At least it would have been quick.* He raised his face to the heavens as he prayed on this, the cruellest of days he had so far endured, but remained silently enraged at the mayor and pastor for letting this madness get so out of hand. His eyes narrowed with contempt as the old men boarded

11

their comfortable carriages for the short trip back to town. They had wielded their power and position to exert control over the townspeople, but it had achieved nothing.

The rain fell harder, mixing indiscriminately with the tears on his face. "Come Ella, we have a lot of packing to do," he whispered in the little girl's ear as he hurried back to town, clutching her ever tighter in his arms. He could not wait for them both to be safely drying by a fire and leave the gossiping of the town behind.

She was all he had left.

Chapter 1

We are not yet what we shall be, but we are growing toward it,
the process is not yet finished, but it is going on,
this is not the end, but it is the road.
All does not yet gleam in glory, but all is being purified. - Martin Luther

Detwang, Germany
July, 1604

The baby struggled for air as the coughing once again took hold. Her mother hurried to remove her swaddling, hearing the dry rasps over the sound of the horse's clopping hooves. She watched in silent horror as her daughter's lips went from pink to blue, unaware she too was holding her breath as she waited for the baby to fill her lungs. She held the small chest to her ear to check her heart was still beating. At last, the baby managed to draw in enough air and some colour returned, followed by broken, hoarse cries. The mother coughed herself, wiping her tears on her sleeve.

The carriage ride was rough and shaky, and seemed to be taking an eternity given it was such a short distance from the town. It was dark outside, clouds covered the moon, disguising how much further they had to go. Her husband leaned forward, putting his hand on her knee. "We will be there soon."

His soothing words could not possibly mollify her at that moment. She nodded, biting her lip. Her maidservant had promised that this farm girl would be able to help, she hoped this trip would not be in vain. It was her baby's only chance.

The horses neighed as their reins were pulled firmly, bringing them rapidly to a halt outside a cottage. The mother rushed from the carriage holding her precious parcel tight while her husband rapped at the door. The coachman held a lantern for them to see in the darkness.

It was the middle of the night and the household had been sleeping. The baby cried, piercing the silence. The mother bounced her baby anxiously, praying she would not start coughing again while they waited. Every second seemed to last an eternity.

Eventually the door opened cautiously. "Hello?" The inhabitant peered into the night, bleary eyed. "Mayor Schulz?" Ernest's eyes widened as he recognised the man on his porch. "Frau Schulz, whatever brings you here?" His voice trailed off as his attention focused on the tiny baby gasping between wails in her mother's arms.

"Ernest, we need your help," the mayor pleaded above the noise. The mother was crying desperately. "Our baby is coughing so badly. She can hardly breathe."

"Yes, of course, come in, I will just fetch my granddaughter." He ushered them in and raced to wake Ella, who appeared moments later, wrapping a robe around her nightdress.

"Forgive me my dress, Frau Schulz." Ella curtsied and reached for the baby. "But this is no time for fancies."

The mother hesitated to pass her baby to the young farmgirl. "Give the baby to Ella." Her husband encouraged her, his hand on her elbow, urging her forward. "That is why we are here."

She handed the baby over uncertainly, a sob of fear caught in her throat.

Ella placed her hand gently on the baby's forehead and held her chest to her ear. The rasp in her breathing was audible, the fever was evident. "Frau, how long has she been like this?"

Barely speaking for weeping, the mother replied, "she has not been well for a few days, but the wheezing only started today. It has gotten so bad that she now turns blue when she coughs."

"Please, wait here, my opa will fix you a drink. Trust me with your baby as if she were my own." Ella dashed for the door where the coachman was standing with the lantern. "Come with me, I need you to light the way."

Ella rushed inside the packing shed, grateful it was the middle of summer, and the night was not cold. She knew the layout of this room by heart so that even in the dark, she was able to follow the familiar path to a long wooden bench on the far side of the room. "Please start the fire and boil some water," she instructed the coachman, pointing to the kettle and stove in the corner. He placed the lantern on the bench next to her and got busy with some kindling.

She lit candles on her bench to give more light. Thankfully, she knew what she was treating, as she had already helped several farming families with the same raspy cough that tried to rob them of their breath this season, especially the younger children. All but one had made it through. She placed the baby carefully in a basket near the bench and swiftly mixed tinctures of feverfew and willow bark together. She first needed to settle the baby by easing the swelling in her throat. She poured the herbal mixture into a narrow metal cylinder and carefully inserted a small plunger into the open end of the tube, tipping it slightly back on itself to hold the precious contents inside.

She retrieved the baby and nestled her firmly in her arm, then skilfully positioned the apparatus as far as she could toward the back of the baby's mouth and squirted the liquid in. When done right, the herbal mixture would travel directly to the baby's stomach, delivering its crucial remedy. When done wrong, the baby would only splutter or vomit and it would need to be attempted again. It was always hard with such little ones, but she'd had plenty of practice. The liquid stayed down while Ella cooed and rocked gently to calm her. Within minutes the baby was breathing slightly better and starting to settle.

She placed the infant back in the basket before crushing up some ginger root quickly with a mortar and pestle. She reached for a pot of thick balm stored below the bench, scooped some out and blended it together; this would warm the little one's blood and move the damp rattling that could be heard in her lungs. Ella loosened the baby's dress and applied the balm to her chest and back, rubbing firmly to liberate the mucous inside. After several minutes of massage, she picked the baby up, placed her over her left shoulder and struck her purposefully on the back three times. The baby spluttered and coughed up some of the thick, heavy mucous that was blocking her airways. Ella made a final mixture of sundew and thyme extracts, squirting this toward the back of her throat too. These herbs, she knew, would help stop the baby from wanting to cough, and dry the moisture from her lungs. She rubbed the balm on the baby's back and chest again, then brought her to her shoulder and liberated more mucus, before being satisfied enough had been moved. The baby was no longer hot and clammy, but her nose was still blocked. "Please, pour me some of that water," she called to the coachman, who promptly brought it to her in a bowl. She rested the baby forward, supporting her weight on her arm, and covered the baby's head and the bowl with a linen cloth. She leaned forward, holding the baby over the bowl to inhale the steam. After a few minutes, she again placed the infant over her shoulder and wiped at her nose until it ran clear.

Content the baby was through the worst, she wrapped her in the swaddling cloth. "Please douse the fire and take us back," she asked the coachman, who promptly did as he was instructed.

Ella cradled the baby on her arm with her chest facing downward to allow any remaining fluids to run out. She was now sleeping calmly, undoubtedly worn out, but much better than when she had first arrived close to an hour ago. The coachman grabbed the lantern and led them back toward the cottage.

🐞 🐞 🐞

As soon as Ella left with their little one, Ernest had set about trying to make the mayor and his wife comfortable.

"Please sit." He motioned to a short bench that ran along their common room wall. He flitted around swiftly, lighting some candles, then raced into the kitchen to get the stove burning, placing a kettle filled with water on top. He was only gone a moment, returning to his guests quickly, but frowned briefly when he noticed they had not moved. "Ella has treated several children in this village with the same cough just this winter gone." He strode over to the anxious couple and escorted them toward the seat. "Let me make you some tea, I'll be back in a moment."

As Ernest left the room a second time, he watched the mayor take his wife's hand. She was crying quietly, a handkerchief pressed firmly to her nose, her knuckles white. Her knees jittered. The mayor placed their folded hands onto her lap, and they stilled.

After several moments, Ernest came back into the living room with earthen mugs on a wooden cutting board. "It has been an unusually good season on the orchard this year." He smiled tightly, hoping to ease the tension in the room.

"Tell me, what does your granddaughter do, exactly?" asked the mayor, his brow furrowed. "To treat people, I mean."

Ernest tried to quiet his nagging fears as he considered how best to explain. He knew the town council was averse to the traditional use of herbs for healing, so why arrive in the middle of the night seeking treatment for their baby if that was the case? He passed them each a mug of steaming tea, which they cupped as tightly as if they had just been handed hope, then pulled a chair toward them as he observed the nervous couple. They were both quite young, compared to him. The mayor was somewhere in his mid-thirties, his face only just starting to show the lines that came with age and worry. His wife would have been in her early twenties, just a few years older than his granddaughter. "Ella uses herbal extracts, or balms. Sometimes teas." He took a sip from his cup. Neither of them had touched theirs yet. "Your tea, for example... I gave you both some chamomile, it helps you feel more relaxed. If I made it stronger, it would help you sleep. If you were having a lot of trouble sleeping, we could give you something stronger again, an extract, or tincture of the chamomile instead. They taste quite bitter, but the extracts are much more powerful than the teas alone, and work like medicine." He sipped again, motioning for them to do the same.

"What will Ella be doing with my baby?" The mother gazed up at him warily, her eyes rimmed red from crying, her voice unsteady.

"Frau Schulz..."

"Please, call me Katherine."

Ernest nodded. "Katherine, with this cough, I expect the first thing she would be doing is trying to soothe your baby. She would most likely start with some herbal extracts that will reduce the fever and take away some of the pain. When they are crying like that, it just makes it harder for them to breathe." He contemplated the treatment he would provide. "After that, she would probably be trying to warm her lungs, and clear some mucus." He bobbed his head once, confident in his explanation. "Please, try your tea, it will help calm you." Ernest could sense her apprehension. "I can only imagine what you must be feeling right now, trusting a young stranger with your baby at a time like this."

Her breath caught as she looked at him. She sat rigid and tense, holding his gaze for the briefest moment before dropping her face toward her hands holding the mug. Her tears won out.

He leant forward and tried to still the shaking in his voice as he reassured her, "my granddaughter will be doing her best."

They sat, for some time, not speaking. Katherine let out the occasional sob while her husband rubbed her back gently. Sipping their tea was the only distraction that marked the moments as they waited.

Eventually Ella came back into the cottage with the baby sleeping peacefully in her arms.

Katherine's relief was palpable as she jumped up to check on her daughter closely. "You did it." She caught Ella's eyes, wonderment glowing from within. She reached out to take her treasured bundle back eagerly. "You saved her." She leaned down to kiss her baby gently as a smile replaced her strain.

"Keep her body facing down, with your arm here." Ella positioned the baby in Katherines arms the way she had been holding her. "It is important to keep her nose and mouth forward, to let the fluid run out."

She nodded silently, at ease now her baby was breathing so peacefully. Ella stroked the little one's cheek as she slept. "What is her name?"

"Clare."

"A beautiful name for a beautiful baby. You must be very proud."

Clare's skin had already returned to a pale pink. "How did you know what to do?"

Ella guided her back to the bench considerately and sat next to her. The mayor rose hastily to give them space. "Frau Schulz…"

"You have just saved my daughter's life. Please, call me Katherine."

"Katherine." She smiled briefly. "Clare has, or had, the same cough I have experienced in our local village more than I would have liked this year." She wiped at the baby's mouth as some fluid ran out. "This cough tries to take the young, but she will make it. Please rest here tonight in case she struggles again. We have a spare room already made up, just across from mine."

Katherine glanced up to her husband who bobbed his head in consent.

"Thank you for saving our daughter," he addressed Ella, then strode over to Ernest, who stood quickly and shook his hand. "I cannot thank you and your granddaughter enough. I shall head back to town now, but I will send my coachman back with appropriate attire for my wife to wear tomorrow. Could you accommodate him too when he returns?"

"Of course." Ernest gazed around their living area; a flush of heat bloomed in his cheeks. Their modest cottage would have been no match for Mayor Schulz's luxurious manor. "We only have the hide on the floor and a spare blanket, but he is welcome to use them."

The mayor regarded the offering and tipped his head politely. "That is all we can ask under such short notice, thank you." He retraced his steps quickly, bending to kiss his baby on the forehead and his wife on the cheek.

"I trust all will be in order here with you," Mayor Schulz addressed Ernest as he made his way to the door. His coachman opened it. "Again, truly, my sincerest gratitude for what your granddaughter has done." He bowed his head and left into the darkness of the night.

"Come," said Ella to Katherine. "Let me show you to your room. The best thing we can all do now is get some rest."

The night had been uneventful, the whole house slept well into the morning. Ella dressed quickly and went to the packing shed to prepare some balm and herbs for her visitors to take with them. When she re-entered the cottage, she saw Katherine at the table cuddling her baby as the comforting smell of pancakes wafted through from the kitchen. It was not often her opa cooked pancakes, but it was not every night the mayor's wife stayed over either. He was obviously trying to accommodate her in a style she must be used to.

Katherine appeared in complete contrast to how she had the night before. Not only was she a lot more serene than when she had arrived, but today she was dressed far more appropriately for her position. Her gown was made of a finely woven pale blue linen, and she wore a large, stiff ruff around her neck. Her eyes were only half a shade darker than her dress, her blonde hair pulled back high and tucked neatly under a lace-edged coif. She had small, pleasant features, a face that belonged to a gentle heart. Clare's cheeks glowed a healthy pink as she slept contentedly, swaddled in a beautifully embroidered blanket. A carry basket was positioned next to the leg of the table.

Ella drew her chair up beside them. "How did she feed?"

Katherine beamed. "Very well, thank you. She is so much better." She crooned at the baby sleeping soundly in her arms.

Ernest walked in with plates of pancakes for everyone, including the coachman, who joined them at their small table. He placed a bowl of stewed apples in the centre with a spoon for serving, along with a saucer containing freshly cut strawberries. He dashed back to the kitchen, returning with a breadboard full of mugs, placing a cup of tea in front of each of them. "Peppermint, to wake us up," he suggested.

Ella couldn't help but notice a slight strain to his voice, a jittering in his movements. Perhaps he felt awkward about their humble offerings for such an important guest.

After breakfast, Ella placed a bottle of herbs in front of Katherine along with a small jar. "I noticed you coughed a bit yourself last night while sleeping. We need to treat your cough as well as baby Clare's," she explained. She motioned toward the brown bottle of liquid stoppered with a cork. "Here is some medicine that will make you both better. You will need to take this." Ella held the metal tube she had used last night out in front of her, so that Katherine knew what she was referring to. "Use this to measure out how much to take. These herbs are quite strong, so you need to make sure you both take the right amount, and you will need this cylinder to help get the mixture to the back of Clare's throat, otherwise she will just spit them back out again. I have marked here, for where you need to draw your herbs to." She pointed to a notch she had scratched into the side of the plunger, showing how far up to draw the liquid. "And this one here is for Clare." She indicated another mark higher up, so the plunger would be pulled out only a little way and the dose measured would be much smaller. "This is the same tincture I used with Clare last night. Make sure you each take it twice a day until it is all gone." Ella demonstrated how to draw liquid into the chamber of the metal device to the different notches, and then squirt it back out. "You will also need to rub this balm on Clare's chest and back, three times a day until the cough has totally cleared." She removed the cap from the jar of pungent salve for Katherine to smell it before re-capping and handing it over.

Katherine's nose crinkled as concern washed over her face.

"Do you think you will be able to give Clare the mixture?"

"Ah, I am sure one of my maidservants will be able to help." Katherine blushed. "They are probably much better at this sort of thing than me."

Ella reached for her mug of tea. "If it is not too bold a question, can I please ask why you came to me in the middle of the night? Do you not have a much more learned physician in town?"

Katherine pursed her lips. "Ah, yes, well, the physician in town, he…" She fiddled with Clare's blanket, as if taking her time to find the right words. "Let me just say, his methods are a bit extreme for a baby. I also think he is a little too fond of a drink to treat a baby at night, if you know what I mean."

Ella nodded. No one would want a drunkard treating their child, but Katherine's description of his methods was curious. Perhaps it meant stronger medicine, treatment she was clearly not comfortable with. "But how did you know to come here?"

"Ingrid, one of my maidservants, grew up around here. She was with me yesterday afternoon and then again last night when Clare took a turn for the worse. She told me you would know what to do. It is lucky my husband inherited this land, your apple orchard, so we knew exactly where to find you. I am sorry we had to call at such a late hour, but I am so glad we did."

Ella's heart warmed. "Ah, Ingrid. We used to play together. She works for you now?"

Katherine hummed. "Yes, and her husband too, in our kitchen."

"I am pleased to hear she has found her place in town then." Ella reached over to pat Katherine's hand. "I am happy to help. I'm so relieved you made it here in time." She held her arms out for the baby. "Here, let me give her a dose this morning, to see you on your way."

Katherine handed Clare over, readily now, watching on as Ella skilfully administered the medicine and rubbed the balm on her chest and back. Once finished, she swaddled Clare firmly and passed her back to her mother.

Katherine held her baby close, but her eyes lingered on Ella. "What you do, it is most foreign to me. I have never seen this type of healing before."

Ernest cleared his throat and piled their plates. It was most unlike him to be fussing like this, his hands appeared to be shaking.

"And yet it worked so well," Katherine continued, giving Ernest a sweet smile to acknowledge his efforts. She bounced Clare gently as she settled. "What does your village physician think of your approach?"

Ella's brow furrowed as she tipped her head to one side. "Ah, we don't have a physician in the village."

Katherine's head rocked back and her eyes widened. "Well, who…? I mean, do you…? Oh, but of course, that's why Ingrid told me to see you specifically. So, you help everyone the same way?"

Ella nodded, her lips curling into a smile. "I know I'm only young, but I have been treating others for many years now." She tilted her head toward the kitchen where a cluttering could be heard. "It was my opa before me."

Katherine's brows raised and her mouth puckered into an o. She bobbed her head politely, clearly trying to disguise her surprise, then bent forward to tuck her baby tenderly into the basket. She packed the remedies and cylinder carefully as well. "It is time we took our leave. Thank you again, so much, for everything you have done. I will not forget your kindness." The coachman came over to pick up the basket, carrying his charge protectively. She grasped Ella's hands in hers and gave them a gentle squeeze of thanks.

Ella and Ernest followed them outside. The mayor's carriage was quite distinctive, the mayor's wife and coachman even more so because of the way they were dressed. Most of the locals had barely more than open carts, so it was impossible to miss, even from some distance. Their orchard ran back a fair distance, but their cottage was close to the common road, and their street frontage disproportionately narrow, like many of the farms around them. As their guests loaded their possessions, Ella observed her closest neighbours standing on their porches to get a better view of what was going on. Her visitors would soon have the villagers talking.

The carriage had barely pulled away when Ernest grabbed Ella by the arm firmly, his forehead creased with lines as he led her back inside the house briskly. She span to face him, her brows furrowed, what had she done wrong?

The moment he had closed the cottage door, he let go of her, removed his cap and scratched his head. His face had drained of colour, whiter than his hair. "What were you thinking?" his voice quivered. "You used your herbs and balms on the mayor's baby." He started pacing, his breathing short and rapid.

"Well, what was I supposed to do? Leave the baby to die? That would have been dreadful." Her lips trembled. "You saw how they arrived last night! They were desperate for help. I am sure we were their last resort."

Ernest ran his hands down his face and inhaled deeply before replying, "you do not understand the townspeople. They are not like our friends around here." He sat down at the table and rubbed his temples, sighing loudly. "Sometimes you are as damned to do something as you are to do nothing," he muttered, almost to himself. He raised his face to Ella, his colour returning slightly. "I am sorry my dear girl, I know it was not your fault. It is just these people can interpret our actions so differently. What if the baby had died?"

"You know that baby had no hope without my help. Her only chance was for me to try. We have seen it in our village just winter gone, the baby we lost and the others we saved then. All we can do is go to church on Sunday and be grateful by the grace of God that she made it." She crouched at his knees and held his hands, catching his eyes with hers. "But to do nothing would have been a sin, and I could not do that to an innocent baby, she has done me no harm. You taught me better than that. The mayor, he is our landlord, we live well off this land of his we tend to. I could not refuse them. Not him, nor his wife or their baby. I just did my best; the mayor and his wife seemed incredibly grateful."

"I know, my dear girl." He pulled her toward him and hugged her tightly. "You remind me more of your mother every day." He stroked her hair and kissed her on the forehead, his movements still unsteady.

Ella drew her face back, tears moistened the corners of her eyes. "My healing has always made you happy Opa. I only mean to bring a smile to your face, never scorn."

Ernest sighed loudly as he stroked her cheek. "I am sorry I got so agitated, it was all a bit of a shock. I did not know they knew about what you do here, or that they would be willing to trust their baby to your care."

She raised herself up properly, straightening her apron and tidying her hair under her cap. "I am more surprised than you! I thought the physician in town promised modern remedies. What do you think Katherine meant when she described his methods as extreme?"

"I have heard they draw blood and force vomiting in these cases," he explained, his voice breaking, as if he knew more about their approaches than he cared to share. "I can understand why she would not want to put her little one through that type of treatment."

"Oh my," gasped Ella. That did seem extreme, and not at all effective compared to the way she had treated others with this cough.

"Well, it would seem some of the old remedies still have their merits." His expression softened as the creases of concern melted into kindness. He drew himself up and tucked his shirt into his breeches. "I hope you got some rest my girl. It's harvest time, and we've an orchard to tend to."

Chapter 2

It is always necessary that the substance or essence of a person be good
before there can be any good works,
and that good works follow and proceed from a person who is already
good. – Martin Luther

Ella woke early the next day to the sound of wood being chopped, her opa already busy with the axe outside. She yawned, still catching up on the sleep she had missed the night before last. Her rustic windows warped the shape of the fluffy white clouds, but it appeared to be a pleasant enough day. Even though the weather was still fine at this time of year, they always needed a steady supply of firewood for cooking. Her opa would be making sure their woodshed was overflowing before winter arrived.

She dressed quickly in a pale brown skirt and beige shirt, tidied her long hair into a neat bun, and went to have breakfast. There would be no pancakes for her today, it was back to their staple of porridge. After eating, she donned her boots and went to milk the goats. They were normally free to roam and kept the grass short, but today she would be trading wares and consulting with locals around the village, so she had penned them in their yard last night as she did not want to waste her morning chasing them around the orchard. The nannies produced more than enough milk for their yoghurt, cheese, and butter, while the two biggest male goats were used to pull her cart.

Their kitchen was compact but functional. A bench sat in the middle, its shelves all but empty beneath. She tsked, realising there was much restocking with preserves needed before autumn descended upon them. The walls were lined with rows of shelves filled with an array of jars and culinary herbs. The bench which held their washbowl housed a shelf where they stored their bowls and spoons beneath. She poured the fresh milk she had collected into a large earthen pot, then added a scoop of the leftover yoghurt from the day before, stirring it through with a wooden spoon until it became smooth. She secured the lid in place and left it to set in the warm slice of sun coming through the small window, then washed the breakfast dishes and milking pail and left them to dry.

The path to the packing shed was short and familiar. The shed itself was more than twice the size of their entire cottage, and where they stored their apples during the harvest. Most of her time was spent in there stewing apples or preparing her remedies when she was not stuck up a tree picking fruit. She gathered an assortment of herbal tinctures, dried herbs, and balms from beneath her work bench and packed them into a crate, then placed them in her cart waiting outside. She packed another crate with apples, then collected several vegetables from their garden and loaded this into the cart as well. Lastly, she ducked into the chicken coop to gather what eggs she could, wrapping these carefully in a small basket lined with linen. The hens clucked happily at her ankles as if promising more tomorrow. She made sure they were fed then latched the hut and placed the eggs into the cart as well.

Packed and ready to go, Ella ran between the rows of trees in the orchard until she found her opa, now up a tree picking apples, a contented smile on his leathery face.

"I'm heading out now, I'll make sure that I'm back before dark," she called up to him.

He climbed down his ladder briskly and gave her a brief hug and a kiss on either cheek. "Make sure you get out to see Friedrich, he mentioned he needed more balm last week at church."

"Yes Opa, I'm taking him a herbal tincture as well."

"Stay safe my dear. I'll see you tonight, you know where I'll be if you need me." He tipped his chin towards the tree and chuckled before ascending the ladder and getting back to work.

She marched back down the gently sloping hill to the pen, collecting the two stocky billies and setting the rest free to meander around the farm. Once they were dressed in their harnesses and attached to the cart, she set off to the cottages nearby.

The road was well worn, as it was the main thoroughfare leading from the city of Rothenburg to the surrounding hinterland. While the houses directly around Ella's cottage were relatively close by, they became more spread out once she had travelled past their church. It was a lovely day; there were plenty of butterflies flitting about, and the sweet, slightly dusty smell of freshly cut grain lingered in the warm air. The faint sound of sheep bleating came from the farming land behind her as she walked.

Her first stop was at a tidy cottage across from them and down a short stroll to the left. She tied the goats to a fence post near a patch of green grass and went to the cart, gathering some goods to trade in her basket and placing a jar of herbs in her apron pocket. She approached the large wooden door and knocked lightly.

It creaked open slowly and a familiar face appeared. "Ah, Ella, what do you have for me today?"

"Hello Leo, I have a cabbage, apples and some eggs." She motioned to her basket. "I have also come to check on Inge. How has she been?"

"A little better, thank you. I will take these." He reached for her basket, flashing her a broad smile. "Let me just get you some fish." He strolled back into the house, calling for his wife.

A grubby faced child dashed up to Ella, grabbing her around her legs and nearly knocking her over. "Ella! Did you bring me some applesauce?"

She grinned as she ruffled his golden hair. "Not yet, we are still busy picking. But I promise I will, in a few weeks." His mother hobbled slowly toward the door with a baby nestled in a sling across her chest.

"Ella, how are you?" Inge spoke in a slow, dreary voice. Her hair was caught loosely in a plait hanging over her shoulder, dark circles sat beneath her eyes. She opened the door wide and motioned for Ella to come in. "Leo," she called, sounding exhausted even this early in the morning. "Please make us some tea." She lowered herself into a chair awkwardly, her hand supporting the baby dozing contentedly in her sling.

Ella's heart pinged, it seemed like Inge could do with some of that sleep herself. "I have some more herbs here for you, do you need them?" She sat at the table, reaching into her apron for the jar of dried fenugreek seeds and placed it in front of Inge. "How has your milk been?"

"Much better, thank you." Inge pressed at her breasts absentmindedly. "Thank you so much for your help." Tears welled in her eyes. "This birth was so difficult, not like Mikkel at all." Inge glanced over at her son, playing happily with his wooden spinning tops in the sunlight coming through the window.

"Hey," Ella cooed. "It will be alright." She reached over to take Inge's hand. "Your baby is healthy, your milk is in, and you are mending well."

Inge nodded, a lone tear running down her cheek. "I still feel so tired all the time, and sad. I cry a lot. I think Leo is getting worried."

Ella stroked her hand and tipped her head toward the cart out the front. "I have another type of tea that will help. Liquorice root, nice and sweet. It will make you feel better."

"It will not affect my milk?"

"No. In fact, I think your baby may even like it." She grinned as she leaned forward to peek into the sling, rubbing the infant's cheek tenderly with the tip of her finger.

Inge smiled wearily. "Thank you, Ella, so much. You do not know how much I need you. This whole village needs you."

"Don't be silly." She shook her head and waved away the notion. "We all need each other. We all play our part in contributing to our village."

"No, it's true. My mama died giving birth to me, and I know you struggled to keep me in this world as Lily drew her first breaths. I've heard the midwife a few villages from here uses stones and chants, and not as many babies get to greet the morn. If I did not have you, I dread to think what may have happened…" her voice trailed off as she struggled to hold back her tears.

Leo came back into the room with Ella's basket hanging over his forearm, along with two cups of tea. "Here you go." He placed the cups in front of the women, shooting Inge a worried glance. He cleared his throat and pulled out a wooden box, lifting the lid and folding back a thin piece of cloth to show Ella the smoked fish inside. She smiled and thanked him as he put the box back and placed the basket on the floor beside her chair. He gazed again at Inge and sighed heavily, his lips pressed firmly together, before moving to rest his hand on her shoulder and squeeze it gently.

"Oh Leo, they look amazing. I smelt you smoking them yesterday and could not wait to call around today. I was hoping you had kept me some." She spoke ebulliently, trying to cheer the mood.

"Speaking of yesterday…" Leo's voice lifted. "Did I see the mayor's carriage leaving your house in the morning?" At this, Inge brightened. They both focused keenly on Ella, waiting for an explanation.

She sipped at her cup, knowing she was going to get this as she called around the village, almost grateful for the distraction as it seemed to ignite Inge. "Yes, they arrived during the night. Her baby was very ill with that horrible cough, but we got to it in time. She was lucky, her baby should make it through."

"What was she like? What was her dress like?" asked Inge, her eyes wide. The mayor's wife was akin to royalty in these parts, the mayor was a landlord over several of the farms.

Ella paused. How best to describe Katherine? "She was a mother during the night, and a mayor's wife the next morning. She is very pretty, with kind eyes, but is still very young, only a few years older than me at a guess. There must be at least ten years between them. She was only wearing her nightdress, well it appeared to be a nightdress, whatever, it was still much fancier than mine, with a cloak over the top. Her baby was struggling to breathe by the time she got to my cottage, she must have left in a hurry to arrive dressed so informally. The baby's name is Clare. She had the most beautifully embroidered blanket I have ever seen. It had tiny flowers and bees stitched in, it must have taken her hours to make."

Leo scoffed. "Or someone else to make." He bent to kiss his wife on the forehead. "I am heading off to fish for the day, I will not be back until dusk tonight. I have left some nets that need mending by the back door, if you can please make sure they are repaired today?" he asked softly. From the way he asked, it was apparent Inge must not be keeping up with the myriad of household chores.

Inge had slipped back into sadness, nodding indifferently, her eyes downcast. "Yes, of course. I shall just finish my tea."

"Thank you for visiting, Ella, please stay for another cup. Inge could do with the company." He glanced down at his wife with a gentle shake of his head. "Just see what you can get done, hey?" He turned back to Ella. "Give my regards to Ernest." He strode over to kiss his son on the head, still happily playing with his toys, and left.

"Do not worry Inge." Ella reached out to hold her hand. "Let me just fetch that licorice root. It will make you feel so much better straight away." She dashed outside with the basket and fish, placing the box carefully underneath some of the other vegetables she had to trade. She hunted around in another crate for the herbs she had packed earlier. The goats were munching happily at the grass on the side of the road, in no rush to leave. She found the jar she needed and headed back inside, noticing Inge still sitting at the table, staring off into the distance. Silent and pale as a statue, she had not moved. "I will just go through to the kitchen and make some more tea."

Ella came back to the table a few moments later with steaming mugs in her hands. "Here, try this." She placed one in front of Inge, willing her to drink. She made small talk as they sipped, relieved to see Inge's smile returning before it was time for her to leave. She wandered over to Mikkel and stroked his hair. "Be good for your mother and help her with those nets please."

"I will for some applesauce." He beamed broadly at her, a couple of gaps in his teeth waiting for new buds to grow through.

"Soon." She grinned at the spritely boy. "But only if you help." She winked at him and let herself out.

It was a decent half hour walk before she would arrive to the next cottage on her trip. She had been enjoying the pleasant sunshine, dreaming about a stroll in a far-off field, her hands grazing the tips of grasses, the goats merrily plodding along. She did not notice the rattling of the carriage until it was almost right behind her. The goats bleated and edged quickly from the side of the road as the driver pulled the horses to a halt, blocking their way forward. She squinted up to the door, shielding her eyes from the sun with one hand, unable to make out who was inside.

It was a few moments before the man's voice called to her gruffly. "Ella Baumann, I've been looking for you." The carriage door swung open eerily.

She instantly recognised it's inhabitant, the Rothenberg pastor, such a bitter old man. His belly was round, his beard grey. He was wearing a black biretta to disguise his bald head. He was supposed to be a man of God, but he was always so rude and treated her like she was little more than dirt beneath his shoes. She had no idea what his problem was with her, perhaps he was like that with everyone. Luckily, he did not visit their village often and her local pastor was so welcoming by comparison. She curtsied politely, hesitant to speak.

"I have been informed of your actions the evening before last. I would not want to hear that you think you can run around playing God, now. Or worse."

"No Pastor, of course not. I was just helping the mayor with his baby."

He cleared his throat. "If that is what you call it."

Her brow furrowed. What was that supposed to mean?

"You would do well to leave true healing to the man of science in town. Use your plants to flavour food and pretty your garden, they have no place in the betterment of health. You women with your herbs and chants do more harm than good. I see you are peddling more nonsense in that cart of yours." He gave a low growl as he surveyed her goods, a mixture of vegetables, bottles, and jars, then mumbled, almost to himself, "I thought we ran your type out of this hinterland years ago. You'll amount to nothing more than your mother."

Ella had to bite her tongue not to respond. He had clearly said that loud enough for her to hear and would have known how much his words would sting. She had never known her mama but loved the thought of her all the same. Drowned, her opa had told her, when the great floods came through. She was wiser than to talk back to a man as spiteful, and with as much power, as he. "Is there anything I can help you with, Pastor? If you do not mind, I have a lot of fruit and vegetables to trade with the locals, and I don't have the luxury of a carriage to speed me on my way."

"Bah!" His face drew into a snarl. "I've more pressing things to do with my time than waste it on the likes of you." He closed the door and leaned out the window. "Know this, girl... I'm watching you." He tapped on the side of the door. "Driver, take me to the rectory."

The carriage rattled away, leaving Ella in a cloud of dust. How a man like that could wear a white collar and preach the words of the bible she would never understand. She directed the goats back onto the road, her thoughts muddled by the encounter. It was not the first time the Rothenburg pastor had made disparaging remarks about her mama. Each time she was left wondering what he knew, and how that could have anything to do with the way he always treated her. He was such a grumpy old man who should have retired from his service many moons ago. She tried to busy herself with identifying the wildflowers growing at the side of the road to calm her racing mind, refusing to let that discontented old crone ruin her trip around the village on such a lovely day. Bees buzzed contentedly and birds were chirping, flying from shrub to tree.

She finally arrived at her next stop, a hut, somewhat rundown with a large barn to one side. The cottage was in need of rendering and several coats of paint, while the exposed timber beams showed considerable rot and the roof would need re-thatching before the cool of autumn set in. A well-fed horse strolled casually within the fence line, if one could call it that. It was more an assembly of posts with logs resting in between, some of them slanting so precariously it would not be long before it was not an enclosure at all. She tied the goats off at one of the sturdier poles and ducked under the log above. She clicked her tongue at the horse who meandered over to greet her, then stroked its nose before patting down its front flanks to check its right shin. She felt up and down the horse's leg while it whinnied comfortably.

"She's mending well." An old man approached her, waving toward the horse. His shirt was half untucked, his pants rolled up to his calves. He walked slowly as if trying to hide a limp. "Can't say the same for me." He chuckled merrily.

"Friedrich, how are you?" Ella patted the horse again before moseying over to hug the old man. "Are you not getting better? I have brought you some more balm."

"My body is not able to repair itself as fast as my horse these days." He shook his head. "But I cannot complain, it was quite a decent fall. We are both just fortunate you could help."

Ella thought back to when Friedrich's cart had hit a large rock in their path a few months ago, throwing him to the road and causing his horse to stumble and scratch its front leg badly. She had treated both of them at the time by splinting their injuries and giving them a balm containing comfrey and calendula. Since both man and beast were given the same care but the horse was healing faster, they had become the brunt of a few well-meaning jokes amongst the locals. "Are you well enough to take our apples into town soon?"

"Of course." He ambled over to the horse and ran his hand along her mane. "I'm sure Missy here would like the trip. It might just take us somewhat longer than usual."

"That's fine, we are glad you have recovered," she said, genuinely. "Is one gulden for two trips enough?"

"How about I throw the first two trips in for free? It is the least I can do."

"Thank you. Let me just fetch you some herbs and more of that balm." She went to her cart to retrieve a glass bottle and small pot she had prepared earlier. "Here you go." She handed them over, smiling warmly. "The cornflower extract will help your body mend faster. Take a spoon full each morning and night."

He bobbed his head toward the remedies in his hands. "Thank you for coming all this way to check on us, I know it is a long walk with only two legs to carry you."

She chuckled as she went back to pat his faithful horse. "Always a pleasure," she gazed at the sky, "and it's such a beautiful day to be out, compared to being stuck up a tree. Can you come over next Thursday? We will have plenty of apples packed and ready to go by then."

"Thursday, of course. Lovely to see you dear, and thank you, again." He placed a light kiss on both of her cheeks and bade her farewell.

Ella spent the rest of the day trading wares with the locals, many of whom consulted her about their health. She provided teas, tinctures or balms as the need arose. The word had spread about her visitors faster than if she had set flame to the fields. She repeated the story about the baby several times, and they had unanimously asked, 'but why come to you?' Each time she explained what Katherine had told her, her curiosity grew at just how different the town physician's treatment must be, since townsfolk had never ventured out to the country for medical help before. Only a couple of the locals had made the trip into town to buy wares and consult the physician while there. They reiterated what Ernest had explained: treatments were aimed at expelling liquids by forcing bleeding, sweating, vomiting, and even clearing of the bowels. No wonder the mayor had sought her help! One villager confided in her: *'the physician in town does not think much of the traditional ways of the country.'*

The sky was turning pink as she arrived at her last stop for the day, her nearest neighbour's farm. While most of the houses in the village were tall buildings almost triangular in shape, this home was a much more ramshackle affair. It had started out like the others but had had many single cottage-style rooms added on as the family expanded over the years, the roof of each section made tall and sloping and connected to the one before. The external walls of some sections had exposed timber beams while others did not, the render and paint varied in colour from piece to piece. From a distance, the roof appeared jagged, much like the teeth on the blade of a saw. The latest section, added only recently, was to accommodate the oldest son, now married with a baby on the way. It was welcoming and lived in, built to suit a loud and loving family of one girl and five boys, ranging from nine to twenty-one years of age. It was a busy farm where they grew oats, beans, rye and spelt, it also had a generous fallow area that served to house their pigs. There was a stream running through the property, so it was often used as a common area for other farmers with sheep and cattle as well. A sizeable barn sat at the border between their property and Ella's orchard, sunflowers fringed part of the fence line between the two. They had lived side by side for as long as she could remember, this cottage and its land as familiar to her as her own. She tied off the goats and trotted past a chicken coop, sending its occupants clucking and scattering.

"Ella!" One of the boys called out to her from the other side, his head bobbing up from the commotion. He was busy with some pails full of food scraps. "So good to see you, I was wondering when you would be calling by. I will go fetch Tomas, he is out the back field with the pigs. Go on in and see mama, she has some ham for you."

She entered the cottage happily. "Hello, Julia?" she called out as she strolled toward the kitchen.

"Ella dear, so good to see you." Julia wiped her hands on her apron as she came out into the hall to greet her. They hugged warmly. "You get prettier every day." She stroked her cheek and straightened the cap on her head. "How have you been?" She led them both back into the kitchen where she was busy cutting vegetables. She had a gentle, round face that despite the hardship of farming life with a large family, always seemed adorned with a welcoming smile.

Ella loved Julia like a mother, she was the closest to one she had ever known. "Oh my, I'm tired now. I've been wandering around the village doing the trading today. I had a run in with the Rothenburg pastor earlier, he's such an awful man."

Julia brought her blade down sharply through some carrots. "Don't worry about him, he's just a bitter old man with a grudge."

"He mentioned my mama again." Ella drew her lips into a tight line, tears threatened to emerge. "He spoke of her as if she were worthless. I really wish I could remember her." She sniffed and wiped at her eyes.

Julia put down the knife and moved over to Ella, reaching for her hand. "I never knew her, but whenever Ernest mentions her, it is with great fondness. He always says how much you remind him of her, and you are most definitely not worthless."

Ella tried to form a smile.

"We have all lost someone special in our time, it's just the way of the world. It is unfortunate you were so young, but you have always had us. I may not have given birth to you, but I've certainly been there to help you grow into the woman you are today." She squeezed her hand tightly, smiling broadly. "I know I'm proud." She stepped back into position, slicing more vegetables.

"Thanks Julia." Ella's heart warmed at the bond they shared. She had been more than a suitable substitute for the mother she had never known.

"So, tell me, Ella," Julia asked, mischief sparkling in her eyes. "Did I see the mayor's wife leaving your house yesterday morning?"

"Yes." She folded her arms across her chest and leant on the bench, exhaling loudly. "Is there nothing else this village can talk about?"

Julia smirked. "No. So you'll just have to tell me all about it now."

She filled Julia in about the night's events while she made them both some dandelion tea and waited for Tomas. She patiently answered the same questions she had heard from all those she had visited: what was she like? What was she wearing? What was the baby like? Having the mayor's wife visit was probably the most sensational event the locals had seen for some time, save for old Friedrich being thrown from the cart last spring. But quiet and uneventful was good, it was how she liked it to be.

Eventually Sarah, the only girl of the family and second youngest, ran inside, dirt dropping from her boots all over their wooden floor. Her hair was in long, golden braids, her apron and face covered in muck. She was almost as much one of the boys as her brothers. "Ella," she cried, running over to hug her tightly. "Tomas is out the back field, they are fixing a fence where the pigs were getting out, so he cannot leave Papa right now. He is very sorry, but he wanted me to ask if he could come and see you tomorrow?"

Her heart sank, she had hoped to see Tomas after such a long day. She pasted a smile on her face to hide her disappointment. "Of course. Tomorrow I must get back to picking apples, but I would dearly love to see Tomas if he could call by in the afternoon?" Her cheeks grew hot at her choice of words. She started fiddling with her nails.

Julia grinned knowingly, her eyes crinkling at the corners. "I will send him around to see you after he has finished his daily chores." She came from around her side of the bench to give Ella another hug. She kissed her on both cheeks and rubbed her arms tenderly. "Say hello to Ernest for me."

She tried to avoid Julia's eyes. "Yes, I must get back now." She curtsied shallowly and rushed out the front door. It was only when she got back home that she realised she had forgotten to ask about the ham.

Chapter 3

There is no more lovely, friendly and charming relationship,
communion or company than a good marriage. – Martin Luther

The sun was low in the sky the next day as Ella emptied her last bag of apples into the crate inside the packing shed. It had been a perfect mid-summers day in the countryside, a gentle breeze had stopped the heat from becoming overwhelming as they worked. A yellow glow was cast over the orchard when a familiar outline came into view through their mottled windows. She threw off her collection bag and ran outside to greet her favourite neighbour, tucking her hair behind her ears and wiping her face and hands with her apron as she went.

"Tomas, you made it!" She hugged him tightly around the waist, her head barely reaching his shoulders.

Tomas picked her up in a warm embrace. "I missed you, my beautiful girl." He lowered her to the ground gently, kissing her briefly. "Am I getting taller or are you shrinking?" He played with the few strands of hair that had escaped her cap, twirling them affectionately.

"Go easy! When we were ten, we were almost the same height." She squeezed his arms admiringly. He was strong and muscular from his work on the farm and seemed to be getting taller long after she had stopped growing. "Hey, you will never guess what happened the other night."

"Oh yes, I would. It is all the village has been talking about. They say you conjured up one of your potions and drained the mayor's baby of the evil inside." He waggled his fingers in front of her face, as if casting a magic spell.

"Oh Tomas, stop that." She slapped him playfully on the shoulder. "You know it was only the herbs and me doing what needed to be done."

"Ow, you're going to give me a bruise." He rubbed the top of his arm.

She put her hands on her hips. As if she could ever hit him hard enough to hurt. "Well, mind your manners then," she said mockingly. "Thank goodness it all ended well, but it did not get me out of picking apples though." She groaned and pointed to the many full crates inside the packing shed. "It has been a good season. I will be stewing for weeks when we are done with the harvest."

"Can I have one?" He helped himself to a juicy looking apple, just one of the many hundreds that sat ready to be taken into the town to be sold at the markets. "Hey that reminds me, I have something for you."

She ran her eyes over him keenly, he did not seem to be holding anything other than the apple. His linen shirt was surprisingly clean, and he smelt as if he had just bathed – or at least did not smell as if he hadn't. His blonde hair was overdue for a cut, shaggy in parts, only partially brushed. She loved it when his curls were long enough to twist around her fingers.

"Where?"

"Not here, obviously." He rolled his eyes at her, sighing in jest. "Come with me." He grabbed her by the hand and led her to the barn that lined the border of their properties. "In here."

They hurried inside and flopped on the stack of hay at the back. The barn smelt fresh from sprinklings of crushed peppermint placed in each of the corners to keep the rats away. "Hey, remember when we used to climb up there?" He pointed to the floor above, where more hay was piled neatly. A rickety ladder was used for access but did not make it look very inviting.

"All too well," she moaned. "Remember when the ladder slipped?"

He grinned and tickled her sides. "More like you slipped."

She laughed, pushing his hands away gently. "However you wish to recall it, I remember quite clearly that the ladder slipped." She pursed her lips, challenging him to reply. "We used to climb up there and play for hours. Whatever happened to my knight in shining armour? Weren't you supposed to save me from the dragon and take me to your castle?"

A smile tugged at his lips. "We got older and more sensible."

"And falling down started to hurt too much." She giggled and rolled into his arms. They laid together, cuddling, staring at the planks of timber above them. She was not sure exactly when their friendship had developed into courtship, and then to love. Its transition had been seamless, blossoming sometime in their early teens. She broke the quiet by sitting up and peering at him with squinted eyes. "Hey, didn't you say you had something for me?"

He sat up and brushed some hay from his shirt. "Why, yes I do." He grinned, one eyebrow raised. "Close your eyes and hold out your hands."

She did as she was instructed, her lips curving seductively. She felt the cool touch of a heavy glass object being placed into her hands and opened her eyes. They sparkled with delight at the jar of honey he had just given her. "Oh Tomas, can I have some now?"

"Only if you save me some for later." He pretended to take the jar back off her, but she whisked it safely from his reach.

"Where did you get it?"

"My father traded a ham hock for a tray of jars. I made sure I kept one for you."

She untied the string holding the waxed linen lid in place, dipped her finger in, and slowly sucked at the tip, relishing the sweetness. "You want some?" She held the open jar out for him to enjoy too.

"I may be a pig farmer Ella, but I'm not a pig." He pushed it back toward her, chuckling. "I'll wait to have it with some bread, thank you. Oh, and I got you something else." He rose quickly from the hay, retrieved a nearby pail and placed it at her feet.

Her eyes widened in anticipation. She hastily put the lid back on the honey jar and rest it in hay so it wouldn't tip, then wriggled forward to look inside the bucket. She unwrapped a linen cloth and glimpsed the golden mass inside. "Is this…?" She gasped at the gift, a huge pail of beeswax. "Where did you get it?"

"When I told the beekeeper who the honey was for, he gave this to me. He had been saving it for you, he knew you would want it for your balms. He and his wife are eternally grateful for the joy you have brought into their house."

"Ah, Kristopher, and baby Josef. Is he doing well?"

"Which one?"

She smirked. "Josef, the baby. I am sure Kristopher is doing just fine if he is out selling his honey. Did you see Helena?"

"No, I only saw Kristopher." Tomas wrapped the present up and settled back down beside her. "He says both Helena and Josef are doing well, and may come to see you soon if they need your help to make another baby. I think they are trying now." He winked at her.

Her cheeks warmed and she dipped her eyes as her blood tingled inside. Oh, how she longed to make a baby with Tomas. Her heart ached at times with the sorrow of her past and loneliness of growing up with just her opa. She scolded herself momentarily; she should be grateful she'd grown up with Tomas' family beside her, they had always welcomed her as one of their own. She reached over for the jar of honey and busied herself by dipping her finger in for some more. "Will you come to my house night after tomorrow? I shall make us dinner and we can enjoy sweet bread and honey for dessert."

"Absolutely, I'll be there. But will there be any left by then?" He scoffed as she scooped another finger full of honey into her mouth.

"I might leave you some," she teased then glanced over toward the barn door. "Hey, it is dark outside, I really must get home. I'm a bit exhausted from picking apples and the mayor's visit. We still have several weeks of harvesting ahead." She stood, shaking the hay from her dress and apron, keeping one hand firmly on the jar of honey. She walked toward the barn door and peeked outside. "A clear evening, the air is still warm." She gazed upward. "Look at the moon, it's leaning but not tipped over yet. We'll have two or three clear days before some rain, there is still so much fruit to pick." She groaned, tired at the thought of all the work ahead. "So, dinner, two nights from now, you'll come?"

"Yes, I'll be there. I'll bring some beer too. Will I see you at church tomorrow?" He caught up to her at the door, handing over the pail of beeswax.

"Of course, I'll save you a seat?" She took the bucket eagerly, causing her shoulder to drop sharply as she countered its weight.

"Sure, I don't want to sit with my brothers anyway, they only start snoring and it is really embarrassing when people stare at us." He reached for her hand. "Do you want me to help you home with that?" He motioned to the bucket. She was a small woman, and it was rather heavy.

"It's alright, I need to build my muscles to keep up with you." She smiled up at him fondly. She reached out to hug him with her free arm, angling her face up for a final kiss.

Their lips met briefly but lovingly, his arms firm around her, holding her close.

"I'll see you tomorrow then." Ella stepped back, ready to walk into the night.

A grin flashed across his face. "That pail is nearly as big as you, my beautiful girl, be careful."

She poked her tongue out but was grateful for the gifts. She headed slowly back to her cottage, leaning somewhat, to support the large pail as she tottered along. After several paces, she swivelled around and watched Tomas close the barn door in the moonlight, missing him already.

The St. Peter and St. Paul church of Detwang was the most impressive building of the area. It had stood for hundreds of years already, originally built grand by the Catholics with few changes during the reform to Lutheranism. It still held much of its original features including an elaborate carving of the crucifixion above an altar and alcove at the front. The grand arch and round stained-glass windows on the eastern wall bathed the congregation that had gathered in rainbows of light. The church was more than large enough to accommodate the entire village and surrounding hinterland locals, with around twenty long pews downstairs and an extra gallery of seating upstairs. The ornate pipe organ was a feature added during the Lutheran conversion, its music a beautiful and joyous part of the service. Some were standing while others were seated, but all were greeting each other eagerly, catching up on their week. Everyone was expected at church on a Sunday – only injury or illness excluded one from attending.

Ella sat next to Ernest in her finest dress, which, like others in the village, did not differ greatly from her regular apparel albeit longer and cleaner. Women were without their aprons and added flat lace collars in summer or linen cloaks in winter, while men wore shirts or jackets that fit firmer compared to their loose shirts used when farming or fishing. She listened to the music being played, saving the space beside her.

Tomas arrived just before the service started, squeezing past several locals as he moved along the row then kissed her gently on the cheek as he sat down. They rubbed shoulders and his finger stroked the back of her hand, sending tingles up her spine.

The villagers sung as one, their service full of hymns they mostly knew by heart. She could not read, nor could most of the villagers as far as she knew, but the songs were sung regularly and taught from mother to child so all could join in. Julia had sung the hymns to her children and Ella many times as they were growing up.

Once the initial part of the service was completed, their pastor ascended the staircase to the pulpit, an impressive, raised structure made from cherry wood, inlaid with gold embossed diamond-shaped framework and gilded spirals. Thank goodness he was so much nicer than the pastor from town. Above the pulpit was an intricately carved sounding board which amplified his voice to ensure everyone could hear him easily. It also made him appear to hover over the congregation and bring him closer to God. He was relatively young, in his early thirties, and had joined their community only five or so years ago with his young wife and two children after the previous pastor had passed on. The overall impression of him standing there, on this raised and grand structure, made him the centrepiece of the church, almost regal in his white robes reserved for Sunday. "Today the gospel's teaching was that we must love thy neighbour. For each of you turn to another and see the good in each other. We are a village that is here for all, there is no evil or devil among us. I stand here before you, proud of what we have built, not from stone or wood, but from love and support, and a genuine desire to see that each has what they need to survive well, in this our farming community." He surveyed his congregation, a village that really did encompass the virtues he extolled. "God has blessed us with fair weather and bountiful crops yet again, so that we may all live and prosper from these times. Let us rejoice in His kindness and celebrate with each other at the blessings we share." The sermon continued for some time in a similar manner, not heavy in its message but certainly lengthy in its content.

Tomas pulled faces at Ella, making her snigger. Her opa nudged her more than once, putting a finger to his lips, motioning for her to be quiet.

After a communion service and more hymns, the service was eventually over. The village people moved outside, milling out the front of the church to catch up with each other before they would head back to their cottages for an afternoon of rest. It gave them the perfect opportunity to spread the local news, and Ella knew she and her visitors would be a topic of discussion, so wanted to be on her way quickly. "Opa, I'm going to head home, I don't really want to have to retell Katherine's visit yet again."

"Ernest, may I walk Ella home?" Tomas asked for his consent even though it was not really necessary. The whole village knew of their affections. When they weren't working, wherever you saw one of them, you usually found the other close by.

"Go ahead, I want to catch up with Tomas' father about the coming season. Make sure you get to those vegetables, Ella, don't just hang about in the barn all afternoon."

She let out a loud sigh then leaned over and kissed him gently on the cheek. It was all work and no play with him sometimes. "I thought Sunday was supposed to be a day of rest."

He grunted, a hint of a smile on his lips. "It is, from picking apples. Time to give the vegetables some attention instead."

"Yes Opa. I'll see you home later." She held out her hand for Tomas to take it.

They strolled through the church yard, dotted with gravestones of various ages and states of decay, some were sadly almost new. As they reached the road and made their way toward their homes, he bent down to pick some flowers growing at the side of the path and handed them to Ella. "For you, my lady."

"Why thank you, Herr Wolff," she addressed him formally, smelling the cornflowers he'd just given her, fluttering her eyelashes.

"I've got to work later today," he said, sounding somewhat frustrated. "The pigs have knocked the back fence down, and they are going to either get out and run away or cause havoc in the rye crops. Papa and I were working on it the other day, but it looks like they've damaged it further along as well. You are so lucky you only have to worry about picking apples."

She studied her roughened hands. Her nails were short and chipped, bits of dirt always remained lodged firmly underneath regardless of how hard she scrubbed, signs she worked on a farm. She thought of Katherine's hands from the other night, so soft and smooth by comparison. It was obvious she did not have to do any manual labour or household chores. "That's fine Tomas, really, I always have some mending and washing to tend to at home. I need to weed the vegetable patch and herb garden today anyway as they're growing out of control. Can I still pick up that ham? Your brother said you had one for us?"

He chuckled. "Never get between Ella and her food, hey?" He squeezed her belly, stopping her in the path. "Hey, you know the sermon today?"

"Yes?"

"Well, I must say, all that talk about loving thy neighbour… you make it easy to respect the word of the bible." He glanced over his shoulders to see if anyone was nearby, then clasped her hand in his and raised it to his lips, kissing it gently. "I know I love my neighbour."

Her cheeks warmed and she nibbled at her lip. "Hey look." She rushed over to a fencepost, where a ladybug was bumbling along merrily in the midday sun. She carefully picked it up and handed it to Tomas who held out his hand to take it. "Make a wish, you know they're a sign of good luck."

He watched the bug waddle in his palm. "There is only one wish I want to make," he said, his eyes fixed firmly on Ella. He blew the bug away and wrapped his hands around hers. "You know how special you are to me." His face became serious. She was not used to this from him, their relationship was usually very playful. "I was wondering if we could... if you would..." He dropped to one knee, her hands still in his.

She gasped, one hand escaping to cover her mouth. "Tomas, are you asking me what I think you are asking me?"

Tomas stared deeply into her eyes. "Yes." He cleared his throat and gave a lopsided smile. He closed his eyes, inhaled deeply, then opened them and started again. "Ella Baumann, would you do me the honour of marrying me?"

She whooped with delight, jumping on the spot then pulling him back up and kissing him fiercely. She leapt into his arms, wrapping her own around his neck, hoping they were far enough from the church so that no-one else was within sight or earshot. "Oh Tomas, yes! I was beginning to think you'd never ask." She kissed him longingly.

He beamed and placed her back down gently. His expression grew stern. "Whoa now, hold on a minute. There are customary rules that must be followed. I should have asked your opa first, so I still need to do that, and then I need to visit the mayor. You know our union must be approved before we can wed."

"Yes, I know." She squinted at him teasingly. "But I just wanted a taste of what I'll soon be feasting on." She licked her lips for good measure, tempting him to kiss her again.

"Oh, my beautiful girl, you are making this difficult for me." He held her arms at her side. "I don't want our neighbours talking about us any more than they already do. I want to make sure they respect you. Please let me get the mayor's approval, and then we can make our engagement public." He kissed her lightly on the lips and reached for her hand, leading her on as they enjoyed the sunshine.

Birds twittered in the background while a comfortable silence settled between them, broad smiles fixed firmly on both their faces at the confidence they now shared. Her thoughts drifted to the mama she never knew, but so often missed. How she wished she could share this moment of happiness with her; she gazed at the sky, hoping she was smiling down from the heavens. "Please, let me be the one to tell Julia of our good news?" She blinked a few times, whisking away the dew that had formed in the corner of her eyes.

He put an arm around her waist and kissed her cheek, near her ear, sending a tickle up her spine. "Yes of course, once your opa has agreed, but I think she already knew of my intentions."

She giggled and leaned into his arm as they walked, arriving at his house shortly after. He ran inside and collected the ham, which had been wrapped in cloth and left out for her.

It was only a brief stroll further to reach her cottage. She let out a slight groan, the morning had passed too quickly. "Wait here," she instructed, tapping him on the chest. She put the ham in the kitchen and dashed to her bedroom, where she fished through her top drawer for a fresh handkerchief she had embroidered. On top of her cupboard sat two small brown bottles which she unscrewed, one at a time, dabbing a few drops of each onto the soft cloth to impart their aromas of lavender and geranium. She hurried back outside. "Take this and think of me." She handed the keepsake to Tomas.

He inhaled deeply. "Mmm, it smells like you." He tucked it into his shirt pocket and wrapped his strong arms around her shoulders. "I shall sleep with this under my pillow and dream of you, of us, together." He cuddled her gently and kissed her tenderly. "I will see you tomorrow night."

"Tomorrow night," she repeated, and went inside, distracted somewhat from her many Sunday chores.

Whoever could have known what a difference a day would make.

Chapter 4

Beware of false prophets, who come to you in sheep's clothing,
but inwardly are ravening wolves. – Matthew 7:15

Ella woke the next morning rested after a contented sleep. Her first thought was of Tomas; she smiled into her pillow at their decadent little secret. Oh, how she could not wait to call him husband and greet each day with him lying beside her.

Her next thoughts were of the day ahead, causing her joy to dim somewhat. Their orchard was not big, but since it was only herself and opa tending it, it meant several weeks of almost continuous picking depending on how well the crop had run each year. This season had been particularly generous, the rain and sun had yielded more apples than normal, so it was certainly keeping them busy. Many years ago, it had been just her opa doing all the work, but it was much smaller than it was now. As she grew to help, he planted more trees, and now it was one of the largest apple orchards in the area.

The trees were quite mature and tall, making the harvesting harder work with longer ladders, but meant the lower branches were high enough to protect them from sabotage by the goats. They pruned the trees well, late each autumn and early into the winter, to encourage strong growth in the spring. Climbing the ladder would have been near on impossible if she were made to wear the normally thick and lengthy skirts expected of women, so it was not frowned upon by the locals for her to wear a much thinner skirt that finished well above her ankles. There were other women in their farming community that wore shorter and less full dresses, like Ella, for similar reasons. It was only at church where longer skirts were worn out of respect and piety.

She grinned as she thought of the times she envied her opa's breeches and the freedom of movement it gave him. What a sight that would be! It would certainly give the locals something to gossip about on a Sunday. It was thoughts like these that kept her in good humour as she struggled on with the mammoth harvest ahead, certain Tomas would find it amusing too.

It was almost on midday when the mayor's distinctive carriage rolled toward the farm, the mayor's nephew Conrad its sole occupant. He noticed the farm girl instantly, awestruck by how comfortable she appeared up a ladder, not used to seeing a woman do this kind of work. She was quite short, but obviously fit, her hair neatly tied beneath her cap, save for a few strands that held a soft wave and glistened with golden highlights in the sun. He watched as she reached for an apple and twisted it lightly at the stem, leaving that one and moving to another. She appeared to be testing several at a time with a gentle twist and when satisfied, picked a few at once with both hands, deftly placing them in the large bag slung over her shoulder. Breath taken by her beauty, he compared it with his sisters back home. She was much thinner and more graceful in her movements. *A woman like this should be focussing on embroidery or music, not stuck up a ladder in a farm.*

"We're here, Herr Sauer," announced the coachman.

Conrad was unaware how long he'd been sitting there gazing out at her. "O-of course," he stammered. He picked up the basket next to him in the carriage and made his way over to the girl. "Ella Baumann?"

She stopped what she was doing, two apples still in her hands, and turned toward him. "Hello," she said, sounding a little stunned. "Can I help you?"

He watched as she peered over his head toward the carriage, a quizzical expression on her face. *Surely, she could not be mistaking me for a coachman. How repugnant.* He ran his hand around the brim of his tall capotain hat, then brushed its long feather plume. "I am Conrad Sauer, nephew to Mayor Schulz."

"Oh, I'm sorry, I did not know the mayor had a nephew."

"Well yes, he does, and I am him." He was tripping over his words, he did not normally stumble around women like this. His cheeks warmed, he cleared his throat and tried again. "I have recently arrived from Munich. Anyway, I have been sent here with a gift from the mayor, personally."

She flushed and wiped her hands on her apron. "Oh, my apologies Herr…?"

"Sauer," he finished for her. Did she not hear him the first time? He frowned briefly, they must not be big on respect in the country. "Seeing as I have been sent here personally to dispatch a gift, please, call me Conrad." He brought his spare hand to his chest and gave the slightest tip of a bow.

"I was not expecting a visitor. Hold on a moment." She climbed down swiftly. "How do you do." She curtsied politely.

She was so different in her mannerisms to other girls he had met that he was struck silent. She raised her eyebrows, prompting him to continue.

"Ah…" It took him another moment to gather his thoughts. "I have been informed of what you did for baby Clare two nights ago, and have been asked to deliver you this basket, as a token of appreciation." He held it out for her to inspect. Inside was a variety of smoked sausages, sweet breads and cheese wrapped in wax.

She gazed at the feast of treats in the basket, her eyes wide and mouth agape. She had obviously never received such a gift, her face bouncing from him to the basket a few times in surprise. "My goodness, I cannot possibly take all of that."

"Nonsense, you saved Clare's life. My aunt is most grateful and insisted that more should be added." He grinned broadly and put his hand on one of the items in the basket. "Have you tried some of this cheese? You really must, it is most delightful."

"Well, I was just about to break for lunch, would you like to stay and share this with us?" She craned her neck and appeared to be scanning the orchard. "Can I just find my opa? If you like, you can head over there toward the house." She raised her arm in the direction of a most humble-looking cottage. "I will be just a moment."

"It's alright, I can wait." He was enjoying watching her. She was such an enchanting creature so completely unaware of the effect she was having on him. She dashed off amongst the trees, her skirt flicking up to reveal a glimpse of her leg as she ran along. He glanced back at their farmhouse. It was an odd shape, mostly one story with a thatched box section mounted at one end. A most primitive dwelling compared to what he was used to, no wonder she was so dumbfounded by the gift basket.

When they were gathered at their dining table they shared a moment's prayer, then enjoyed a small portion of everything. They savoured the sausage with its rich, smoky flavour then tried the soft, sweet cheese. There was also dried fruit, nuts and some sweet bread.

"Mmm, this is some of the finest food I have ever eaten," commented Ella between mouthfuls.

Conrad raised his eyebrows as he chewed. It was delicious, but not the finest.

"I must say, this is very different to our usual lunch of salted fish, pickled cabbage and goat's cheese," Ernest added with a chuckle.

"Thank you for sharing some with me." Conrad wiped at the corners of his mouth with one of their napkins. He observed Ella happily munching away. Amazing what she could pack away considering her size. "My uncle asked if you could show me around since I'm out here. He is busy in town and asked me to report back with any improvements or changes you have made." His eyes flitted between Ernest and Ella. "How many of you tend the orchard here?"

"It is just us," informed Ernest. "Ella can accompany you on a trip around the orchard. It has been a good season, your uncle will be pleased with what we have done with the land. It is very fertile, and we have planted another dozen trees up the back. They are fenced off, to protect them from the goats, but they are already growing well. They should bear fruit in another four years or so." He rose to leave before adding, "Ella, please take your time showing Conrad the trees and the gardens, and make sure to send him back with some apples for Mayor Schulz."

"Yes Opa." She pushed her chair back and hastily cleared their lunch plates, winking as she leaned in to whisper conspiratorially, "anything to get me out of picking apples for a few hours."

Once tidied up, they ventured back outside. "Our orchard runs from here, all the way back up to there." She demonstrated where the borders ran, from the road to the back of the property. "We have just put the new trees Opa was talking about over yonder, they're still young and won't be producing apples for some time. But the soil is good." She bent to pick up a handful, letting it run through her fingers. "We have been most fortunate with the weather for the last few years." She dusted her hand off on her skirt as they wandered through the grounds. "See how heavily laden the trees are?

We start picking from the outside and the top and work our way in as they ripen."

"There are still so many apples left to harvest." He gauged their work ahead. He could not imagine having to work like this, no wonder she appeared so trim. He reached up and tugged at an apple until it snapped free. "May I?"

"Sure, we have plenty left as you can see, and that's one less I'll have to pick." She grinned and raised her eyebrows.

He smiled at her charmingly. Did he detect a hint of attraction from her just then? The apple crunched loudly as he took a bite. "Mmm, very juicy." He chomped as they meandered along. There was something relaxing about being with this girl. She did not seem to be judging him constantly like he was used to, he could just be himself and enjoy the moment. "Why do you have different plants at the base of the trees?" He bent to touch the top of one he was standing next to, picking a sprig and inhaling its aroma.

"We plant these to repel the pests," she explained, pointing to the bush he was referring to. Lilac buds coated its top, the fragrance delightful. "This is lavender." She sauntered past some other shrubs planted nearby, gracing the flowers with her fingertips. "We use geranium and thyme as well. I like to think it makes the fruit extra tasty, it certainly makes the orchard smell divine. We also have sunflowers on the fence line over there, it attracts the bees to bring pollen to the blossoms during spring." She singled out the tall flowers, standing at the edge of the property. "Have you ever watched a sunflower?"

He shook his head as his heart pumped harder; he could just listen to her prattle on all day.

She smiled enthusiastically, causing dimples to dent her cheeks. "It is quite something. The head follows the sun as it passes across the sky." She pointed from the east to the west, moving her face with her outstretched arm, as if to provide an example. "The seeds are good for the goats, and we also get oil from them. One of the villagers has a press."

He had to force himself to peel his eyes away from her and focus on the flowers she was describing.

She took a few giant strides over some grass growing wildly before her, in the direction of a plot nearest to the cottage. "Over here is our vegetable garden," she called over to him when he hadn't moved. She then moseyed on further, her voice raising its pitch with excitement as she approached another area bordered off. "Over here is the herb garden."

He had to almost jog to catch up, then stood beside her, surveying the generous patch arranged in neat rows before him. He leant on the fence, patting the top of it, almost at his chest. "Why so high?"

"To keep the goats out. They'll eat just about anything they can get to. We let them roam free in the orchard most of the time, it helps keep the weeds down. We don't want them in here though, otherwise there would be nothing left within a few days."

His face warmed. Of course, he should have realised that, how silly he must have sounded. He considered the many herbs this garden contained. "Why, this is nearly three times the size of your vegetable garden!" His gaze drifted back and forth between the two. "Why so many herbs? Surely there can't be a use for all of them?"

"These are the herbs we use to treat the locals." Her eyes shone with pride. The fence was at shoulder height for her. "We also use some of them to flavour our cooking."

"Really?" He flicked his finger toward the tall plants closest to them. "That one there, what is it used for?"

"That is lemon balm, it reduces feelings of nervousness. It is also great in cake, gives it a nice lemony flavour."

"And this one?" It was a bushy shrub with butterflies flittering around it.

"That is hyssop. It is good for coughs and colds as well as stomach upsets. I use it in stews sometimes too."

"What about that one, that one and that one?" He was challenging her now, enjoying watching her come alive as she guided him through their various uses.

She giggled. "Rosemary, great for cooking and when washing the hair; motherwort, for childbirth; and bearberry, that's good for when you, umm." She flushed, her cheeks turning adorably rosy. "Have pain passing urine. Out over there…" She indicated just past the borders of her orchard, clearing her throat and changing the subject quickly, "that is a clove tree. The dried cloves are really good for toothaches."

"I was always told you needed to kiss a donkey to cure that. I endured the pain of a few toothaches without complaining to avoid it." He grinned. His body tingled with infatuation listening to her. "Fascinating!" he exclaimed, eyeing her up and down. Thank goodness she was focused on her herbs and did not notice. He motioned to the herb garden and orchard behind them. "You really grow and tend to all of this here by yourself? How do you keep on top of it all? I've never managed to grow a thing."

"We do most of the work on the gardens during spring while the apples are still growing." She led him toward the packing shed. "Then summer is picking season. By then the vegetables and herbs are well on their way and only need a little attention while we are busy with the apples. I am sure you could grow something if you tried."

"Hmm, maybe," he feigned agreeance, although it was not something he was inclined to try anytime soon.

"I need to go to the forest at the back of the farms to collect some herbs on occasion too. There is not enough room in this garden alone. Some, like the cloves, grow on bigger trees. Others grow out the back fields like weeds. Out here we grow everything we need and trade it for what we don't have with the local villagers."

"I have heard there is a bartering system in place, it is not like the town system at all. How do you get by?"

"We keep what we need, and trade what is left. The apples get sold in town, that keeps us and the farm going nicely."

"My uncle has been showing me the ledgers. You and your opa have done well. I think it was four hundred gulden last year? It looks like you will get much more with this season." He rested his hands on his hips, taking in the bumper crop of apples yet to be picked.

"We have had two very good seasons. It certainly keeps us busy!"

He considered the cost of each of his suits. "You don't find living on that difficult? It would not get you past a few months in the city."

"Ah, but we do not have the need for much out here. We must earn enough to cover rent and a few items for the orchard, and some years that's about as much as we make, but then we may have a few good years and make extra money."

"Interesting." He observed her dress and coif; their funds certainly did not get spent there. "What a simple way to exist." He scanned the horizon, noting the farming cottages dotted around the village and the hillside beyond. They must all live this way. Scraping by on an existence off basic trades was not something that sounded very appealing.

Her brow furrowed. "I could not imagine wanting it to be otherwise." She followed his gaze and the view of the hinterland from their vantage point. "Life is simple here, just the way I like it."

They were silent for a moment, before he pointed back toward the fence around the herb garden. "So, tell me Ella, how does one take those herbs and turn them into that vile liquid I see them shove down Clare's throat?"

She laughed at his description. "That vile liquid contains important medicine from the plant and is what makes a person better. Or animal. We treat both out here, the herbs care not if you are animal or human. Let me show you." She covered the short distance to the packing shed promptly. "This is where I prepare the 'vile liquid', as you call it." She welcomed him in, guiding him past the crates of apples piled in the centre, then led him over to the wooden bench on one side where rustic windows faced out over the orchard. They were not totally clear like he was used to, but instead more like a poorly moulded bottle, alternating thin to thick in parts, warping the view that could be seen. There were several mortar and pestles on top of the bench, and two rows of large pots with lids to one side. A kettle rest atop a nearby stove. Along the top of the windowsill hung dozens of different herbs tied in small bundles, drying in the afternoon sun. Beneath the bench was an assortment of glass bottles and jars in various colours, shapes and sizes. Some were corked with liquid inside of them while others were empty.

His jaw dropped. "My word, what is all of this?" He had never seen anything like it before, it certainly was not like the office of the town's physician. His rooms were lined with shelves containing beakers and vials, Latin names emblazoned in scrawling letters across the front. He recalled the strange animal specimens preserved in ethanol that were lined up across his desk, the crisp smell of unknown chemicals in the air. This shed, the enticing aromas that lingered from the flowers drying at the window, her herbal preparations… so different by comparison. How could a bunch of plants possibly do any good? *Who is this girl? She is simply the most amazing creature I have ever met.* He studied her closely. She had golden brown hair, a few wisps had escaped her cap. She had the cutest smattering of freckles that ran lightly across her nose. Her eyes were not blue, but not green either. They sparkled brightly when she spoke about her herbs. *She's far too beautiful to be trapped in a farming life.*

She blushed and reached up to touch the bunches at the window. "These are the herbs I am drying to make into tea. Some are easy to take that way, they do not taste too bad and are not as powerful, but are useful to keep one in good health. When I need the medicine to do more, I use the extracts, these liquids." She reached below the bench to grab a bottle out of a crate and pulled the cork off for him to smell it.

He screwed his nose up in distaste as it was unexpectedly pungent. There was a tag hanging from the bottle which he caught in his hand. It contained no words, only a picture of a plant. Perhaps she could not read, so this would be her way of marking what each bottle contained. Best not to mention it, it would only embarrass her; he dropped the tag before she could realise what he was surmising.

"The extracts are much stronger in how they work but are more bitter when prepared that way." She recorked the bottle and put it back where she had got it from, then took a few steps over to the bench where a mortar and pestle were sitting. "The herbs are much more concentrated when fresh, so I crush them to express the juices and then put them in one of those pots with alcohol and leave them to brew for a month. If you don't like the smell of the vile liquid when Clare drinks her herbs, you wouldn't want to be here then! They make the whole shed smell bad." She grinned and winked at him.

"After a month, I strain the mixture and pour off the liquid." She bent forward to touch the cork of the bottles below the bench.

"That purple one." He reached up toward a bunch of herbs bundled tightly, hanging upside down to dry at the window. "Is that lavender? That was at the base of the apple trees."

"Yes." She tipped her head as if impressed, he was glad he had been paying attention. "A cup of lavender tea, for example, is good before bed. It will help you sleep. It can also settle a bloated tummy."

He moved closer to the bench. "And this one?" He tapped some white flowers with golden yellow centres also hanging at the window.

"Ah, that is feverfew. It is good in tea for headaches."

He strolled along the bench, his fingers trailing on the smooth wood. "Incredible." He stared at her, his heart pounding. "Where did you learn all of this?"

"My opa. He taught me everything I know."

"And he – where did he learn?"

"His aunt taught him."

"How odd, for a woman to pass all this learning to a man."

She shrugged. "She had no children of her own, I guess she wanted to make sure the healing tradition continued, so taught him instead. My opa was sent to her when he was just a baby after his parents were killed in the margrave war. He was fortunate to survive, he was hidden in a basket and wasn't found for two days."

"Really? That was lucky. What about your parents, where are they?"

She shifted on her feet uneasily. "My mama drowned when I was young. I don't know who my papa was."

"Oh." He fell silent, busying himself with the bottles underneath the bench. He glanced back at her tenderly. To not name a father carried heavy consequences for a woman, why would her mother not name the man responsible? He focused his attention on the workbench and items lined neatly beneath. "What is this here?" He picked up a pot of balm, opened the lid and sniffed cautiously. "Finally, something on your farm that does not stink." He smirked at his own humour.

She smiled politely. "That is a balm, or you may know it as a salve." She came beside him, swiped a pea sized amount from the tub, and smeared it on his skin. "It is just beeswax, sunflower and flaxseed oil now, but I can mix the herbal extracts in there, or other crushed herbs or roots, and then it takes on the properties of those plants." She caught his eyes as she explained.

His skin tingled at her touch. "What sort of things would you use this for?"

"Oh, well, when mixed with chickweed, it is good for itchy skin. When mixed with wintergreen oil it is good for sore joints or muscles. I even use it on animals or children when they break a bone. I mix in some comfrey to help the bones heal faster. It's also good on deep wounds or scratches, it stops them from turning red and swelling." She took the jar from him, put the lid back on and placed it under the bench.

"Is that what you used to make that ginger smelling rub they use on Clare?"

She raised her eyebrows and bobbed her head. "Yes, I mixed some ginger root in with the balm to warm her chest, it helped move some of the mucus that was blocking her lungs making it so hard for her to breathe."

He personally thought Clare's balm smelt so bad it almost made him retch. She seemed pleased with herself, however, so he held back from sharing that. He sauntered over to the stove and kettle, noticing a stack of pots at the end of the bench. "You have quite the collection here. I have never seen this type of healing done before. You say your opa's aunt taught him? What happened to his wife?" She was captivating; he wanted to know everything about her.

Ella at first seemed taken aback by his questions but shrugged and answered anyway. "My oma died giving birth to my mama, my opa never remarried. What about your family? Why did you come to Rothenburg?"

Aha, she was interested in him, he should have known. "My parents are both in Munich. I have come here to learn the ways of the council from my uncle. To be groomed into the next mayor, if you like. Have your family always been apple farmers?"

"Ah, no," she stammered. "My opa grew up in Rothenburg with his aunt. She was a seamstress and healer until…" her voice drifted off.

"Until?" he enquired. He watched her withdraw. Whatever it was, it was clearly upsetting for her to speak about.

She was gazing at her hands, her fingers fiddling nervously. "She was accused of being a witch, Herr Sauer, and was burnt at the stake." Her voice was so quiet it was almost inaudible.

"Well, witches must be purified, if they are to be given a passage to heaven." He repeated the teachings reinforced in many a Sunday service. "The pastor tells us so. Do you not attend church?"

Her eyes narrowed, confusion washed over her face. "Of course I do, but it is not a topic that gets spoken about often in our church."

"Oh?" That was surprising. His pastor in Munich, like the one in Rothenburg, had lectured them at length about the evil deeds of witches and warned them regularly to beware. "Well, did she confess?"

"I am told she did, but opa always disagreed with the judgement." She shuffled in her place. "It is not something we really talk about out here."

She appeared to be dimming, a change of subject was necessary. "So now you continue their practice of dispensing herbs as medicine, but only for good. And what good it did! Clare is doing so well."

Ella brightened. "She was lucky. Our village lost a baby last winter to the same cough, we nearly lost many more. I am so pleased she made it through."

"Well, she wouldn't have made it without you." He stroked her cheek affectionately. "To think, your plants made such a difference."

Ella stepped back quickly. "Opa always says nature provides everything we need, I am just fortunate to have had such a knowledgeable teacher." She moved toward the crates, picking up a basket and filling it hastily with apples. "I should get back to harvesting. There will be rain soon." She passed the basket to him, his hand clutched at hers as he took it. She wiggled her hand away nervously. "Please take these to your uncle, tell him it has been a good year. Our apples should be in your markets soon." She was speaking fast now. "It will be several weeks before I start preserving, but I can send some stewed apples and applesauce to him when ready."

He was not used to girls shying away from him like this, his chest burnt with a compulsion to win her over. He could almost kick himself for making her uncomfortable a moment ago. How he'd love to kiss those lips, feel the warmth of her flesh against his. He restrained himself from reaching out to touch her again, he could not be too overt with his intentions until he had his uncle's permission and a chance to spend more time with her. "Of course," he said, flashing her a broad grin. He reached for the basket of apples as he gazed deeply into her eyes. "Thank you for showing me your orchard, it was very enlightening. I shall let my uncle know how well you are doing and that his gift was appreciated." He strolled over toward the door, then swivelled back, hesitating in its frame. "It has been lovely to meet you, Ella. I would very much like to come and see you again." *Did she feel the same way?* He thought he'd read her signs right, but with the way she just reacted, he wasn't completely sure. He studied her again. *How does one impress a girl like this?* She did not seem to respond to his position of power the way other girls did in the city. Money did not seem to hold the same value to her either.

"You are welcome, anytime." She dipped her head and curtsied. "It is your uncle's land. Please thank the mayor and his wife for their generous gift and check on baby Clare for me."

He tipped his hat, savouring one final vision of her that would have to last, before turning and striding quickly to the waiting carriage. Regardless of how she might feel right now, she would come around to favour him with time.

He would make sure of it.

Ella finished picking apples earlier than normal that afternoon, heading inside to prepare dinner for Tomas and her opa. She washed her hands, face, and neck carefully, dabbing some balm infused with rose petals on her neck and behind her ears. She rubbed a paste of rosemary and sage ashes over her teeth to whiten them, then spat it out before chewing on some peppermint leaves to freshen her breath. She tidied her hair neatly into braids on either side of her head, twisting them into a bun at the back of her neck, and secured them in place with a fresh linen cap. This one she had edged in lace last winter, wearing it only at church or on birthday celebrations to ensure it stayed crisp and clean. Tonight counted as a special occasion, she thought gleefully, as Tomas was going to ask her opa's permission to marry her.

The stew was simmering gently in the kitchen, so she added another log to the fire to keep it burning merrily in the stove. She added herbs she plucked from one of the many shelves to give some extra flavour, then gave it a stir and inhaled deeply. *Mmm, delicious.* She crossed to the bench in the middle of the kitchen to cut the bread her opa had made into thick slices. He almost always made the bread. Sometimes he moulded circles, other times plaits; mostly he made round loaves and cut shapes into the top. Today it was a long loaf, fresh and crunchy, it would go perfectly with the stew.

As she set out cutlery on the table, her thoughts drifted to those of her wedding and the dress she would hopefully wear, borrowed from Tomas' brother's wife if she was fortunate. She was quite a bit shorter, but Julia was so handy with a needle and thread, she would know exactly how to adjust it properly.

Her thoughts were broken by her opa entering the cottage with Tomas following close behind. Tomas had picked her a bunch of wildflowers, holding them out to her in one hand, a large earthen jug of beer in the other. She reached for the flowers giddily and ran to put them in a glass bottle with some water, then brought them back to the table with some mugs and poured them all a drink. They clinked mugs with each other, announcing 'prost' happily, and took a swig.

"So, my dear girl, I smell stew, but I do not see stew." Her opa sniffed the heavily scented air. "Are you planning on feeding us sometime tonight?"

"Yes opa, just as soon as you men make yourselves presentable." She smirked at them playfully, then dashed into the kitchen to serve dinner while they went to wash their hands and faces.

By the time the men came back in, the stew and bread were served and waiting for them on the table.

"The spoons," Tomas commented, rubbing his fingers along the smooth cow horn. "You still have these?"

"Yes." She smiled shyly. "We have not used them in quite a while, and I thought they might be a nice touch with dinner tonight." They exchanged glances, knowing just how much this evening meant. She had taken extra time tonight to prepare everything just so, and even set the table with their finest.

"My goodness, Ella, where did you find these?" Her opa picked one up, inspecting it closely. "I thought these were long gone, it must be years since we've used them. How old were you two when you made them?"

"About twelve." Her cheeks flushed warm at the memory. "It took us all afternoon to craft these out of the old cow's horn. Certainly, too much work to be bothered again."

"Ours were broken many years ago," remarked Tomas. "The young ones were not as gentle with them as they should have been."

"I used to fashion knife handles out of boar tusks," her opa commented, a whimsical gleam in his eyes. "It was a hobby of mine. Your mama used to sew scraps of fabric at my feet when she was just a child while I whittled away." They shared a comfortable silence, warmed by his memories. "Ah, but I have not had time for such folly in many years." He scooped the stew into his mouth with the spoon, followed by a bit of his bread. "Well, at least they do the job. This stew is delicious, thank you, my dear."

Tomas agreed, exchanging loving glances with Ella. She could not wait until she was making a happy home for them in the future.

After dinner they enjoyed some fresh apples, pears and nuts, served with some cheese from the mayor's basket, along with Tomas' honey. She showcased what was left of the gift she had received in gratitude.

"Delivered personally by the mayor's nephew," her opa informed Tomas.

"I did not know the mayor had a nephew."

"Apparently he has just moved here from Munich." Ella stood and gathered their plates. "He was dressed rather like a peacock."

"More like a turkey," added her grandfather, chuckling to himself.

She grinned as she explained, "he had a feather plume in his hat that touched the door frame as he entered. Must have been his first trip to the country." She laughed at the thought. "Well, time to clean up." She had a kettle warming some water on the stove. "Opa, would you please fetch some more water from the well?"

"Yes, of course my dear." He headed toward the door and put his boots on.

"Let me help," said Tomas, standing quickly.

Ernest's raised his brows. "Fetch water? I can assure you I am not too old for that yet."

"I mean, I need to get some for my family too." He hurried to the door with the old man, who was regarding him strangely.

"Alright then. Ella, we are both going to fetch some water," he broadcast, shaking his head at Tomas who was acting more than a little odd.

Ella covered her mouth to hide her smirk. Maybe this would be the moment. "Here, let me get you a bucket." She raced into the kitchen and returned with an extra pail, handing it to Tomas. He touched her hand as she passed it over, catching her heart and eyes briefly. "I will just tend to the fire and get these dishes started," she said awkwardly, before dashing back toward the kitchen.

✿ ✿ ✿

Once outside, Tomas wasted no time. "Ernest... Herr Baumann..."

"Please Tomas, how long have you known me? What is this Herr Baumann? Since when have I ever been Herr Baumann to you?"

"Actually Herr, as of this moment." He cleared his throat and put his hand on Ernest's arm to still him. While he was at least a head taller than the old man, he suddenly felt quite nervous, like a child once again. "Ern... I mean, Herr Baumann, I would like to ask your permission to marry Ella."

Ernest stared at him. He breathed deeply before his eyes glistened and his leathery face moved into its familiar creases around a broad smile. "Well, it is about time, boy! I thought I was going to have to make you ask soon." He slapped Tomas squarely on the back, dropping his bucket to shake his hand cheerily. "Of course you can, you have my blessing. It would make me so happy, knowing you are here to watch after her, be the one to protect her when I am not able to do that for myself. And thank goodness too – I don't know how much longer I'll be around."

Tomas let out a sigh of relief. "Thank you, Herr."

"Enough now, stop with the Herr stuff please, you know my name."

"Yes Herr... I mean Ernest." They both laughed, making the moment more comfortable.

"Have you asked Ella?"

Tomas fiddled with the bucket. "Yes, but I told her we must wait for your permission first."

"Well, you knew I would say yes, surely? Your bigger problem is going to be the mayor. He is very proud of this orchard, you know, and I cannot tend to it myself. There will come a time when I won't be tending it at all."

He brought one hand to rest on his heart and faced Tomas optimistically. "Have you considered taking over here? The mayor should agree to that."

"Yes, Ernest. I hope you will not think it too forward of me, but I have already discussed this with my father, before I came to you. He came up with the idea actually, because he knows what the mayor is like, and that he may be unlikely to approve of our union if I were to take Ella from this land. I know it is customary for the wife to move to the husband's family, but since my father has other sons, especially an older son, he does not need me. It's already a very full house over there." He smiled awkwardly. "If you would permit me to live here and learn from you, once we are married, it would give Ella and I good standing in the community, and a strong and prosperous future. Your orchard is very well established so it would be more than enough of a dowry. I was hoping you would agree to this?"

"Yes, of course, my boy. Excellent plan. You'll be taking care of my Ella and giving your family a fine start to life." He gazed up at the stars and raised his arm quickly. "Look there, a shooting star, a sign of good luck! What a wonderful night. Shall we go back and tell Ella?"

"Yes." Tomas started back toward the cottage, bucket still in hand.

"Ah, Tomas?" Ernest called after him.

"Yes?"

"The water?"

"Of course." Tomas rushed back to Ernest and they continued toward the well, filling their buckets before returning to the cottage and sharing the news with Ella.

Chapter 5

Whatever you wish that others would do to you,
do also to them, for this is the Law and the Prophets. – Matthew 7:12

Everything was so different for Ella the next day: the sun shone brighter, the air smelled sweeter, the orchard seemed greener. She was engaged to Tomas — well almost engaged, now she had her opa's permission — and could not be happier. They need only get the mayor's approval, and since Tomas would be taking over the lease on the orchard, he was unlikely to refuse. To make it even more enticing, Tomas planned to visit the mayor with one of his family's finest pigs as a gift, just as soon as he was granted an audience.

Ella was picking apples happily, totally lost in plans for her wedding, when she noticed a carriage arriving. She paused, perplexed. They rarely received visitors from town, and this would be the second in as many days. The coach was almost as grand as the mayors, but nowhere near as dark. Fully enclosed with velvet curtains drawn back from the open windows, it obviously belonged to someone quite wealthy. She was astonished when a young lady stepped out, her skirt billowing.

The coachman came around to assist her as she dismounted. She surveyed the orchard as she stepped down, her face a mixture of awe and disgust. She was tall and appeared quite imposing with two strands of pearls that sat atop her chest below a wide, stiff ruff. A large feather floated from a pile of raven hair perched high on her head. She lifted the front of her skirts as she wove her way around tufts of grass along the edge of the trees. As she got closer, Ella cringed as she watched her delicate satin slippers get covered in dust. "Excuse me, you there, can you tell me where I can find Ella Baumann?" She spoke with a formal accent, every syllable pronounced distinctly. She fanned herself with a hand ensconced in a finely knitted lace glove. Her other hand was holding a small part of her skirts from the ground, while a rounded leather purse dangled from her wrist. She was quite attractive, made even more striking by her beautiful turquoise dress. Her eyes were blue but unwelcoming, her skin bone white.

Ella was suddenly very aware of how dowdy she must appear by comparison. She put the apples she had been picking into the bag slung over her shoulder. "Hello, I am Ella," she replied. She untucked her skirt from her boots and climbed down the ladder, noticing her opa, at a nearby tree, had stopped to watch this visitor arrive also. "How can I help?" She approached the woman dubiously.

The woman squinted at Ella and her lips puckered. "I am Louise, daughter of Hugo Meier. I have come to seek your help." She leaned in closer and cleared her throat. "On some personal issues," she said in hushed tones. The feather in her hair bounced and waved in the breeze, her skirts were getting dirty from dragging in the orchard. She must have realised the name meant nothing to Ella. Her voice took on a frustrated tone. "Councilman Meier?"

Ella eyed her with suspicion. They would have been about the same age, yet this lady spoke down to her in a way in which she had never been treated from her peers, or even elders from the village.

Ernest approached the women, standing close to Ella. "I am Ernest Baumann, tenant to the mayor. Can I be of assistance?"

"Hmmm, I think not." Louise screwed her face up as she ran her eyes over the old man. "Katherine Schulz, *the mayor's wife,* suggested I see Ella personally." She added extra emphasis on her town connection, as if to imply she was not being given the respect she deserved. "I have, uh, health issues of a private nature, that Katherine insisted Ella would be able to help me with." She glanced disdainfully from Ernest to Ella.

"I am sorry, we are just apple farmers," declared Ernest, adjusting the heavy bag slung over his shoulder. "We are not able to help, unless you are here to purchase some of our apples?"

Ella faced her opa, trying to hide her confusion. They never refused village people seeking her assistance, so why was he behaving this way?

Louise peered down her nose at Ernest, stroking the starched ruff at her neck. "How odd." She pursed her lips so tight her cheeks sucked in as though she were chewing on her words. "I was told Ella could help. I was assured by *the mayor's wife* that she would help. This is his orchard, is it not?" There it was again, the emphasis on the mayor's wife, like Ella would be doing a disservice to ignore this request. The woman played with the pearls resting on her chest, eyeing Ella as she did so, no doubt displaying the chasm of class difference that lay between them.

At the mention of the orchard, Ernest drew in his breath sharply. "My dear, why don't you take the young lady inside and see if she would like some tea?" He turned to Ella, who was bewildered by both his behaviour and that of this woman.

Louise nodded as if to let him know he had made the right decision. Her feather plume seemed to agree with him also, bouncing happily in the breeze.

"Yes, of course, Frau Meier, please follow me." Ella led her to the cottage.

Once inside, she directed Louise to the kitchen table, where Tomas' wildflowers still sat as the centrepiece. She could see Louise gazing at her surroundings distastefully, her eyebrows raised as she took in the humble furnishings.

She span around to face Ella, refusing to sit. "Let me make this clear," she said coldly as she stared directly into her eyes, "so that there is no more confusion."

Ella gulped. "Yes, Frau Meier, how can I help?" She curtsied lightly again to show her respect.

"That is much better." She drew her thin lips into a wry smile. "The thing is, my monthlies. They are…" Her tone softened ever such a touch, she was clearly more than a little embarrassed by the subject matter.

"It's alright, you can tell me. The more open you are with me about your…" Ella searched for the right word, then continued, "…issues, the better I am able to help." She reached over to touch Louise's arm gently, a gesture of kindness, but the lady pulled away as quickly as if she had just been singed by fire.

"I really hope you can, Ella, but how a farm girl can help when a physician has not been able to, I am struggling to comprehend." She sighed loudly and played with her pearls. "I should have known this trip was going to be a waste of my time," she mumbled, just loud enough for Ella to hear. Her eyes again ran around their cosy common room, her lips puckered.

Ella raised her brows. She had never encountered someone so rude, especially since they were, until moments ago, strangers. While this woman clearly had a lot of money, not as much could be said about manners.

"Well, I'm here now, I suppose I might as well get this over and done with. They're painful and irregular, and I lose a lot of blood," Louise spurted out, almost spitting it with distaste. "The mayor's wife told me what you did for Clare and said you would know what to do."

"Of course," Ella assured her. "Please, tell me more."

Louise spoke haltingly and vaguely, seemingly repulsed by her own problem. When she finished speaking, she unbuttoned one of her long cuffs and held her bare arm out to Ella.

Ella stared down, frowning, thinking it a rather odd offering. She reached out to grasp her hand and smiled warmly, if not a little uncomfortably.

Louise's face soured as their fingers intertwined. She shook her fingers out of her hold and gasped. "Whatever are you doing? Don't you need a sample or something?"

Ella gulped, her eyes drifting around the room, her lips drawn tight. "Ah, er, a sample?" She snatched her hand away and rest it in her lap.

"Of my blood. Don't you need to cleanse me, or test it to ascertain the problem or something? How else do you propose to cure me?" The woman rolled her eyes to the ceiling, sighing loudly, as she tapped her foot on the floor. "Good grief, since when did the patient have to guide the physician?"

"Oh, ah, um," Ella stuttered as she chewed on her lip. "That's not how I do things here." She stepped toward the door, her eyes glued on Louise's pained expression. "Please stay here while I go fetch some herbs."

She dashed to the packing shed and poured out some chaste tree extract into a small glass bottle, stoppering it with a cork. She then pulled some dried red clover flowers and raspberry leaves from the bunches drying at the windowsill, crushing them lightly with the mortar and pestle before wrapping them into a linen cloth, just the right size to fit in her palm.

"What are you doing?" asked Ernest.

Ella's breath caught in her throat as she span to face her opa. "Oh my, you startled me. I'm preparing some herbs for Louise."

He came closer and ran his eyes over the bench. "I know what you are doing, but what I'm really asking is, *what are you doing?*" His voice had a restrained calmness to it, barely disguising his aggravation.

"She has been sent here by Katherine. What would you like me to do, send her back with nothing?" Not this again. What was his problem lately with her helping people? "Mama never turned anyone away seeking her assistance, you told me so yourself. You used to say it with such pride, but now, you scold me with reproach."

Ernest raised his head to the rafters, closing his eyes, breathing deeply. He brought his face back to look at her squarely. "I know, and it may have been her undoing."

Ella's jaw dropped. "Opa? Whatever do you mean? Why teach me all these things if you suddenly don't want me to help others anymore?" She let out a loud sigh. What was next, did he want her to stop seeing the locals too? "If you have such an issue with me treating the townspeople, then tell me now, otherwise I do not understand why you keep speaking to me like this, when all I'm trying to do is help in the way that I know best."

He chewed on his bottom lip for a moment before answering, his hands on his hips. "The visitors from town are not the same as our friends in the village. We must be wary of what assistance we give them. They can turn on you as fast as they turn to you." He clicked his tongue. "I cannot expect you to understand. I am sorry, my dear, do your best. You always do." He pivoted and trudged out, his head down, his shoulders slumped. He suddenly appeared older, defeated, more tired than usual.

She shook her head to clear her thoughts and focused her attention on what she was doing. She collected the bottle and the bundle and rushed back to the cottage. "Frau Meier, here you go, I have a couple of things for you. This liquid here, take this morning and night, half a spoonful." She handed over the bottle. Louise wrinkled her nose as she lifted the cork to smell it. "It is best to measure it out and put it in a mug, add some water and drink it, then have some more water to chase it down. It tastes quite bitter." Ella smiled, trying to create some sort of connection with this frosty woman. Were all the women in town this bristly? Katherine had not seemed so.

"And that, what else do you have?" asked Louise, pointing to the linen pouch she still held.

"These are some herbs for a tea." She handed the small bag over. "Drink two cups daily, half a spoonful steeped in each." She reflected on the herbs briefly, then added, "you are not trying for a baby, are you? Not possibly with child already?"

Louise glared at her as fiercely as if she had just been slapped. "I'll beg your pardon, how dare you!"

"Oh, I am so sorry, I did not mean anything by that." Ella glanced briefly at the ground, giving a shallow curtsy in apology. She raised her face reluctantly. "What I mean is the herbs in that tea," she said, tapping the pouch gently to make sure Louise understood, "should not be taken when you are newly with child." She then touched the bottle of liquid. "While the herbs in there will make you more fertile."

Louise drew back, wide eyed, staring at Ella.

It had never been this hard to explain her medicine to someone before. "Um, ah, you see, when a woman's cycle becomes regular, her body takes a baby easier." The cottage walls seemed to be shrinking in on her. This type of response from someone she was trying to help was quite unordinary. Perhaps some people just had strange ways of showing gratitude. "The liquid won't hurt a growing baby, but that tea could, if it is in its early stages."

Louise gazed down to the bottle and bag in her hands, her brows relaxed slightly. "I've not been given medicine like this before. Will they force me to vomit?"

Ella shook her head rapidly. "No, of course not. They are bitter, a taste you are probably not used to, but no, they will not make you sick."

"Then how will I know if they are working? The doctor in town usually takes my blood or gives me something to expel the poisons affecting me."

"Ugh." Ella shuddered at the vulgar description. "You will know, when your monthlies improve."

Louise stared oddly at the remedies she still held. "Are you sure they will work?"

"Mmm-huh," Ella hummed and bobbed her head a few times, cautious not to rattle this woman again. "Many women of our village have needed something similar at one time or another." She attempted a brief smile.

"Right then. Half a spoonful of each, twice a day. Brew the tea, take the liquid with extra water. How much?"

"Excuse me?" Did she not just repeat the dosage back exactly as she had been instructed?

"How much for these herbs, and this… *consultation*?" Louise's voice was sour as she asked, impatiently fiddling with the lace trim at the bottom of her gloves.

"Oh." Ella had no idea what to charge, or what this sort of service or her herbs should cost. "We normally trade goods out here," she offered.

"Well, I pay in coins. So, how much?"

She tried to calculate what her time and the herbs might be worth, noting Louise's frustration growing. It was almost palpable. "One gulden please," she blurted.

Louise sighed and opened the leather purse that had been hanging from her wrist. She pushed one gulden firmly into Ella's palm. "I trust you won't repeat this meeting to anyone?"

"Of course not, that goes without saying," she assured her. "But please, you will need more than what I have just given you. What you have there will last you about a month. It would be best if you could come back and let me know how you are going then, in case I need to give you something different, or more of the same."

"I see." She watched as Louise ran her eyes over their common room again. The woman acted as if a second visit to her quaint cottage would be the last thing she could tolerate. "Can I just take more of the same right now? Here, take this." She reached into her purse and held out another gulden. "How long does this take to work?"

"Around three cycles. Four at most. These herbs work well, they will work for you."

"Fine." She handed over another two gulden. Just how much could she have in that purse? "Take these and go fetch me enough for another three months. I really can't make it out here so often." She smoothed her hair with her hands then patted down her skirt, knocking some of the dust onto the common room floor.

Ella studied the gulden in her palm. She had never been given so much money for so little work. She hurried out to prepare more herbs for Louise. Exactly what it was a councilman's daughter did that could make her too busy to visit again for the sake of her health was beyond her, but still, it was what she had instructed and paid for. Her opa had told her townspeople were not the same as village folk, but she had never encountered anyone quite this different before.

She went to the packing shed and dispensed more of the extract and tea, then raced back to give them to Louise. She bid her farewell and put the gulden safely in the pot they kept in the kitchen to store their spare money, then returned to the orchard and her ladder, climbing a little unsteadily at first, still flustered from the encounter. She placed her bag over her head, acknowledging a nod from her opa, her heartbeat calming as she went back to picking apples.

Conrad pulled his chair closer to the table and tapped his foot as he waited for his Uncle Carl and Aunt Katherine to be seated. The oak dining table in the Rothenburg ob der Tauber manor was generously laid with more food than they could possibly eat, while two servants were in attendance, armed with plenty of wine to top up their glasses. His eyes followed speckles of dust, dancing in the rays of the summer sun shining through tall glass windows, while he held his tongue.

"So, tell me." His uncle spoke as he tore some chicken off the drumstick he was holding. "How was your trip to the farm?"

"Carl, don't talk with your mouth full." Katherine was cutting her food into small squares politely. It was not the first time she'd scolded him about his table manners in front of company. "And use your knife, not your hands."

Carl finished chewing then swallowed audibly. He licked each of his fingers, smacking his lips loudly, before speaking again. "What news do you have for me?"

"I left some apples in your office, Ella was kind enough to send some back. They're very crisp and juicy." Conrad mimicked Katherine by cutting his food into smaller pieces. "They are having a very bountiful crop and have planted more trees at the back of the field."

"That is good news. Ernest has been an excellent tenant for years, he has worked that land since before I was mayor. I am proud to own the finest apple orchard in the area."

"His granddaughter Ella was quite something." Conrad could not stop the smile from spreading across his face. Katherine put her cutlery down with a clink and shot him a disdainful glance. "She truly is the most fascinating woman I have ever met. You should see her up a ladder. She moves as deftly as any working man I have ever seen, more perhaps, because she's young and agile. She picks the apples, not just one at a time, but several in her hands, so small but capable. And she carries so many in her bag, I have never seen a woman work so hard."

"Perhaps you should visit our kitchens or laundry some time." Carl chortled between mouthfuls. Katherine glared at him.

"They plant herbs or flowers at the base of most of the trees, to keep the pests away, and sunflowers at the fence-line, to attract the bees. Her herb garden was huge, and so well-tended. Your gardeners here could learn a thing or two from her. She knew what every herb, seed and leaf was good for, off the top of her head. I don't think this girl can read, but she knew what everything was for, just like that." He snapped his fingers.

Carl put the chicken bones he had cleaned on his plate and chased the meat down with a swig of wine. He tipped his head toward a servant standing nearby for a refill. "Sounds to me like you are more interested in this girl than my apples." He wiped his mouth and beard with the tablecloth, looking sternly at Conrad before continuing. "We are not to have a repeat of what happened in Munich."

Katherine cleared her throat softly. "I think I shall go check on Clare." She moved her chair back while a maidservant ran up quickly behind her to assist. She rose from the table and curtsied shallowly to her husband, then stared down her nose at his nephew. "Conrad," she said admonishingly.

Conrad stood briefly and bowed to Katherine as she prepared to leave, his glare returning her disdain. He sat again, dreading the conversation that was due to begin.

Carl played with the stem of his wine glass. "Leave us," he barked to the servants in attendance, without so much as a glance their way. The servant with the wine, a mousy, frightened-looking young girl, left the carafe at the edge of the table and scurried quietly out of the room with the others.

Once they were alone, he started. "Conrad, you've been here now, four weeks or so?"

"Nearly five."

Carl bobbed his head. "When my sister sent you here, she was very clear in her instructions and what she wanted to achieve. You do realise the opportunities you have available to you, and what waits for you in Munich if you were to return?"

Conrad's face grew hot. He silently cursed his mother for painting him as such an incapable dolt. "Uncle, that was not my fault. You must understand what these wenches are like. Surely you…"

Carl held up his hand. "Your Mother — my sister — had to expel a perfectly good seamstress because of you." He pushed food around his plate, stabbing at a carrot with his knife. "They had to craft a story that the baby she was growing — *your* baby — was from a travelling merchant or some-such to save your family's good name. She sent her away to God only knows where, to fend for themselves. She is totally unhappy with the replacement. Good staff are hard to find, and I've had no end of her nagging letters telling me I must watch over you before you cause trouble again." Carl took a hearty swig of wine and poured himself some more.

Conrad held his own glass out for some, but his request was ignored. He shrank back in his seat.

"Your father practically disowned you for what you did," he added gruffly. "And here you go, prattling on about some farm girl. My tenant, my land too! Well, Conrad, you will stay clear of her. I will not have you defaming her and ruining my relationship with the farmers that tend the orchard so well. Don't forget, they also saved my little Clare." He reached forward and pulled another drumstick off the chicken in front of him. "I would never hear the end of it from Katherine if your poor excuse for courtship should end badly for Ella."

Conrad sat quietly, suitably chastised but not yet ready to concede defeat.

His uncle chuckled and assumed a more conspiratorial tone. "I know what it is like to be tempted, I have certainly had my choice over the years." He chewed and swallowed, then licked his fingers. "But you need to choose your wenches wisely, boy, and you need to be discreet. Make sure it is never someone that cannot be removed without an issue, if you know what I mean." He winked, as if sharing sage advice.

Conrad sat up straighter. "But Uncle, this girl is different. I would be different with her." He leaned forward on the edge of his seat, his forearms resting on the edge of the table. "I would like your permission to call on her, court her properly."

Carl huffed and put down what he was eating, wiping his hands again on the tablecloth. "It is not normal to aim down in class, boy. There are plenty of councillors daughters that would be more suited to you and the towns ways."

"But Uncle, I am not attracted to any of the girls in town. They're all the same, they don't challenge me, I have no interest in any of them."

"You've hardly met any of them," Carl said, sounding exasperated. "Where have you been to meet these town girls?"

"Well, the tavern..."

"The tavern?" Carl interrupted, slapping his hand on the table, laughing merrily. "What kind of girl do you hope to meet in the tavern?"

Conrad smirked. "True, true, but I've also attended a few of your dinner parties, there have been girls of better class there."

"And none of them take your fancy?"

"Not as a long-term partner, no. They've got no real substance." Conrad reached over for the wine, pouring some into his glass. He sipped and gave it a swirl, the way his head and heart were feeling for Ella at that moment. He thought of the girl who had frequented his bed lately, Louise. A councilman's daughter he'd met at one of his uncle's parties. She was a prissy girl who wore large feathers in her hair and always fidgeted with the pearls at her neck. She refused to take the damn things off, even when they were in the thick of it. "I find talking to them rather boring."

"They are women, boy. What do you think they would be able to offer in terms of conversation? It is not like talking with men. Women are there for entertainment, to organise the household, sit and stitch. Their range of topics can be..." He checked around the room, making sure it was just the two of them before finishing, "somewhat limited." He raised his eyebrows and tipped his head.

"Everything was so different with Ella. She was interesting, and compelling." Conrad's words were tumbling out, so buoyed was he by the memory of her standing at the herb garden. "I listened to everything she had to say, and I could have stayed there all day just to hear more."

Carl put his wine glass down and leaned back in his chair. His gaze focused squarely on Conrad. "Are you really quite serious about her?"

Conrad sensed the shift in his uncle's thinking. His pulse quickened, his smile broadened. "Yes Uncle, she is the most amazing girl I have ever met. I want to know everything about her."

Carl put his hand up again. "To marry someone below you in class is not forbidden, but I will not sit here and arrange marriages either." His other hand was still on the table, his fingers drumming lightly. "Did she give you any indication she was interested in you?"

Conrad shrugged. "What is to question? We have money, power, position. A girl of her class would do well to marry a councilman, let alone the nephew of the mayor! All she needs is time to get to know me."

Carl picked some chicken from between his teeth. "This Ella, I have met her a few times. She is a pretty thing, I'll give you that. Good in the garden, but really, just a farmgirl. I don't think she's ever been to our city." He rested his elbow on the arm of his chair with his chin on his fist. "I am sure you could find someone much more suitable in the town here. A girl that is used to finer things in life, one that will not need to be trained in how to behave at court or be reminded of her place. You would lose interest in Ella after a few weeks of her country ways, I am sure. Stay away from that orchard. I would rather you find someone local, a girl born into society."

Conrad rallied. "I have met plenty of town girls already. None have caught my eye, or my heart, like her. I would like your permission to court her, with honourable intentions. You can mark my word." He wanted his uncle to warm to this idea, get him in his best humour. "Here." He strode over to where Carl was sitting, filling his glass for him. "Enjoy this wine, think it over." If there was one thing Conrad was certain of, it was how to play a person and get them on side.

Carl tipped his head in thanks. "I tell you what." He twirled the green stem of his glass, watching the liquid spin inside. "I want you to meet the girls here in town first. Behave yourself, of course." He sniggered and winked. "In two months, if you really can find no-one better in town, and if you still feel the same, I will allow you to court Ella."

Conrad nodded as he returned to his seat. He knew his uncle, and this was not such a bad outcome. There were plenty of local girls he could be 'discreet' with to fill in a couple of months, then he could court Ella openly, and with his uncle's consent. "Thank you, Uncle. Do you want me to fetch Aunt Katherine now, ask her to re-join us?"

Carl laughed out loud. "Now, why would I want to ruin a perfectly good meal with the mutterings of a woman?" He reached for more chicken. "They're all about manners and some such. No, I'll enjoy this meal with just you, my boy. See, it is no different as you get older, women can be useful for some things, but the company of men is often far easier. So, tell me, was this wench in Munich worth the hassle?"

Conrad chuckled as he acknowledged the trouble he had caused, knowing now his uncle saw the light-hearted side of it. "Are they ever? Let me just say, when the conquest makes it too easy, it is no longer as much fun. I was growing bored of her before she told me about the baby anyway. As you say, I should have chosen someone that could be more easily removed. Mother was most displeased."

The two men made the most of their lunch, the good food and wine of the region flowing through their veins. The thrill of the chase was what kept him in pursuit of Ella. The challenge of proving himself to his uncle, the anticipation of wooing Ella, these were the motivations driving him. He knew his worth, and it would not be long until he would win her over and show his uncle the kind of persistence and strength of character he held.

Chapter 6

I should have no compassion on these witches;
I should burn them all. – Martin Luther.

The next day saw another new carriage arrive, then a cart the day after, and another the day after that. Soon enough, there was a new face or family arriving almost every day. Some came in carts, some came by horse. Some even walked from the town to their orchard. Word had spread fast about Ella and her healing herbs, so they came in a steady stream seeking her help for one condition or another. Thankfully, the next lot of visitors seemed much kinder than Louise, and while they often commented on how different her approach to treatment was, and expressed surprise at the remedies offered, all were more than willing to pay or trade for her services and remedies.

There was Carol, Katherine's seamstress. She had sore knuckles and wrists, especially after a lot of sewing. Ella gave her comfrey balm to soothe her joints, and juniper berry tea to cleanse her system. Carol could not afford one gulden but measured her up and promised her a beautiful dress using a fine purple linen. That was more than enough payment, even though Ella could not think of when she'd ever get to wear such a gown. She was still excited at the thought of such a gift, so sent her away with extra balm and tea.

Hans and Magda, the city bakers, were lovely too. They both suffered badly from a burning feeling in their chest that worsened when they lay down. Their laughs were as big as their bellies, their silver hair matched the patches of white flour speckled on their clothes. She gave them a mixture of fennel seeds and marshmallow root to drink as a tea at lunch and with dinner. They gave her a cake with almond and dried fruit, vowing the same each month if her remedies worked well.

Johann, the town clerk, rolled up his sleeves to show her his red welted arms. His skin was itchy, he informed her it was a condition that had plagued him for years. She prepared him a balm of chickweed with calendula, and herbal tincture of milk thistle. He paid her one gulden and came back a week later with his son. He showed her his skin, already so much smoother after just seven days of treatment and could not thank her enough for what she had done.

His son was a very different case. Harvey was a slender boy, much shorter for his age than he should have been, his skin a pale grey rather than healthy pink. She checked his gums and saw signs of recent bleeding. She listened to his chest, which sounded weak rather than damp. She could not tell exactly what was wrong with him but knew there was not a lot she could do. He was a sickly child, his constitution poor. She made small talk with Harvey and then asked Johann to step outside with her.

"Johann, your son…" she trailed off. "I have not seen anything like this before. I am not sure there is much I can do to help. Have you consulted the physician in town?"

Johann scratched at his cheek and scuffed his boot on the smooth stone at her doorstep. "Ah, no." He pursed his lips and clicked his tongue before continuing. "I went to see the good Doctor about my skin some time ago, but he drew great volumes of blood from me, and gave me a bitter tonic that made my bowels loose for several days." His cheeks flushed and he cleared his throat. "It left me in bed for the better part of a week but did nothing to help my condition. I worry that kind of treatment may be too much for Harvey, he is already so weak."

Ella nodded as she hummed her agreeance. "How long has he been like this? So pale?"

The concern on Johann's face increased. He removed his hat and ran his fingers through his thinning hair. "It has been some time now. Perhaps a year, maybe a few months more." He fiddled with the rim of his hat.

She chewed at her bottom lip. "His gums, they are weak and bleeding. Does he have trouble eating?"

"He used to have a good appetite, but now, he hardly eats a thing. He is tired most of the time, and he gets nose bleeds. He says his head aches often, and he gets fevers sometimes. More often he feels the cold terribly." He sniffed softly. "Are you sure there is nothing you can do?"

She felt it prudent to be honest with him. "I have not seen a child like this before. It is like the life has already left him, but not from a fever. I would hate to give you false promises."

Johann's face dropped. "There must be something you can do?"

She thought for a moment. "I can give him some herbs to warm his blood and help ward off sickness, but I don't know if they will do much good." She reached for Johann's hand, patting it gently.

Tears welled in his eyes. Johann nodded lightly and placed his hat back on his head. "I was worried you might say as much." He wiped at his nose with his sleeve. "Thank you for being truthful with me. I have taken Harvey to a few cunning men that took my money and gave empty blessings, but that never helped."

"Ah yes, cunning men, I have heard of them in the villages not too far from here." She shook her head, her heart aching for the poor man. The evil of some people, to take advantage of such a tragic situation.

"Could you at least give me those herbs to try, if that won't make him any worse?"

She prepared Harvey a tincture of ginger and echinacea, and instructions to eat a lot of meat and vegetables. There was only so much she could do for a child with naturally poor health like Harvey, and Johann seemed to appreciate what she was offering. She refused to take any payment; what she was giving would not make Harvey sicker but may not be of any benefit either.

She saw many for more regular cases: difficulties sleeping and feelings of sadness, tiredness was common too. There was even one woman who blatantly informed Ella that her husband was unable to perform – right in front of him – much to his embarrassment. She treated them all with kind respect, and they paid her what they could.

There were also some irregular cases. It took her by surprise, on more than a few occasions, what some visitors thought she would be able to assist with. There were those who came asking her for amulets or tokens to ward off evil. She was under no illusion as to what her remedies could help with physically, compared to what faith was better equipped to help with spiritually. There were those with strange beliefs that sought her advice on even the most personal of matters or asked her to rid them of bad luck. Odd what some people thought her herbs were apt to conjure. There were even couples who sought her help to fix their marriage. As if a rhyme or jumble of words could change fate, or the minds of others! Why would they think she was capable of casting such spells? That erred too close to magic, and sorcery was forbidden by their religion, she would have no part in it, and did not believe in blessings given by anyone other than her pastor.

She'd suffered so much loss before her memories even formed to think a wish or totem held anything more than empty promises. She counselled these people with hesitation, instructing them to seek guidance from the church instead. With a man as bitter as their town pastor, however, she should not have been surprised her welcoming nature must have been so much more inviting.

A chill ran down her spine at the thought. Whatever would he think of his flock straying so far from his grace, and what would he do if he found out it was her they were running to?

Ernest watched the townspeople come and go with a silent tension growing inside. He always sensed a time like this may one day come and started regretting his decision to teach Ella their healing ways. When he had first moved out to the country, he had picked plants and brewed tinctures only as they were needed to help the local villagers. As Ella grew, and her skills seemed natural, he had taught her everything he knew. Now she was even more gifted, and better at treating others, than he had ever been. He felt safe helping the people of the hinterland, they had never regarded what he did with superstition like when he had lived in town. He had seen no harm in Ella continuing in the tradition, until now, since word had spread so widely and so many strangers had come to visit.

He was sitting on a crate in the packing shed, a beam of late summer's sun warm through the window. He was needing to sneak away from the orchard more often these days to take a brief rest. His chest felt tight on occasion, his breathing short at times. At least with so many visitors, Ella was too busy to notice. He did not want to mention anything to her, did not want her to worry. He consoled himself knowing she had Tomas to care for her should anything happen to him.

He ambled over to the long bench, scouring the many boxes of herbal tinctures Ella had prepared and stored beneath. His eyes rested on a tag with a picture of hawthorn berries, knowing they were good for the heart. He reached for the bottle, uncapped it, and took a small swig before sealing it again tightly. He would sneak it inside, put it next to his bed, and start taking it regularly. That should ease the pain.

He came back to sit in the sun, kneeling forward to rummage through his toolbox slowly, as he did not want to anger the ache in his chest that had just settled. It was just a few moments before he found what he was searching for: a carved box, his fingers graced the top almost reverently. He pulled out the pouch inside and then the knife from within, its blade glinting in a ray of light. He unscrewed the base, a boar tusk with his delicate engravings, and poured out two small beads it contained. He examined them closely, a smile playing on his lips as he recognised the clay ladybugs Leyna had once made. He let them roll in his palm for a moment, his heart initially warm from the memory. How proud she would be of the woman Ella had become. If she were here, she would tell him not to worry, that Ella could handle herself and was happiest, like she had been, when helping and healing others.

But that was the problem, she never heeded his warnings, and now Ella was exposed to the same kind of risks. He saw more of Leyna in Ella every day, and that was what worried him the most. He huffed; his jaw clenched. How he wished he'd done more to protect his precious Leyna. He should have yelled on the bridge that day, he should have ordered them to stop. His eyes welled with tears, and he forced himself to slow his breathing, the ache in his chest brewing as he relived the pain of losing Leyna. He'd never forgiven himself for not speaking out all those years ago, but then, if he had, where would Ella be today?

He exhaled deeply, then kissed the ladybugs in his palm and placed them ever so carefully back inside the handle, screwing it on to the knife to keep the memories protected. He put the blade in its pouch, inside the box, and then back into the base of the tool chest. He had tried so hard to protect Ella from what could be such a horrible world out there, raising her in the country so they could enjoy a peaceful life with locals they called friends. Any one of these strangers could bring with them the type of danger, an accusation even, that could not be easily resolved. Even though it had been many years since he had been to the town, he remembered all too well the type of irrational punishments they used in the city.

Everyone in the region knew about his aunt's confession and conviction, the fate of a witch was common knowledge. Only the elders in town would possibly remember Leyna though. Since she had drowned at the dunking, she was considered innocent, and the events that led to her death never mentioned again. He tried to shield Ella from the pain of knowing more about it, because it never needed to be shared. Let Ella hold on to only happy stories about the mama she had never known. It was an untimely death caused by the town mayor of the time, and that even more ridiculous pastor. The mayor had passed many years ago, but the pastor of the town still lived. Growing older and more bitter with time, he never took the blame for the death of Leyna as he should have.

With so many visitors of late, Ernest worried how long it would be before Ella may come under the scrutiny of the hierarchy in town, as had happened to his aunt and daughter. Everything Ella was doing seemed so innocent right now, but his concern grew as to what her help, and the ever-spreading word of her abilities, may lead to.

He shook his head, his troubling thoughts circulating once more, the unending loop of what he should have done, knowing that it could have been worse, whirred around faster and faster until he forced his mind to stop. He placed his hand over his heart; no good could come from dwelling on the past.

Better to get back to the apples and keep his eyes on Ella. She was his world, and so long as he drew breath, he'd make sure she would not suffer the same fate as Leyna.

🐝 🐝 🐝

A few weeks later at Church, the pastor stepped up to the pulpit and surveyed his congregation with a grave face. "People of Detwang and our surrounding hinterland, I have some concerning news that I sadly bring to you today." The villagers glanced hesitantly at each other, a humming buzz like bees already building. "I have been informed of some unfortunate events in Wurzburg." He gripped the pulpit as he spoke, openly struggling with what he needed to share with his community.

"Two weeks ago, a young lady of their town was accused of being a witch after an altercation with a soldier." The pastor watched as the elders nodded in agreement. "Under interrogation, she admitted to making a pact with the devil, and named five others of the town as her accomplices. They were all taken into custody and, on questioning, admitted they were guilty of witchcraft too.

"The accused confessed to midnight gatherings, pacts with the devil, riding horses to exhaustion and drying up milk from the cows. There have been many cattle losses in that area, and the group took full responsibility." He paused for a moment, bending his head forward and shaking it in sorrow. The gathering started to talk amongst themselves. "All six were burnt at the stake this past week. A most horrible way to go." His eyes grew moist with tears, he covered them with one hand momentarily and took a few deep breaths. "Even if they were guilty, we must remember we are all children of God. We should look instead at how they were tempted so far from grace, such that we can protect our communities from that sort of inhuman desire." He again remained silent for some time as he boldly fought to compose himself.

Ernest sat in the congregation, the anger he had buried sixteen years ago threatening to resurface. He thought of his aunt and his daughter, who went through similar trials and accusations, knowing they made no such pacts with the devil. He doubted these people from Wurzburg had any conversation with the devil too, yet it had not mattered for them either. Once accused, there was little you could do to clear your name and walk away free. To be named a witch was equivalent to a death sentence, no matter the truth or outcome of a trial. Tears welled in his eyes, he dabbed at them with a handkerchief, pretending to blow his nose.

"I find myself in a difficult place, having to inform you of this. But I also want to deliver an important warning." He made eye contact with random members of the crowd as he spoke. "I know you all have your superstitions, and I caution you from letting them take hold of your better judgement, they'll only muddle your mind. There are some of you who may gather without due ceremony, and I urge you to take caution that others, outside our village, may consider that chanting or honouring a false god. Save your prayers for your dinner tables, your bedsides and our Church. Any meetings you have, be aware that others may be watching, waiting, to see if our village and lands have been infected too.

"Be careful with seeking out amulets for luck or false protection, or blessings to that effect, as it is often the conjuring of those who would rob you of your gulden, instead of rid you of your sins or bad luck. All of these practices and beliefs only show your faith is not strong enough in God, that

He is not almighty enough to grant you the protection you desire. There are some who seek help and advice from those trained to give it, as well as those who are not." His gaze settled on Ella.

Ernest felt his chest tighten. There it was again, the pain, the shortness of breath. He wondered if it was from the mounting tension of the town's visitors, or his advancing age. Perhaps it was a bit of both. He tried to focus on the pastor's sermon as he inhaled deeply and waited for the discomfort to ease.

"We must make sure we protect the members of our village whose ways may be incorrectly scrutinized by others hoping to gain power or control over our freedom and liberties." He raised his eyes, taking in the broader gathering. "Let us now make peace with each other and be there for our brothers and sisters in these troubled times, amen." He bowed his head in silence, ending his sermon abruptly.

The gathering repeated 'amen' and dispersed from the church, the gossiping having started before many had even left their pews.

🐝 🐝 🐝

"I heard she had red hair."

"I heard they flew at night."

"I heard they come to you in your dreams."

The pastor wandered amongst the crowd, shaking his head, hearing the rumours build, grow, take a life of their own. It was always the way with these sorts of things – people's superstitions and fears always won out over common sense. People were so ready to believe in a supernatural force of evil, as if fear compelled them to stray from the word of the Lord. He sought out Ernest and Ella, standing at the fringe of the crowd. Ernest's voice floated over the din, a discussion about crops and yields with other farmers, and the pastor tried in vain to catch his eye.

He did, however, manage to draw Tomas' attention, who was standing with the group, before breaking away to join him. "Pastor, I was wondering if I could have a word with you, ask you to write me a letter to the mayor?"

"Yes, my child." He leaned in close and spoke quietly, so their conversation became private. "Actually, I need to have a word with Ernest and Ella after everyone has gone as well."

"Of course." Tomas agreed, whispering in reply, "should I be worried?"

The pastor swivelled to his left and then his right slowly, waving to the locals whilst checking that no one loitered close by. He gazed up at the sky, pointing at the clouds and rocking on his feet, to make it seem like their conversation was about nothing more important than the weather. He leaned in again, speaking into Tomas' shoulder. "There have been murmurs coming from the town." He stepped back, slapping Tomas heartily on the back with one hand, and shaking Tomas' right hand with the other. He made his voice audible to more than just those nearest to him. "I look forward to meeting with you later, for this letter to the mayor. Should we be excited as to what it might contain?" He swivelled his head to the locals, raising his eyebrows and smiling broadly to ensure several people had caught his words.

This had the desired effect, setting the rumour mills alight with much happier news. Locals stopped discussing the witches and started muttering about Tomas and Ella instead. Mumblings of, "it's about time," and, "I wonder if a little one is on the way," rippled through the crowd like wind blowing across water. The pastor smiled to himself. Their visit to his office would not cause further discussion now.

It had taken some time for the villagers to disperse with so much to discuss. Tomas, Ella and Ernest gathered in the rectory located behind the church. It was a modestly furnished room with a basic wooden bookshelf and chairs, but it was small, such that when the pastor entered, there was not space for another person. He sat behind his desk, interlocking his fingers.

"Thank you for coming to see me today. I want you to know you are in a welcoming and safe place with me."

The group nodded. Ella's hands rested apprehensively within her lap while the men sat fiddling with their hats.

"I have asked you here, as there have been some people in town that do not agree with Ella's treatments."

The trio sat quietly on the other side of the desk for a moment before Ernest commented. "Ella has told me of most of the visits, I believe she has acted appropriately."

Ella bobbed her head in agreement but remained silent.

The pastor mumbled his consensus. "I am sure she has, we in this village know Ella always does well. But there are some in the city that are, perhaps, fixated on more scientific approaches, and do not approve of the business coming to the country. It contradicts what they are trying to achieve. While Ella's ways appear to be more effective, it suggests that the work of a country girl is more powerful than what the university teaches. That not only undermines the learnings of those far more educated, but also the council's decision to adopt Galenic medicine as a way of moving forward."

Ella glanced over to her opa, as he cleared his throat. "So, what would you have us do? Refuse those who seek her help?"

"It is not my place to suggest that any of my flock should turn away those in need, especially when assistance can be provided." He shuffled some papers on his desk, tucking them under his bible, and moving the whole pile to the left. "I suppose what I'm really saying is to be careful. Be sure of what you are doing, do not give them any room to suggest that you are making false claims or promises. Be especially wary of those seeking answers you cannot provide, and stay away from those that think your services extend beyond the use of herbs for the betterment of health."

Ella nodded, her eyes bright. "I have seen some of the people you speak of, Pastor. I have told them I am not able to assist with those sorts of matters. If they ask for a blessing, I refer them to their church. I understand what you mean." She leant forward in her chair. "May I enquire, from whom have you heard these rumours?"

He seemed at first somewhat hesitant to say. They waited quietly for a few minutes before he spoke. "You are aware of the pastor from Rothenburg?"

Ernest's face reddened. "That old crone. Why can't he just leave us alone?"

Ella's gaze shifted down to her hands, her voice sad. "He has never liked me. I don't know why." She lifted her face back up to the pastor. "But I am sending these strange requests to see him for counsel. Can he not see I am trying to support the teachings of the Lord when asked for blessings or charms?"

The pastor shrugged, his palms faced the ceiling. "There is no controlling the thoughts of others," he offered as an explanation.

Ella thought on this for a moment. "Well, I will just have to be more careful with the people that ask for what I cannot provide."

He tipped his head from side to side as if mulling this over. "Mmm, yes, there are some that make their superstitions obvious, of them you have grown wise to recognise. But people do what people are prone to, and that is, talk. For many, each time they speak of a matter it grows bigger and more important than it was before. It is not only those who make their objectives known to you that you will need to be mindful of, but in fact all of those who visit you."

She frowned. "Surely not everyone?"

"Unfortunately, yes." He leaned back in his chair, resting his hands on its arms. "I heard of a boy, barely six years old, that accused his mother of flying to him in a dream and taking him around to taverns, stealing their wine barrels. He told this story to another child, who in turn told his mother, who reported it to their council. It happened in Oberstetten. The woman was taken into custody and interrogated under some force, I do believe, and this all happened on the word of her six-year-old son."

Ella's eyes grew wide, she gasped. "Was there something wrong with that child? It was merely a dream."

He leaned forward, steepling his fingers and resting them on his desk. "That is my point, Ella. There are some who are so caught up by their fears and misbeliefs that all sense and reason abandon them. If a boy of six can speak of a dream that lands his mother in gaol for questioning, a farmgirl offering herbs to heal the sick can land in hotter water from a disgruntled old pastor."

Ella caught her breath as his words sunk in. She raised her hand to her mouth, shaking her head slowly, turning to Ernest for support. She watched as he clenched his fists, his hands resting on his knees. His face grew hard, she could sense the fury he was holding in.

The pastor continued. His message had hit hard as a warning. "You cannot stop these townspeople from coming to see you, Ella, but you can practice more caution. Do not give them room to find fault in what you do, and never charge them more than you would be willing to pay for the service you provide."

The group sat quietly for a moment. Ernest placed his hand on Ella's arm and turned to her, his eyes misty. "Our pastor is a kind and clever man. He is only trying to protect you. Perhaps we keep you away from some of these townspeople. Maybe you should only continue to treat those who have already been to visit."

Ella sat there, stunned into silence, then nodded slowly. "It will be hard for me to turn people away. When I treat others, it makes me happy inside; I'm loved and needed. It's only ever been Opa and I, so it's nice to be needed by others. I feel that I was born to this role, to help others, just as much as you were born to be a man of faith." She shifted her gaze from the pastor to her grandfather. "Opa, you are wise, you can see the truth in people far better than I. Maybe you should greet those who come to visit first, and only permit those you think are of a good nature to seek my help. I can tend the trees at the back of the field or keep to the packing shed when we see townspeople approaching."

The pastor nodded sagely. "I think this would bode well for all." His face softened as he spoke to Ella. "If you are careful in this way, you will still be helping those who are truly in need and deserve your special abilities." He leant over to a drawer and retrieved some paper. "Now, I believe you have come here to ask me to write a letter to Mayor Schulz?"

He smiled as he dipped his quill in some ink. "May I enquire as to the nature of this letter?"

Ella beamed as Tomas grasped her hand, the mood in the room became suddenly joyful. "I have asked Ella to be my wife, and Ernest has agreed. I would ask that you please write a letter to the mayor, seeking an audience with him to grant us permission."

"This is much happier news." The pastor started writing, then paused, one eyebrow raised at the happy couple. "May I ask if there is an urgency to this union?"

Ella's cheeks grew hot as she dropped her eyes quickly to her lap.

Tomas replied, "no Pastor, in fact, given our lengthy courtship, we want to wait until next spring, or even summer to wed, so as not to give the village any extra fodder on which to gossip. They already whisper about us enough, I want to make sure they know there is no rush." Tomas reached for her hand and brought it to his lips for a brief kiss.

The pastor let out the breath he was holding. "Wonderful news indeed. I shall finish writing this letter for you today, and make sure it is on its way to Mayor Schulz tomorrow." He rose from his chair, prompting Ella and the others to join him. They gathered at the door, the pastor shaking the men's hands and bowing his head to Ella as they passed. She curtsied politely as he clasped her hand in his. "Thank you for meeting with me and being so open to discussion. Now go, enjoy the sabbath, I hear you have quite the crop to attend to."

It was only a few more days before the pastors' warnings rang true. A most conspicuous couple arrived on an old cart pulled by a small horse. She was a rather round and haughty woman, her hair tied back in an untidy bun that was barely contained within her coif. He was a frail man who hardly filled out his tall frame. She had large, poorly mended patches in her skirt, while the man's shirt was almost threadbare. Her mannerisms did not match with their appearance, it was abundantly clear she thought more of herself than her drab standard of dress would suggest. Ernest grew wary the moment he saw them. He stopped picking and climbed down from his ladder to greet them at the gate as he did not want them near Ella, or even to set foot on his property. He had no time to warn her or have her hide in the packing shed as they had planned, so he silently hoped that she had seen this couple arrive and stayed out of sight.

The woman dismounted with great difficulty, making quite a fuss, no doubt to gain attention. The pair walked up to the gate, arriving just as Ernest did on the other side. "We have come to see Ella Baumann," the woman demanded. She clasped her hands beneath her drooping bosom and sighed discontentedly.

"She is not here at the moment. Is there something I can help you with?"

"Unless you can conjure up a spell to help my husband return to work, I think not." The woman shrugged, clearly unconcerned about broadcasting their private problems to a stranger. "We have been most unfortunate of late. I have been told on good accord, that for a fee, Ella could help rid us of some bad fortune. I have an amulet here." She fumbled to remove a necklace from around her neck, squeezed between her breasts. It had a boar tooth on it; Ernest watched as she unscrewed the top to show that it was hollow inside. "I need her to give us a token for me to place inside this tusk, and a blessing to bring us good luck."

"I am sorry, Ella cannot help with those sorts of things." He shook his head and started back up the hill.

"Can you give us some mandrake at least?" she called after him, scrambling along the fence line. "To help my husband, you know…" She was beginning to sound frustrated, even desperate.

"Frau, I do not pretend to know much about these things." He swivelled back to face her but did not go any closer. "However, I do know that mandrake can be a dangerous root indeed. It is not something Ella would use. Her remedies are much more gently enticing." He pivoted again, making his way back toward the trees. "I bid you good day, Frau," he called over his shoulder, waving his hand as he left.

The woman raised her voice, clearly annoyed now. "We were assured these were things Ella could help us with. You come back here at once, or else I shall have to report what I have heard to the council."

Ernest halted in his tracks. He turned on his heels to face her again.

"That's right," she nodded, speaking with an air of superiority, bringing her puffy hands to her rounded hips. "I shall also let them know that you charged me good coin for bad magic. Now find that girl and bring her to me."

Ernest removed his hat and studied it, chewing on his lip, then stared at the woman and stroked his beard for a moment. He was about to put her in her place, then thought better of it, replacing his hat, waving her away and continued back through the orchard.

"If you won't get that girl to help rid us of our bad luck, then I shall curse you and your field with the same," she spat out, before letting off a stream of profanities.

Ernest kept walking, hoping Ella had kept out of sight. The woman was making enough noise for their neighbours to come outside and see what the commotion was about. As he neared the trees, he glimpsed the toe of a boot beneath a large shrub of lavender. He smiled and busied himself with picking apples just above Ella's hidden crouched form, to completely shield her from view.

Eventually the woman left. The cart rolled away slowly as the horse struggled with the weight of its passengers.

"I do not think even mandrake would be effective if you were married to a woman like that," chuckled Ernest, making Ella smile. "Now off you go, back to your picking. It's getting late in the season."

Ella stood, brushing herself off. "Yes Opa, thank you. I would not have liked to have met with her." She headed back to her earlier position in the orchard, and Ernest retreated to his.

The autumn cold was arriving early, and he could not help but shiver at the change of season and turn of events.

Chapter 7

*Men cannot do without women. Even if it were possible for men to beget
and bear children, they still could not do without women. – Martin Luther*

Conrad busied himself learning the ways of the town council, which
would see him work his way toward a senior position in due course. He was
first put in charge of checking the town ledgers and scheduling the mayor's
appointments. Within a decade, he would sit righteously as the next mayor,
having earnt his place through family position and commitment, and
preferring Rothenburg ob der Tauber to his birthplace Munich any day.
While being related was no guarantee, the experience he would gain and the
connections he could grow over time would see him seated as mayor when
the time came, he just knew it. His opportunities in Munich would never
reach this high, his father being just one of the many councilmen of that area.

He received letters calling for appointments with the mayor daily. One
of his tasks was to go through all these requests, grant those worth an
audience permission and schedule it in, and deny, gracefully, the ones that
were not. He was only in this role a week when he received a letter from the
Detwang pastor who penned correspondence for the locals, since most of
them were not able to read or write for themselves. This particular letter
requested a meeting with the mayor for a young Tomas Wolff seeking
permission to marry Ella Baumann. He screwed the letter up into a ball and
threw it in the nearest bin. That request would go unanswered. He would
simply let them wonder for some time why there was never a reply… letters
were known to get lost or misplaced all the time.

The next week, however, came a similar letter with the same request. This time Conrad made sure it was denied, penning a response that the mayor was currently attending to more important local matters and the villagers should focus on their harvesting duties. Two weeks later he received another letter of request, and when that was denied too, he received yet another two weeks later again. Each he denied in a polite but non-descript way, preventing the audience with the mayor and any possibility of an approval. This Tomas Wolff would not get his chance to win the mayor's permission for Ella's hand in marriage before he'd had his.

Conrad stayed true to the promise he had made his uncle, being socially active at all required events and making an effort to meet with many fine women of the town. He stayed discreet, as requested, cavorting with a few of the local girls on occasion, and Louise all too often. Even though he found her quite boring and self-important, she knew how to please him in the bedroom, so he continued meeting with her despite his better judgement. A man of his age and position had needs which were eagerly fulfilled by girls seeking status from a comfortable marriage. How foolish they were to think that opening their legs was a doorway to his heart, with so much choice around. He would need to start being careful with Louise nevertheless, as her father was an important council member. She was also a bit too friendly with his Aunt Katherine for his liking, so would not be one that could easily be dispensed if she were to find herself in a delicate position. While she was keen to frequent his bed quite regularly, he did not want her thinking she was assured a permanent place there. There were many times where he would lie with Louise and wish it were Ella instead.

He opened his diary on a Monday, late in September. He had circled it and written 'Ella' beside the date, marking the two months he had promised his uncle that he would wait, before approaching the subject of courting her again. Not a day had gone by where he did not think of her and wonder what she was doing. He often found himself daydreaming of the moment when he first sat watching her from the carriage, picking apples, the sunlight framing her angelically. The absence from her had made him more excited about seeing her again, and now his uncle had no grounds to refuse him.

He hurried down the hall to his uncle's chambers where they could talk in private, knocking at the door as he opened it, impatient to have the conversation. "Uncle, good day." He bound into the room, barely pausing to bow. "It is nearing October, which means it has been two months."

"Ha-ha my boy, it's been thirty-six years for me." Carl raised his eyes briefly when Conrad entered, then hastily returned his attention to what he was writing.

"I mean, it has been two months since I came back from meeting Ella, and now I would like your permission to court her publicly. You asked me to wait two months, and I have."

"I also asked you to find a nice town girl." He put his quill down and gave Conrad a once over. "Haven't you been courting Hugo's daughter, the prissy one. What was her name?"

"Louise. Yes, I have seen her once or twice." The lie slipped from his tongue all too easily. It had been far more often than that, but if his uncle thought it was rare then he was proud of his deceit. "I am not serious about her. She has been someone to fill time in with, nothing more."

"I hope you have been discreet?"

"Yes, Uncle." He smirked at the thought. What they did together could never be described as discreet. "But now I'd like to see Ella."

"There really is no other girl in town that you would rather?"

Conrad shook his head and waited silently for his uncle's approval.

Carl interlaced his fingers and chewed on his bottom lip, then eventually nodded. "Very well. You have done as I asked, so you must have lasting feelings for her. It is Katherine's twenty-fifth birthday next week, and I am hosting a dinner party in her honour. Go visit the orchard tomorrow and ask Ella to attend, as our guest. Let us see how she behaves in town for a few days, if her feelings for you are reciprocated, and if she is worthy."

Conrad smiled broadly. "Thank you, Uncle." He bowed deeply, darting out the room rapidly to organise the carriage.

It had taken them a full two months, but the harvesting was finally complete; it would soon be time to start preserving. The elders of the village had predicted this would be a particularly cold and long winter, so Ella wanted to be ready early, in case they became stuck inside their cottage for weeks on end.

She was busy in the garden, her hands full of herbs, readying some extracts and drying others for use in teas. Today she was preparing tinctures of thyme, great for sore throats and coughing, and sage, ideal for a range of digestive issues, which she had found incredibly common amongst the wealthier townspeople. Tomorrow she would start brewing some saw palmetto, a tried-and-true remedy for men both young and old, and was hoping the weather would hold out for her to trek through the back fields, beyond the village, to collect some milk thistle the day after that. It was good for those who drank too much. She grinned, thinking how common a past time that was for many of the locals and townspeople as well. Enjoying wine and beer in copious quantities was at least something all classes seemed to have in common. She had checked the sky earlier, there were wisps of clouds in a rippled pattern, somewhat like fish scales, indicating rain would be coming in a few days. So far, however, there were no heavy or dark clouds on the horizon that would suggest wet weather was more imminent. She was looking forward to the hike, as Tomas would be going with her to help collect some herbs and try his luck at catching a hare. Ella was keen to spend time alone with Tomas, away from prying ears and eyes, so they could just be themselves, and talk about their future.

She had two large pots atop the bench in the packing shed and a fire was crackling steadily in the stove, warming the space as she worked. This stage of brewing started with pre-crushing the herbs to release their juices, then adding the herbs to a pot filled with a strong alcohol base. It was then covered and stored for a month, stirred occasionally in that time, and the liquid strained off into bottles for storage. She had picked thyme and sage to work on that day, as they were both particularly pungent; might as well get the stronger smells out of the way at the same time.

It was on one of the many trips between the packing shed and her herb garden when she saw it, causing a chill to run down her spine and goosebumps to bristle on her arms. On top of the roof, in broad daylight, was an owl - it was an omen of bad luck to see one during the day. She paused, checking around her warily. A cold wind blew, the goats bleated in the orchard, but it was otherwise silent, nothing else seemed out of place. Her grip on the herb basket tightened, and she took a few steadying breaths to calm the anxiety that bubbled in her belly.

She returned to her work, picking more herbs, trying to keep her mind busy. She headed back into the shed, crushed the herbs, and added them to her waiting pots, having all but forgotten about the omen when she heard knocking on the door of the shed.

She spun around quickly to see Conrad standing in the door frame.

"Oh my, you startled me." She jumped and put her hand to her chest. He was dressed far too well for a trip to the country, in a dark brown quilted doublet and cape, with a long feather tucked into the side of his felt hat. His dark blonde hair sat in neat waves beneath, short enough to tuck into his outlandishly large collar, which was starched to stand up and out, half folded. He had a moustache and beard that ended at the corners of his mouth, his cheeks were clean shaven.

"Ella, how I've yearned to see you again." He rushed over beside her and grasped her hand.

She withdrew it nervously, "I-I am sorry, Herr Sauer, I did not realise you would be visiting today."

He leant in beside her, his hand resting on her shoulder, his breath warm on her face. "Call me Conrad, please."

She nodded her ascent. Her cheeks grew hot at his touch, her pulse quickened.

"What are you doing today? I was wondering if you would like to go for another wander around your orchard?"

She stepped back from him and motioned to the many herbs on the bench, and pots she was preparing. "I'm afraid I am far too busy for that." She smiled politely, "I do not want to appear rude, but I really do not have the spare time to just go for a stroll. I'm preparing some herbs for bottling, and I have more to filter and pour off yet." She blinked rapidly as her heart started beating faster.

He stepped closer to her again, resting a finger under her chin, lifting her face to meet his. "Well, I come with some great news. It is Aunt

Katherine's twenty-fifth birthday this weekend, and I have been asked to come out here and invite you to attend."

Ella's thoughts buzzed. A town party! How often would an invitation such as this present itself? Her eyelashes fluttered as she brought a hand to her forehead, finding some loose hairs and tucking them behind her ear. "Why, thank you, but I have no way of getting there."

Conrad persisted, smiling broadly. "That's alright, I have my uncle's carriage. Aunt Katherine insisted that you come. Not just for the evening, but stay for a few days in town, see how you like it."

Ella paused. She had never been to town before and was fascinated no end by the folk who frequented the farm. "Well, it would be nice to see Clare again, and Frau Schulz," she admitted. "How many nights is she asking me to stay? I really must get back next week to start preserving the apples and make applesauce. There are still a few weeks work in all of that." Whatever would Tomas think if he saw her standing here like this with another man, so close?

"I'll be here on Friday to pick you up, and I can have you back on Sunday afternoon." He grinned and winked at her as he added sarcastically, "my uncle was very insistent that your applesauce should not be affected by a party."

She smirked, almost flirtatiously, then checked herself for behaving so. "Trust me, it will be here waiting for me no matter what. But yes, I would love to go. I will have to check with my opa." She wiped her hands on her apron.

He rubbed her arm affectionately and gazed deep into her eyes. "I can ask him for you, as the message did come from the mayor and his wife directly, so I am sure he will agree. You did save their baby, after all."

"Thank you, Conrad." She gave a shallow curtsy. "Please thank Frau Schulz. I look forward to seeing her and baby Clare on Friday."

"I look forward to seeing you on Friday." He reached for her hand and brought it to his lips.

He was quite an attractive man, she had never noticed the blue of his eyes like this before. She caught her breath and pulled her hand away. "I'm sorry, I am, um..." Unable to say she was engaged without the mayor's approval, she struggled to find the right words readily. "I am spoken for," she explained courteously, as she clasped her hands in front of her dress.

"Oh, I see." He tipped his head to her considerately, holding his hat in place along with that ridiculous feather, and paced back toward the door. "Friday then."

She watched him leave before returning to her work. She had never been to town, so might as well enjoy it for what it was worth. At least if she went, she could ask the mayor for an audience with Tomas directly. But first, she had her duties to attend to, and since that now meant a lot of extra visitors and people to care for, she really needed to focus on brewing and bottling more herbs in preparation for the coming cold season.

She continued working away until the day gave way to dusk, the light dimming through the packing shed windows, a sign that night was fast approaching. She tidied up her bench and pulled the packing shed door behind her before heading toward the cottage to make dinner and work on some mending. At least with a short trip into town, she would get a break from these never-ending chores.

Two days later Ella pulled out her heavy winter coat and boots. It was a cold, windy day for late September, and she needed to get to the back fields while the weather still held out. It would be raining later, she could sense the heavy damp in the air, but it was already getting late in the season to be picking the milk thistle, so could not be put off any longer. She had not had time to get out earlier, not with all the visitors and extra brewing she had needed to do to keep up with demand. Still, it was a hardy plant, and it was the seeds of the flowers as well as the leaves and stems she was after, so there was sure to be plenty to collect.

She packed her biggest basket with bread, smoked fish, apples and some pickled cabbage and peppers, along with her pruning shears and gloves, and headed over to Tomas's house. She knocked on the door, bobbing on the spot to keep warm. It was certainly chilling off fast.

The door opened promptly. "Tomas, Ella is here," called Julia, welcoming Ella inside. She enveloped her in a warm hug. "There may be rain later, I hope you won't be out too long?"

"We'll be more than half the day, we need to make the trip worth it. I'll keep my eye on the weather though, it should be dry until late in the afternoon. I have my winter coat and boots," she explained, knowing Tomas' mother worried after her as if she were one of her own.

"Hey beautiful, so good to see you." Tomas came over to her, kissing her lightly on the cheek and squeezing her hand. "Let me just grab my coat and the traps."

"Here," said Julia, reaching for a clay pot. "Take some beer, it will at least warm your insides." She passed it to Ella who took it gladly.

"Thank you. We'll see if we can catch a hare today, maybe keep that fire going for a roast tonight?"

"Can I come?" Sarah came rushing into the room, hugging Ella around her waist and gazing up at her pleadingly.

"Not today, Sarah, it is too cold." She could see Sarah's disappointment, but she had her heart set on spending the day alone with Tomas.

Sarah pouted. "But I've come with you on other trips."

"I need you to dig up some vegetables and get them ready for our roast. If we don't manage to catch a hare, at least we could enjoy some vegetables tonight." She reached down to straighten Sarah's cap.

"Not fair. I'll only let you go if you bring me back a present." Sarah stomped her foot and folded her arms.

"We'll see, shall we?" She was uncertain of what she would be able to find, it was too late for blackberries or cherries, perhaps she could find some flowers for them to press.

"Don't be such a brat," said Tomas as he strode back in, large traps slung over his shoulder. He was wearing a thick calf-skin coat lined with sheep's wool, underneath he wore a knitted woollen sweater.

"Oh, Tomas, I like your jacket, I may need to borrow that today." Ella rubbed her hand along his sleeve.

Julia grinned. "Why thank you, Ella, I will see what I can find to make you one similar. Maybe show you how?" Julia did not work the farm, her hands were full raising the children, making what clothing she could, and keeping them all fed. "Well, off you go, the weather is not going to hold off forever. Good luck today you two, be careful." She kissed them both on each of their cheeks.

They passed through the gate at the far corner of Tomas' farm and ventured out through the fields beyond. Wild grasses free to grow tall blocked the wind, making the trek much warmer, until they came to the edges of the field where it met the forest. Tomas set his traps at the natural border that formed where the grass thinned out – only four – as they were quite heavy to carry. He bashed the sizeable pin into the ground and pulled the trap open, its iron jaws made bare, then covered the chain and metal brace carefully with loose dirt. Ella cut apples into slices, which he placed just inside the trap as bait. They laid their traps randomly at the rim of the forest, then started searching for some milk thistle and what else may be around.

"So, what exactly are we looking for?" he asked. He had been to the back fields with her before, but she always led the excursion. They usually left earlier in the season when there were all sorts of berries and fruits to gather as well. Sometimes they even went a few times during the warmer months and brought Sarah when the weather was pleasant.

"Over there." She pointed to a particularly wide-spread patch of milk thistle. "That's it." It was a tall plant with a bright purple flower on top and spiky bracts around the base of the flowerhead. The leaves were green with white veins running through them.

"Looks like just another weed to me," he said.

She nudged him on the arm. "That, my dear man, is far more than just another weed." She placed her basket down gently, put on her gloves and grabbed her pruning shears. She marched over to the milk thistle, picking out the sturdiest stems. "See here?" She traced the lines running through the leaves with her finger. "This is why it has its name. It is said this plant is so good for you, that it contains Mary's milk." She cut it with the shears and snapped the stem in front of him, causing a white fluid to ooze out. "It is rich in this liquid, and that is why we are harvesting it." She pointed over to the basket. "I brought Opa's gloves, you will want to put them on. It might look like just a weed, but it's very spiky and will cut your hands as you pick it."

They started harvesting the thicker stems and leaves. "Is this good anymore? It looks a bit wilted." He held up a large head.

"Let me see." She reached for the flower. It was a vibrant purple, but its petals appeared damp and sagging. "It's still useful." She crushed it in her hand, several brown seeds came from inside. "These are great to chew on." She put a few in her mouth and munched. "Mmm, crunchy. They are also really nice brewed as a tea. Here." She handed him a linen pouch. "If you find more, please crush them and collect the seeds in here."

He watched her move, collecting the plants. "How do you remember all of this?"

She winked and flashed him a cheeky grin. "Impressed?" She reached over to another thick stem, clipping it easily. "I don't know, how do you remember when to plant and sow your crops, or how to build fences, or what your pigs need?"

He laughed. "Pigs don't need much, that's for sure." His eyes were glistening. "Really, how do you remember all of this?"

She placed her hand on her hips, her lips curved to one side. "I guess some people are just meant to do certain jobs in their life. This is mine." She bent to collect more stems, speaking over her shoulder, "besides, it is such a good feeling to be able to help people. Please don't think me silly, but when I'm treating others, it keeps the memory of my mama warm in my heart, even though I never knew her. Being a healer like she was, well, I hope I'd be making her proud. I hope I make Opa proud." She gathered the plants into bundles and wrapped thick pieces of twine around them. "When I was a little girl, I would draw the plants when I could, and went with Opa whenever he foraged. He taught me how to grow the herbs and what each was good for. Besides apple farming, it's all I've ever known." She tied a knot and pushed the herbs firmly into her basket, taking out their food to make room for more. "When it's all you have ever known, it's not hard to remember something."

"I suppose." He handed her a bundle he had bound together. "Ella, have I ever told you how amazing you are?" He sauntered over to her, put his arms around her waist and effortlessly lifted her off the ground. "I love you so much, I cannot wait to begin a life with you." He kissed her longingly then placed her back down gently.

Her cheeks flushed. "Well, Tomas, I should bring you out here more often. Seems you have developed quite an appetite." She giggled, her belly full of butterflies. "Should we take a break to eat?" She flattened out some grass, using his large coat as a blanket, then knelt down, spread out the food, and plonked the pot of beer firmly in the middle.

They feasted quietly, protected from the wind by the grass, enjoying the twitter of the birds chirping and the rustle of leaves, feeding each other their lunch and enjoying the ale. They had just finished eating and were enjoying a moment's rest when a loud 'snap' rang out from nearby.

"The trap!" Tomas was on his feet as fast as lightning, racing toward the sound. "Come here, quick," he called out to her. "You should see the size of it, it's huge!"

She raced over to stand beside him, admiring the catch. "Wow, that should give us all a feed!"

He picked up a jagged rock, hitting the struggling hare over the head squarely to put it out of its misery, then unclasped the trap and strung it up on a nearby tree. He cut its throat to bleed it out. "It tastes better if you do this straight away," he explained.

She cringed and gagged. "I think I'll go back to the milk thistle," she said, dashing away in a hurry.

Sometime later, Tomas strode over as she was bundling up another pile of herbs, tucking them into the basket. The traps were hung over his shoulder as he held the hare up as his prize. "One hare as requested for my lady." He placed it on top of the basket, its meat exposed neatly. "I also found these." He held a branch of juicy round berries proudly in his other hand.

Her blood ran cold as she recognised what he was holding. "No!" she screamed, pulling the branch quickly out of his hand and throwing it away, forcing him to nearly drop the traps.

"Woah, what?" His eyes were wide, his mouth open. "They looked so good. I was surprised to see berries out here so late."

"Did you have any?" Her heart raced.

"What?"

"Did you have any? Any of the berries?" She raised her voice, panic boiling in her blood.

"No, beautiful, calm down. They're only berries."

"No, Tomas, they're not only berries." She pointed at the branch she had thrown. "That is deadly nightshade. They are very poisonous. Two of those berries will kill a small child. Ten can easily kill a man." She wiped her forehead to remove the beads of sweat that had formed. "I'm sorry I yelled," she said, slowing her breathing. "They really are deadly. Opa has always warned me against them, he had a bite of one once, he said it made him feel groggy straight away. They look delicious, and they are said to taste quite sweet, like a blueberry, but they kill quickly." She reached out for his hands, inspecting them closely. "Did you get any juice on your hands? You have to be that careful, it can get into cuts and poison that way too."

"No, I just picked the whole branch. Thought it might be a nice surprise." He put the traps down carefully and chuckled. "I won't touch anything out here again without your permission." He held his hands up in mock surrender. "Should I ask you about the mushrooms I found then?" He winked at her and grinned.

"Tomas!" She jumped on him, giggling as she pushed him to the ground and kissed him fiercely. "Don't you ever leave me, you adorable man."

"I don't intend to, my beautiful girl." He held her tight. "But really, there were some good mushrooms over there." He jabbed his thumb over his head, back in the direction from where he had come.

She got to her feet and dusted herself off. "Fine then, let's go take a look, but please don't touch anything unless you know what it is."

He brushed himself off and grabbed his coat and the basket, now full. He picked up the traps, slinging them over his shoulder while she carried the pot, the beer almost gone.

They strolled over to the edge of the forest to where he had found the mushrooms. "These here," she explained as she dug them out. "These are good. They're small and round at the top, the stem is straight and thin, and if you check inside…" She picked one up and broke it open to show him. "The frill is brown. These are safe." They collected as many as they could and wandered on to where another patch of white buds was growing. "These I'm not going to take my chances with." She picked up a stick and used it to push one out of the ground. It had a stalk that bulbed near its base, with a cone shape at the top. She poked at it until it split open to reveal its frill. "See how its white inside?"

He nodded. "Does that mean its poison?"

"Not always," she explained. "But it could be. You also need to avoid any that are orange or red. *If the frill is not brown, leave it in the ground,* is what Opa always says. You could miss out on some good mushrooms that way, but you also won't get sick."

THE INNOCENT WITCH

"I'm all in favour of that." He picked up the basket. "We can't fit any more in here anyway, we might as well head back."

"Yes." She glanced up at the sky, grateful the weather had held out this long. "Thank you so much for helping me today, it's been a lot of fun." She laughed at him lovingly. "You almost killed yourself with some deadly nightshade and poisonous mushrooms, so it's certainly been amusing."

"Well, I learnt not to touch anything in the wild without you letting me first." He grinned. "I love spending time with you beautiful, it's always... eventful."

She nudged him tenderly and they headed home. She had kept a few of the better milk thistle flower heads to press with Sarah when she got back, that should keep her happy. They would be enjoying roast hare and vegetables tonight, perfect with a few sprigs of thyme and rosemary. She thought briefly of her coming trip into town, and how it would take her away from spending time with Tomas. She was not so sure about going now.

If only she could take it back.

Chapter 8

A good tree cannot bring forth evil fruit,
neither can a corrupt tree bring forth good fruit. – Matthew 7:17

Ella twirled around their living room as if she were a princess in the beautiful purple gown Carol, Katherine's seamstress, had made in return for her balms and herbs. "Oh, Opa, this is the finest dress I have ever owned, just look at the stitching." She rushed over to her grandfather, holding a sleeve out for closer inspection.

"Yes dear." He glanced at Tomas and rolled his eyes. "I'll never understand women."

Tomas laughed, grabbing her and spinning her around in a merry dance. "You are so beautiful, Ella. You better be careful with all of those councilmen at the party, I do hope you'll come home to me."

"Oh Tomas, I'm going to miss you terribly. There is no one who could take your place." She gave him a peck on the cheek. "Besides, I'm too in love with this dress to even think about anyone else, including you." She tapped him on the nose and giggled.

"If the sleeves were any puffier, you would need to turn sideways to walk through doors." Ernest raised himself slowly from his seat to replenish his cup of tea.

Ella stopped dancing for a moment and gazed sideways at her sleeves. They were indeed puffed out, then fit firm to her wrist from just above the elbows. Her fingers traced the delicate silver lace that ran around the bottom edge of the bodice and the short collar around her neck, which was lined in a pastel pink. She even had a matching purple cape and cap. Unlike her other skirts which sat just above her ankles so she could move freely around the farm without stepping in the hem, this one ran the full length to the ground. "Lucky it is long, look." She lifted her skirt to reveal the farm boots she wore beneath.

"Oh, goodness, my beautiful girl, do you not have other shoes?" Tomas scoffed as she sniggered, it really was a sight to see big boots under such a pretty dress.

"No, as a matter of fact, Herr Wolff, I do not." She spoke poshly, dropping the front of the dress to cover them back up. "I have not needed formal shoes until now, not even for church. Who can walk in those silly things anyway? These are much more comfortable for dancing and walking, see?" She pranced around the room again to demonstrate how well she could move, even in her large footwear.

"They're much more sensible in both the town or country anyway," huffed Ernest, sitting down heavily in his chair. "You'll want the extra height of those soles when you walk through the city streets." He smirked to himself as he sipped at his cup.

She paused mid-twirl to face him. "Why, what do you mean?"

"Oh, my dear, you have so much to learn." He chuckled. "In the city, there are a lot more people, and a lot more waste. Where do you think it all goes?" He raised an eyebrow at her.

She thought for a moment then screwed up her face. "Ugh, disgusting. Surely not?"

Ernest guffawed, clearly enjoying himself now. "There's plenty of *scheisse* in the town, and not just in the streets."

"Opa!" she gasped and covered her mouth with her hand. It was not the type of language he used often.

"Well, it sounds like your boots will be of good use to you then." Tomas laughed heartily then peeked out the window when he heard a carriage arrive. "They're here. Are you ready to go?"

"Yes." She picked up her basket by the door. "I've packed my nightdress and underclothes, as well as my perfume and the gifts for Katherine. I do hope she will like them."

"What did you get her? What does one get a mayor's wife anyway?"

"I made her some balms mixed with dried rose and geranium petals, and a bottle of flowers in alcohol, the way I make my perfume. I also stitched together some small sacks and filled them with dried lavender for her to use in her wardrobe and drawers."

"Nice." Tomas bobbed his head as he helped her with the basket.

"Please be careful." Ernest's voice was suddenly grave. "You know I am not keen on this trip, but I understand why you would want to go. It is a big deal to be invited to the birthday of the mayor's wife. Make sure you keep to yourself, don't speak out of turn, and remember that you are their guest."

"It will be fine, Opa, really."

"Don't trust anyone, they are not like the village people out here. Be mindful of our pastor's wise words." He rose out of his chair and squeezed her tightly. "Please make sure you come home safely on Sunday."

She thought briefly of their meeting with the pastor and his warnings. She nodded her agreeance, returning his embrace, then moved to Tomas, wrapping her arms around him tightly and kissing him sweetly.

"I will miss you so much," he whispered in her ear. "I love you with all my heart."

"I love you too," she replied. "I will be doing everything I can to get an audience with the mayor arranged for you." She stepped back, holding his hands and looking deeply into his eyes. "For us."

He leaned forward and kissed her again. "Go, have fun. Make sure to eat some of that good food and drink extra wine for me."

She walked out to the waiting carriage with Tomas and her opa behind her. Tomas handed the coachman the basket who loaded it diligently.

Conrad stood beside the door of the carriage, his cape fluttering in the wind. He wore a high capotain hat with a tall feather plume puffing from the top. His jacket was bright red with split sleeves, his white shirt could be seen beneath. His breeches were red too, drawn in tight just below his knees. Both jacket and pants were edged with a gold trim, while his stockings were unbelievably white and the buckles on his shoes were gleaming. How he could keep his hose so white were beyond her, the best they could manage was a pale beige in the country. She could not help but notice the way he was eyeing off Tomas, a self-satisfied smirk on his face. He climbed into the carriage first, leaving the coachman to help her mount the steps.

She stuck her head out of the window and waved as they set off. When they were out of sight, she leaned back in her chair and tried to relax, gazing out at the Tauber river, still as glass in the chilly autumn air. She gasped in awe when the reflection of Rothenburg ob der Tauber's protective walls came into view on its motionless surface, rushing over to the window to take the view in properly. The walls were incredibly tall – almost as high as the steeple of her local church – and daunting, stretching as far as her eyes could see in either direction. "Oh, my word, I never realised the wall was so big from this close," she exclaimed. Her cheeks warmed as she voiced her thoughts aloud, what a naïve farm girl she must have sounded.

Conrad grinned smugly. "They are impressive, but I have so much more planned for you to see on this trip." He was watching her closely for some time, making her feel more than just a little uncomfortable. Eventually he sat forward, his elbows resting on his knees, pointing out toward the wall. "It is almost a full wegstunde long, and completely surrounds the city. It takes nearly an hour to walk if one was so inclined." He sat back again, running a hand down his feather plume. "Have you never been to the town before?"

"No, Opa does not like the city, even though he grew up inside its walls. He says we have everything we need in the country, so we have never bothered."

"Have you not wanted to visit the town for yourself?"

A smile played on her lips as she remembered her spirited attempts to draw her opa to its walls when she was just a child. "I did when I was younger, but not now. We have always been too busy tending the orchard or catching up with villagers. We have never had any reason to come to town and no one to visit." She did not want to sound ungrateful or disinterested, so added, "well, this trip is of course very different, and I have been invited."

"Yes, you have, and I must add, it is quite the honour." He tipped his head to her as if to emphasise his point. They swayed gently inside the carriage as it rumbled on pleasantly. "We can go for a wander inside the wall later if you like, it provides some great views over the town."

Her eyes grew wide as she stared back out at the imposing structure. "We can walk along the wall?"

"Yes, there is a path inside that goes the full way around. I was not joking when I told you how long it takes to cover its full distance." He smirked, raising his eyebrows a few times. "I have done it myself more than once." He leaned forward and put his hand on her knee. "Common people are not allowed to, of course, but it is different when you are related to the mayor." He winked at her.

She wiggled over toward the window to shake his hand away and break the moment. Two sets of tall wooden gates opened as they approached; Ella gazed out and up in wonderment as the carriage slowed to pass through, marvelling at the work that must have taken place to build this wall originally, not to mention what was needed for its upkeep. Her thoughts flicked to their humble cottage and the repairs her opa had made over the years. That would be nothing compared to a structure this size. The clip-clop of the horses' feet echoed on the cobblestones as they passed through the arches and into the town itself. Ella kept staring out the carriage window the whole time, her jaw dropped and eyes wide.

While the outside of the stone wall was almost impenetrable, the inside was completely different. It housed a covered walkway and timber railing that ran the length between each watch tower. Guards sat casually, chatting at stations along the wall. On either side of the street ahead of them were rows of impressive gabled houses, some of them with shopfronts, many with exposed wooden beams stained in bold colours. The buildings were rendered and painted in pastel shades, making the city appear welcoming and friendly. It was not at all spaced apart or in the washed-out earthy tones of her farming community. What must all the towns' people have thought of her quaint cottage when they came to visit? Her small village, all she had ever known, was such a homely place, but barely a tiny bud in a posy of bright flowers compared to the many coloured houses that stretched out before her.

"There is the town hall," Conrad pointed it out as they passed by. The driver continued along before heading right towards more imposing towers.

She turned to face Conrad, confused. "Where are we going? Is the mayor's manor not above the town hall?"

"I want to take you on a short tour of our town first." He moved over toward the window where she was sitting, bending forward, his face close to hers. He reached out and took her hands in his, not seeming to notice her resistance. "First, we are heading to the grounds of what was the castle. It was flattened by an earthquake a couple hundred years ago and is now one of the most beautiful parklands you will ever see, even at this time of year. I thought you would enjoy what they have done with the gardens, since you are so good with your own. You will need to return and see it in spring when it is flowering." He winked and stroked her face tenderly.

Her heart raced. There was a tingling under her skin that she had only experienced before when Tomas touched her in the same way. She bit her bottom lip and closed her eyes; how easy it would be to get swept up in all this attention. When the carriage came to a stop, she almost jumped out, relieved to remove herself from temptation.

Conrad was quick to catch up and led her through more towering gates. He greeted a man clearing leaves near the entrance. "Hello, Herr Neumann, this is the young lady I was telling you about. I have come to show her around." He beckoned her to come forward and she curtsied to the caretaker. Conrad appeared to be parading her like some sort of prize.

She strode forward quickly to explore the garden, admiring the variety of plants and statues placed strategically throughout the grounds. A flock of birds flitted amongst the trees, their trills sweetly lilting.

Conrad ran up behind her. "What do you think?"

She span around, her arms outstretched to take it all in. "This is amazing. I had no idea that gardens could be planted like this purely for pleasure." She strolled along the stone path, studying the variety of herbs and shrubs set amongst the many hedges that formed distinct patterns around the base of each statue. Trees stood tall at the edge of the gardens in varying stages of autumnal change from yellow to red. The sun's rays dappled through, casting an ethereal glow.

"If you come over here and look out there," Conrad said, striding briskly to a short wall and pointing into the valley, "you can see your village."

She wandered over, humbled by the tips of the trees and rolling hills spread out before her. She gazed toward her village, barely noticing as Conrad's arm rested on her shoulders. It resembled a toy town with white sheep dotting the green of the land. The church was conspicuous compared to the rest of the buildings, and she used its location to try to find her cottage and Tomas', but there were a vast number of trees standing between her and that part of the dale. Her heart sank, it would have been nice to see familiarity from within this very foreign place. She suddenly felt the weight of Conrad's arm around her and a sinking churning in her belly for behaving so comfortable in his presence. She ducked and twisted herself away, her hands clasped firmly in front of her skirts.

"Come, wander with me through the gardens for a bit, and then we'll take a stroll along the wall." Conrad caught up to her, reaching for her hand but dropping it to his side when she did not return the gesture.

The garden was beautifully manicured and well cared for. Even at this later stage of the season there was hardly any leaf debris, it would have to be cleared daily to stay this tidy. She glanced around, curious to see how many gardeners were in attendance, but realised even the caretaker had made himself scarce to give them time alone. They meandered beneath a trellis covered in rich red leaves, while lavender dotted the green hedges. The yellow of some smaller shrubs offset the rainbow of colours before her. "I have never seen a garden with such a mixture of plants. So many different colours and sizes." Ella moseyed along, touching the leaves and late flowers as she spoke. "The planning it must have taken to arrange everything like this." She studied the hedgerows and sections where bulbs would regenerate, and gaps where flowers would no doubt be planted fresh when spring returned.

They ambled along for some time, Conrad finally giving her some space and plenty of time to absorb and appreciate her surroundings. They eventually made their way back toward the carriage, but as they approached the archway to leave, she gazed up at an eery oval face sitting high above them on the wall. Thick black lines ran from the mouth of the mask down the stones below. "What is that?" she asked, her eyes wide.

"They used to pour hot tar from within that part of the wall, through the mask, onto anyone trying to breach these gates," he explained.

She glanced up again, bringing her hand to her cheek. "Oh my. The older men of the village have sometimes mentioned the wars that plagued these lands." She narrowed her eyes to inspect it closely. It was one thing to hear her elders talk about the wars, but it was very different to see remnants of the violence left so markedly behind. "You certainly know the town's history well."

"I am to be the next mayor, you know, so understanding the past is an important part of planning for the future." He led her past the waiting carriage to a wooden door at the base of a watchtower and knocked loudly. "Come, this is how we get to the pathway inside the wall." He held out his hand to her as the door was opened, a guard recognising and greeting him straight away. Ella followed, but picked up her skirts to busy her hands, careful not to show her boots beneath. He did not appear to notice her deliberate rejection as they ascended the stone staircase.

They wandered along a section of the wall while the coachman followed along below. She considered the sea of houses spread out before her. "I've never seen so many houses," she gasped, her hands gripping the handrails. The roof peaks appeared like large arrowheads pointing to the heavens, while a maze of streets ran before her, leaving narrow gaps woven through the tapestry of the town. She could not imagine how many people must live here, she had only met a handful in her lifetime compared to what this city must hold. A dull clopping of hooves could be heard from far away, giving the city a heartbeat of its own.

"Come along Ella," Conrad called as he promenaded along the wooden pathway, guards tipping their hats to him and Ella as they passed. "Herr Sauer," they muttered respectfully. He seemed increasingly pleased with himself each time he was recognised. He rubbed the top of her arm unexpectedly and leant in close, his breath hot on her ear. "See, being the mayor's nephew has its advantages."

It sent shivers up her spine with him so close. She should be flattered but instead, began feeling apprehensive. She really wanted to make the most of her visit to the town, but his expectations were exceedingly obvious, and she was unsure how to handle his advances politely.

They descended the stairs at the next watch tower and boarded the waiting carriage. The driver took them directly to the town hall and mayor's residence. When they arrived, Conrad stepped out promptly and pranced up a few of the stone steps. He placed his hands on his hips, as if he were surveying the square, waiting to be noticed. He was hard to miss in that outfit, his feather plume a dancing exclamation mark that forever hung above his head.

The coachman dashed over to help Ella out of the carriage, then raced up the steps to hand her basket to Conrad, who frowned at the offering, as if it were below him to be taking it. "Don't be fooled by how quiet it is today," he called back to her, studying her possessions oddly. "Tomorrow the city will come alive with the markets."

She stared, wide eyed, at the long steps of the town hall and the many archways leading into the building. It was bigger than the church of Detwang and a few of their cottages put together. Above the arches were two more stories of building erected from stone, with three more rows of windows in the steepled roof above that.

He descended a few steps to stand beside her, linking his arm around hers. "Come on then." He led her up the stairs and into the building where a maidservant took her basket from Conrad with a curtsey. There were lavish rugs in the entry covering the wooden floors that ran the length of the hall. A grand wooden staircase was off to the right, a runner lining the centre. They went upstairs and marched along to what must be the private quarters, where he led her into a generously appointed room that would have been bigger than the kitchen and common room of her cottage back in Detwang. "The guest room," he informed her. "One of our finest." A fire was burning, the room was delightfully warm. Her basket was already there, placed next to the robe. He strode through to the windowed doors on the other side, opened them and stepped out onto the terrace. She followed him and leant over the balcony, observing the carriage below and the rows of stone steps they had just ascended. The terrace was huge, with long flower boxes housing evergreen plants and winter blooms.

"What are they growing here, with winter so close?" she asked, rubbing the soft leaves between her fingers and thumb.

He raised his eyebrows. "You don't know what they are? I thought you knew everything about plants," he commented, imperiously.

She nudged away the urge to roll her eyes, shaking her head instead. "No, I only know what I've been shown to grow. I did not know there were plants that still flowered so well in the approach to winter. In the village, we might find the occasional wintergreen leaves and berries, but that's about as much as we see when the weather turns cold."

"Well, your trip has not been wasted, you've discovered something new!" He sounded delighted with himself. "You shall have to ask Aunt Katherine if she knows, or perhaps their gardener."

His pompousness was becoming tiring. She pasted a smile on her face to hide her displeasure as she gazed up toward the sky then back around the terrace. "It's glorious out here. Do you come out here often?"

He shook his head. "No, I'm afraid I'm usually far too busy for casual strolls like these. By the by, my room is on the other side of the hall and down a few doors." He winked at her. "Not too far from yours."

She held in her sigh, his attempts at affection were bordering on frustrating. Standing in the garden with a view of Detwang had been enough to remind her how much she loved Tomas, and that it was his arms she was longing to be in. "Can we climb up there?" she asked, pointing to a tower. A portion of its wall curved into the courtyard.

"Why yes, and it is a most incredible view from the top. Come with me." He again held out his hand, but she clasped hers firmly in front of her skirts.

They went back inside, latched her door and enjoyed the heat of the warm room briefly before leaving it again to walk along the hall to the tower door. Cold air greeted them as they entered the base of the tower stairs, there were no tapestries or soft furnishings in here. The staircase wound around a central pillar, which was made of stone, but appeared almost as if it were twisted silk. Windows were dotted around the walls to let in light as they ascended; from the top they really did have an incredible view of the city centre. She could see people crossing the town square, commuting in the final stages of daylight. Music and loud chatter wafted up to them from the side of the town hall, and there were several people heading in that direction. "What is down there?" she asked, pointing toward the noise. It was out of sight, so wherever the townspeople were heading, it could be heard but not seen.

"Ah, that is the tavern." He smirked and came to stand beside her. She shivered, causing him to draw his cape around her and pull her in close. "In most towns, the tavern is below the street, or across from the town hall. In Rothenberg, the tavern is on the side of the town hall. Makes it easier to get to." He loosened his embrace to play with his feather plume. "Actually, I am to meet there tonight with Uncle and a few of the councillors to go over some plans for the town. I have arranged for you to dine with Aunt Katherine, I trust this will be suitable?"

Ella nodded and stepped away, relief running through her. He evidently had the wrong idea about what this visit might mean. "That would be perfect, as I have some presents to give her."

"Oh, how thoughtful of you." He did not sound at all interested.

Ella could not take his company, or the cold, a moment more. She dare not shiver again, nor stay alone with him if she could help it. "I am sorry, I am frightfully chilly up here. The view is beautiful, but I had best wash up for dinner." She swivelled on her heels quickly and headed back down the winding staircase to the landing below, not waiting for him to follow. Once inside, she trotted briskly down the hall, hoping she was heading in the right direction.

He managed to catch up to her quickly. "I trust you enjoyed your first day in town?"

"Yes, thank you for showing me around." She curtsied politely but kept moving.

"Oh, we have so much more to see, and of course we have the special dinner for Aunt Katherine. Rest up tonight, you'll need your energy for tomorrow." He grasped her hand and pulled her back toward him, bringing her fingers to his mouth to give them a kiss.

She was too slow to snatch her hand away in time. "Conrad, I think you have the wrong idea..."

He put a finger to her lips. "There now, do not rush your thoughts on this. I must go now, important business to attend to. But look forward to the morning, there is more of the town we shall explore and lots of time to talk." He kissed her on the cheek and whispered in her ear, "I cannot wait to see you again, I shall think of you tonight." He stepped back, then winked and tipped his hat before he dashed away.

She wiped her fingers on her skirts, trying to erase the memory of his touch. She was more than a little perplexed by his persistence. Surely there must be other girls in town that would take his fancy and be a better match? She shook her head to clear her thoughts and entered the beautiful haven of her room.

Once alone, she finally had a chance to appreciate everything she had seen, and where she was staying. The fire warmed her quickly and she delighted in the exquisite furnishings. The bed was huge, it had four posts covered with carvings that resembled vines complete with leaves and berries. The wood was stained and highly polished. It was dressed in a mint green velvet quilt with matching curtains that were pulled back at each side with a gold trim. She had never known these types of cabinetry or trimmings existed, it was all so elegant. She sat on the bed, stroking the plush fabric. The floor was timber with a large rug covering most of it, while a low padded bench rest at the foot of the bed. The wardrobe was another stained oak masterpiece, with carved posts up either side to match the pattern of the bedposts. The fire was crackling away happily on the centre of the far wall facing her, its frame ornate. Extra logs sat neatly in a rack to the side. To the left of the fireplace was a wide ceramic wash basin and jug atop another oak cabinet. She opened its doors and found rolled up pieces of thick, luxurious cloth. She took one out, unravelled it, and rubbed her fingers in its thick weave, realising it must be a washcloth. She poured some water in the bowl, noting it was surprisingly warm, the fire must have been burning in this room for quite some time. She started to wash her hands, face, ears and neck, enjoying the feeling of the washcloth and the warmed water so much that she decided to wash her whole body. She soon realised she would need to find a maidservant that could help her de-robe. Her dress, as elegant as it was, had a long row of buttons up the back – totally impractical for dressing, or undressing, oneself alone. She dried her face and hands on another of the fluffy hand towels and headed out to find a helper. Now on her own, she could not believe how much of the building she had missed before. Timber panels ran halfway up the walls, all of them edged and highly polished. Dotted on either side of the hallway were several painted portraits and elaborate tapestries of the local countryside, town, and elders. It was almost silent in here, only a mumble of the noise from the outside entered in, muffled by trimmings and the decor. She was almost at the end of the hall when she ran into a young maidservant, taking just a moment to recognise her.

"Ingrid?"

The girl was shocked at first, then curtsied.

"Ingrid? Don't be silly!" She leaned forward and hugged her tightly. After a few seconds, the embrace was reciprocated, somewhat cautiously.

"I can't believe you are here." Ingrid pushed back to take in Ella's appearance. "Your dress, it is gorgeous. Where did you get it?"

"Carol made it for me."

Ingrid shook her head, she did not seem to register the name.

"Katherine's seamstress, Carol, I believe she works here too?"

"Oh, Ella, do you have any idea how many people work here? I could not possibly know them all by name." She reached out to hold her hand, patting it softly. "I heard what you did for the mayor's baby. I did not realise you were to be our village visitor."

"How have you been? How is Otto?"

"He is good. He works hard in the kitchen, but we are starting to make a life here. We would like to try for a baby, but we need to serve here for some time before we can make enough to survive in the town on our own."

"Are you glad about your decision to move?"

Ingrid paused, glancing around before she answered in a whisper, "sometimes yes, sometimes no. It is very different here, and not always in a good way."

"Oh." Ella was saddened to hear this from her childhood friend. "I always remembered you and Otto talking so big about your dreams for a modern life in the city. Are things not working out?"

"It's mostly alright, it's just taking a bit longer to reach our goals than we thought it would. Everything here is so much more expensive than we had expected." She linked arms with Ella as they dawdled back from where she had come. "Is your room to your liking?"

"Oh yes, it's the most amazing room I have ever seen. Actually, I was wondering if you would be able to give me a hand with something?" She swivelled, pointing to the row of buttons doing up her dress.

Ingrid chuckled. "Haha, a prisoner in your gown?"

"Yes, I'm afraid so. Feel this linen." She lifted up part of her skirt and the girls rubbed it between their fingers. "So soft," they said together, their fingertips gracing their lips as they giggled like children.

"Most of Katherine's gowns are made of similar fabric. Come, let me help you out of it."

On entering the room, Ingrid started undoing the many clasps.

"So, tell me, what is it like here? Do you have a room like this?"

Ingrid snorted. "Of course not! I share a room a fraction of this size with three other servants. My bed linen is the same as what we had back in the village. I am not even allowed to spend time with Otto except for Sundays after church. Even then, I am only allowed to spend the first Sunday evening after my monthlies with him. It is their way of, hmm… controlling things."

Ella's heart sank for a moment, she would hate to be separated from Tomas for that long. Her belly suddenly churned, she was quite disgusted with herself for how she had behaved with Conrad earlier, she should have put a stop to him sooner. "That must be hard."

"It was at first, but we made these sacrifices to move here. Frau Schulz is lovely to work for, not too demanding. I get to look after Clare most days for a short while. Herr Schulz is, well, like most men of this town. We are saving hard, and Otto is getting quite a good reputation for his cooking. In a few years we will have enough to move out and rent a room, and he will be able to get a job in the tavern or a hotel. It will be worth it in the end." She nodded, as if trying to convince herself as much as Ella.

Like most men of this town. What could she mean? She had so far only had a brief encounter with the mayor and short meetings with the men who visited at her farm. Conrad was the only man from town she had spent any decent amount of time with, and her tolerance of him was already wearing thin. Were they all like him? "Tell me Ingrid, how do you find Conrad?"

The dress, totally unfastened now, dropped to the floor in a circular heap of layers. Ingrid helped her step out of the pile, her underclothes still in place, and assisted her with her boots. She at first seemed distracted by her footwear, then Ella realised she was hesitant to comment.

"Ingrid?"

"It really isn't my place to say. Why, are you considering him as a suitor?"

Ella gasped, her cheeks grew hot. "Good heavens, no. Actually, I have some exciting news, but you must keep it to yourself."

Ingrid's eyes sparkled. "Yes?"

She moseyed over to the basin and started washing her arms and shoulders, sliding her loosened underclothes this way and that to freshen up as much skin as possible. She grinned, enjoying keeping her friend in suspense. "Tomas and I are to be married."

"Oh Ella, that's fantastic!" Ingrid rushed over to give her a squeeze. She reached into the cabinet to retrieve a hand towel and helped dry the areas Ella had just washed. "When? Where will you live? Are you planning babies?"

"Slow down." Ella grinned. "Our union has not been formally approved by the mayor yet, so you must not tell anyone. I am hoping to get an audience with him while I am here, to organise a time for Tomas to come ask him. Our pastor has sent several letters for us, but the replies have always been that he is too busy." Washed and dried, she stepped over to her basket and retrieved some of her rose and lavender perfume, dotting it behind her ears and at the base of her neck. "We are hoping the mayor will approve for

Tomas to move to our cottage and tend our orchard. Opa is getting quite old now, and I can't take care of all that land on my own."

"Well, I hope it all works out for you, I really do." Ingrid helped Ella back into her dress and commenced fastening all the buttons up again.

Ella searched around the room inquisitively. "Tell me please Ingrid, where is the chamber pot?"

"Haha, country girl Ella! That is not how it is done in this household."

"They don't need to go?"

Ingrid laughed. "Of course they do, silly! It is just they do not often use a chamber pot. I will have to get you one."

"If they don't use a chamber pot..." She scoured her mind for various options, but had to ask, "what do they use?"

Her dress all done up now, Ingrid stood in front of Ella with her hands on her hips and a smirk on her face. "Come, I'll show you."

Ella did not have her boots back on, but no-one could tell with her long skirts covering her feet. They moved soundlessly down the hall until they reached a door in the wall. Ingrid tipped her head at the handle, so Ella pushed down hard and opened the door. The first thing she noticed was the cold air rushing in. Her mouth dropped open as she stared at a timber seat with a hole cut out of it, where the air was coming from. Next to the seat was a pile of torn up rags. "What is that?"

Ingrid reached for the door, closing it briskly. "It's called a garderobe. You sit on the seat, do your business, and it drops to the water at the bottom. It can be a bit chilly in winter, but no need for a chamber pot."

Ella tittered as she entered for a second look. She stepped right in this time and peered through the hole in the seat to the snake of a creek running below. She laughed out loud, covering her mouth to stifle the noise as she re-entered the hall.

"If you think that's something, wait till dinner tomorrow night."

"Why, they aren't going to use this in front of each other, are they?" She gasped. Everything here was so different, she did not know what to expect next.

"Oh no, silly." Ingrid giggled, then stopped herself abruptly, gazing around. "It's just that, well, you will see all sorts of interesting behaviours when the nobility of the town are together. They will all be, how do I explain? Let me just say, they will be very formal, and showy. Each one likes to make sure the others know how very wonderful and important they are, but no-one is allowed to out-do the mayor. They are not like the people in the village."

"I guess dinner will be quite interesting, then," said Ella, almost absently, still distracted by the shock of the garderobe.

"Here, let me escort you back to your room, and get you settled in." Ingrid led her by the hand. "I'll go and get you that chamber pot." She smiled, reassuringly. "It will only be an hour or so until I need to come collect you for dinner with Frau Schulz anyway."

Ella clasped Ingrid's hand tightly, grateful for the assistance and friendship. "Thank you, Ingrid, for your help, and making this feel a little less strange."

"Oh, wait for it, you'll see plenty of that tomorrow night." She sniggered, leaving Ella at her door feeling even more nervous about what was yet to come.

Chapter 9

We will commit sins while we are here,

for this life is not a place where justice resides. – Martin Luther

It was just before six when Ella was shown into a wood-panelled dining hall where Katherine and two servants were already in attendance. The table was long with carved legs and matching chairs, it could have easily seated twenty or more people. It was set with fine ceramic plates and silverware, while fancy glasses with green stems sat waiting, already filled with wine. The room was pleasantly toasty, a roaring fire was burning brightly and stunning velvet drapes, almost the height of the room, were drawn to keep the heat in. Paintings and embroidery decorated the walls.

Katherine rose from her seat as she entered, coming over to Ella and hugging her briefly. "I'm so glad you could make it."

"Thank you for inviting me." She juggled the presents precariously as she tried to return the embrace.

"Come, sit." They moved to their places at the table while servants assisted them with their seats and laid napkins over their laps. They were positioned at one end of the grand table, adjacent to each other.

"I have some gifts for you." Ella laid the neatly wrapped package before Katherine. She bit her lip and fiddled with her thumbs while she waited for them to be opened.

"Oh, really? You did not have to do that." Katherine leaned forward to untie the ribbon holding the bundle together. She studied the gifts one at a time, smelling the balms and perfume. She dabbed a few drops on her wrists and neck. "What are these?" She held up the little sacks filled with lavender inquisitively.

"You put them in your drawers or hang them in your robes. It will give your clothes a fresh scent."

"How lovely, I have not seen these before." She sniffed at the small bags again, then placed them gently on the table before reaching forward to take Ella's hand and clasped it tightly. "As if saving my daughter's life was not enough of a gift, your presents are truly lovely. Thank you."

"You are welcome." Ella's cheeks warmed.

"Now shall we enjoy an evening without the men to hold us back?" Katherine giggled, waving at the servants.

They dined on roast chicken and root vegetables, the wine flowing as easily as the conversation. They talked of Ella's trip to the garden, her fascination at the furnishings, and baby Clare's development. Despite their difference in backgrounds and status, a firm friendship was founded.

They wandered through the great hall after dinner while Katherine explained the history of some of the portraits and tapestries. "Our families have known each other for more than one hundred years. My father was a councillor to the previous mayor."

Ella, emboldened by the wine and comfortable in Katherine's presence was intrigued. "Is that how you met Herr Schulz?"

Katherine hummed as she nodded her ascent. "I am indeed fortunate to have married so well."

Ella tipped her head to one side, thinking of Tomas. "What is it like, to be married? Did you court for long?"

Katherine's cheeks reddened and she had a far-off gleam to her eyes as she reminisced. "You would have noticed the considerable age difference, no doubt?" She reached out to stroke a tapestry as she spoke. "I was just sixteen when he first showed interest. My parents of course encouraged the pairing. He was not mayor then, but he was one of the previous mayor's closest advisors." She strolled along the hallway. "Marriage is not so bad most of the time. I need to hold my tongue on occasion, but he has provided well for me, so I cannot complain. He dotes on Clare terribly." She smiled delightfully, turning toward Ella. "How about you, are you interested in marriage?"

Ella's face warmed and she gazed down at the richly embroidered floor covering; it was a mixture of sepia whorls and red roses. "I cannot wait to start a family. It has only been my opa and I for as long as I can remember, so I want several children to fill our farm." Her lips curved at the thought as she brought her eyes up to meet Katherines.

"Well, I believe you may find a part of your wish granted this trip," Katherine stated, much to Ella's surprise. What could she possibly know? "Come, I believe supper will be served in the dining hall by now."

Katherine led the way back, Ella following diligently behind, relieved she was not expected to remember her way around. They shared dried fruit, nuts and some more wine before Ella retired to her room eagerly, if not a little dreamily. She was again assisted by Ingrid out of the dress, who hung it carefully in the robe while Ella changed quickly into her nightgown and climbed into the inviting bed.

Ingrid added another log to the fire then drew the velvet curtains closed around her. "I'll be back to help you in the morning, sleep tight."

She barely heard her leave before falling asleep.

Ella was sitting on the edge of the bed, her hair brushed and hanging in a loose wave, when Ingrid knocked at the door the next morning and let herself in. She was only in her undergarments, but the room was comfortably warm.

"How did you sleep, Frau Baumann?" Ingrid marched briskly over to remove the wash bowl and jug from their place and pulled back the curtains at the door.

Ella, surprised at how formally she spoke, swivelled around and noticed Ingrid was not on her own. Another maidservant entered with a pewter tray of sliced fresh fruits and a pastry topped with stewed apple. A small pot and cup were also set out. The maidservant placed these silently where the wash bowl had been and proceeded to clear the chamber pot, while Ingrid pulled the velvet curtains back from around the bed, tying them neatly at the head posts.

Ingrid went over to place a log on the fire and stir it up. It had almost burnt down overnight but Ella had stayed exceptionally cosy, especially under the velvet blanket with the curtains around the bed wrapping her in like a cocoon. Once the other woman had left the room, Ingrid came over to help Ella with her hair.

"How proper you can be." She giggled at Ingrid. "I had the most amazing sleep. I think it was the extra wine I had last night at dinner." She stifled a yawn.

Ingrid unravelled her plait and brushed her golden-brown hair. "Glad you enjoyed yourself. So, what do you have planned for today?"

Butterflies were busy in her belly about what may lay ahead. "I believe Conrad is going to take me into the town, show me around."

"More like show you off, if you ask me." Ingrid almost muttered under her breath as she fixed Ella's hair into a low bun.

Was she being ridiculed or warned? "Whatever do you mean by that?"

"Let me describe it this way," Ingrid started, as she retrieved the dress from the robe, laying it on the ground in a neat circle for Ella to step into. "Conrad likes to think he is perhaps more important than he actually is."

"Hmm." She hummed as she smirked. "I think I am discovering what you mean." The girls giggled.

"Come now Ella, you must eat, wash and get dressed, for I believe you are required downstairs in less than one hour."

"Oh my, well if I'm *required*, I guess I should do as I am told." She chuckled and made her way over to the tray of breakfast. Everything was presented so elegantly, it would be hard to face simple oats each morning when she returned. Her opa had never served breakfast like this, the rare occasion when he made pancakes was considered a treat! She would have to prepare something this extravagant for him and Tomas one day. Her heart beat faster as she thought fondly of the man waiting for her back home, trusting her, allowing her to make this trip. She closed her eyes and set her mouth firm, resolving to make it clear to Conrad that his advances were not appreciated. She opened her eyes and crunched into one of the pastries, its buttery sweetness rolled blissfully on her tongue. "Mmm," she hummed, almost subconsciously, holding it out to Ingrid for a bite.

Ingrid waved her hand and shook her head. "Don't mind me," she mumbled, "I'll be back shortly to assist you with those troublesome buttons."

Once fed and dressed, Ella made her way downstairs to the grand area of the town hall where Conrad was already waiting. He was dressed in a deep maroon jacket with matching cape and breeches with another pair of his impossibly white hose. His black shoes had brightly polished buckles and there were red ribbons tied just below his knees. His ruff was starched and stiff around his neck and the plume of his hat was bright enough to match the ribbons on his legs. He must have a room just to house his clothes, where could he possibly store them all? While his hats and the feathers seemed quite ridiculous, she had noticed a few men around town wearing similar adornments yesterday. Their attire would be so impractical for a day's work in the country, while it was evidently quite normal here to want to look like a turkey. She grinned at her own joke, but Conrad misread it as delight at seeing him.

"A pleasure as always to see you, Ella." He frowned at her dress. "Is that the same gown you were wearing yesterday? Is it the only thing you own?"

She glanced down to hide her face and pulled her cape around her shoulders. It was the only dress she could wear into town without looking like the hired help, and she had been so proud to wear it yesterday and again today. Back home they changed only when their clothes were dirty or smelt bad, since washing was such a time-consuming task, and the thread became bare the more often it was cleaned. The linen of this dress felt so delicate on her skin, and it was the most stylish item she owned, but his snide remarks now made her face burn with shame. She bent her neck forward and took a sniff – after washing yesterday she certainly smelt fresh, so what was his problem? "Well, yes, it's the only dress I have good enough for a visit to the mayor's manor," she snapped. "I am from the country, we do not have the luxury of just sitting around and stitching, nor do we have the means to spend all day admiring our latest clothing."

He cleared his throat, clearly aware he had upset her. "Well, we shall have to remedy that before this evening." He gazed around and up. "You there," he clicked his fingers as he called to one of the maid servants scampering along the hallway above them. "Come here at once."

A young mousy woman scurried down the stairs and curtsied to Conrad. Ella recognised her from bringing breakfast and clearing her room that morning. "I want you to see Frau Schulz and ask for a dress suitable for Frau Baumann to wear this evening."

"Yes, Herr Sauer." She bowed her head deeply while she backed away, then hurried back up the stairs.

"Now, shall we?" Conrad held his arm out for Ella. She took it, hesitantly, as he led her from the building toward the waiting carriage. The square in front of the town hall was coming to life with stalls and canopies being erected, while pens with live animals and carts of fruit and cheeses were being wheeled in. He assisted Ella as she stepped into the carriage. "We will come back to the markets in an hour or two." He sat across from her, a broad grin splashed across his face. "The markets will be in full swing by then, and you will get to see all sorts of exotic fruits and foods available." He reached over to touch her knee and tried to take her hand, but she moved away just in time, so his hand grasped at nothing more than air. He smiled tightly, then added, "I will make sure I take you to the stall where they sell your apples." He winked and settled back in his chair, one ankle resting on the other knee as he gazed out the window.

Ella pasted on a smile to hide her growing distaste. As the carriage started moving, she leant out the window to observe the sky above and to the north. "It will be windy today, with rain later. Do they run the market when the weather becomes unpleasant?"

Conrad sneered at her. "How could you possibly pretend to know what the weather is going to do? It looks fine to me." Conrad raised his eyes toward the patchy clouds. "It's just like every other day at this time of year. Cold and grey."

"See those clouds over there," she said, her finger pointing in the direction of her gaze. "They are streaky, like a horses' tail caught in the breeze. It indicates wind is on its way." She gestured further back. "Those clouds over there, they look full and heavy at the bottom. Not as fluffy as these above us now." She leaned out of the window, considering the sky once more, then sat back inside. "It will not even make it till noon before the weather turns bad."

"Oh my, so the clouds speak to you now, do they?" Conrad raised his eyebrows at her a few times and grinned smugly.

She tried to swallow but her throat felt thick. "I am sorry, Herr, but everyone in the country knows to gauge these weather signs. Many use the moon or watch for animals moving in certain patterns as well. It is an important way for us to plan our days. We need to work when the weather remains clear or make the right kind of preparations when it shows signs of turning bad." She stared out the window so he could not see the tears pricking at her eyes. "I am no more special or able to speak with the clouds than any other farmer of my village." She spoke quietly now, silently wishing the day would pass fast.

They travelled for a few minutes, the ambience in the coach frostier than the air outside, before Conrad knocked on the roof. "Driver, stop the carriage." It pulled slowly to a halt while he put some gloves on, reaching over to pass her the thick coat that lay beside her. "I thought you might like a short wander through the town before we head back to the market?"

Ella smiled tightly. *Anything to get me out of being stuck inside with you.* "Yes, that would be lovely, how thoughtful of you," she answered curtly. She dressed in the coat and stepped outside with the help of the coachman.

Conrad reached for her arm, but she declined it politely. His brow creased. "Remember, this is my town I'm showing you around. You were so proud of your quaint farm, now it is my turn. This is where real opportunities can be made, and futures changed. We have such a bigger population than you rural folk are used to." He put one hand on his hip and waved the other before him as he spoke, "this part of town is called Plonlein, it is one of the prettiest parts. That road over there heads toward an exit from the city." He indicated toward a path leading down. "All entry and exit points are well guarded, so you have nothing to fear while here." He pointed ahead. "Up here is a delightful bakery with the best bread and pastries the city has to offer."

Despite the company, she could not help but find this an absolutely enchanting town. Beside her was a building rendered in blue, a lattice was covered in dense foliage, even at that time of year. Above her head swung a curved, wrought iron frame holding a sign declaring it was a tailor. Before her was a yellow rendered building with bright curtains being pulled back by a smiling inhabitant who waved, a wooden sign on its wall claimed it was a butcher. Further ahead she noticed an imposing clock tower, it must have been five or six storeys tall, with a generous arch allowing people and horses to pass beneath. On the other side of the street were more rendered houses with pitched rooves and exposed beams. She gazed around with her jaw dropped and eyes wide, trying to capture its beauty.

She tried to make light of the moment, perhaps thaw a bit of the tenseness between them. "I had some friends move here from Detwang, they serve in the mayor's household now. Until this moment I had not understood what could have drawn them to city life, but this really is something."

They entered a pink building with a sign in the shape of a gigantic rolling pin hanging out the front. A few locals were inside, lined up patiently to purchase the items on display. It smelt of freshly cooked bread, just like her cottage did when her opa baked, only stronger and sweeter.

Conrad sauntered to the counter, ignoring the people waiting, and addressed the man serving. "I'll have two of your little chocolate cakes with cream, thank you Herr Becker."

The man finished with his customer then nodded to Conrad. He stilled when he noticed who stood beside him. "Ella?" He wiped his hands on his apron and came from around the bench to hug her tightly. He called out over his shoulder, "Magda, Ella is here, come see."

A buxom woman came through a doorway that must have led out the back. "Ella!" She waddled over to hug Ella then stepped back and dusted her off, since they were both now covered in flour. "Hello lovey, thank you so much for your herbs, we both feel so much better."

Ella beamed at the familiar faces. "It is my pleasure, Frau Becker. So good to see you. So, this is your bakery?" She glanced around. Racks of bread in various shapes and sizes lined one of the walls, while a display case sat at the front to one side, filled with small and large cakes. A serving bench was located in the centre of the store with a pot of cream and pad of butter.

"Do you like it?"

"It smells divine! I cannot wait to taste more of your baking."

"Well, it would be possible if we had some service." Conrad coughed in a feeble attempt to make himself visible. "I take it you know the Beckers?"

Hans returned promptly to stand behind the counter and reached for the cakes, while Magda disappeared quickly around the back. He split the delicacies open and spread them generously with cream that had been whipped so thick it stood in stiff peaks.

"Hans and Magda have come to visit me from time to time," explained Ella as she moved closer to him.

"Perhaps I shall need to be of poor health to get more of your attention," said Conrad sarcastically.

Ella struggled to hide her scowl, her distaste for this man was burgeoning on loathing.

"No one should wish poor health on themselves Herr Sauer." Hans put the lids on each of the cakes and passed them over. "On the house, for our dear Ella." He winked at her, an endearing smile on his face.

"Thank you, Hans." She curtsied lightly and bit in without hesitation. "Mmm, delicious!" she exclaimed, crumbs in her hand and cream at the corners of her mouth.

"Come Ella, so much more of this town to see." Conrad all but pulled her out of the shop by the elbow with his free hand.

"I'll see you next week before it gets too cold," called Ella over her shoulder as she was being led away. She must conduct herself in a more demure manner, she admonished herself, as Conrad had an undeniably scornful manner when he was not the centre of attention.

They strolled quietly for a moment, Ella devouring the cake with pleasure, Conrad barely touching his. "So just how many other people in this town do you know?" he asked dryly.

She chewed and swallowed her mouthful before speaking. "After I treated baby Clare, a lot of your towns people came to visit."

Conrad scoffed. "A lot of this town? Ella, you silly country girl. There are over six thousand people in this town. So, you've had *a lot* of this six thousand come visit you?" He sounded each of his words out pointedly.

Oh my, that is an incredible number of people living in one place. "Ah, well, a few then," she said humbly. "I simply meant that it felt like an awful lot of people from town had come to see me. There have been at least one or two new faces every couple of days for the last few months. We rarely get any visitors from town, so it has been busy by comparison." She bit into her cake and chewed slowly, focussing hard on its flavours to prevent her tears from escaping. She thought she had made a helpful difference to a few dozen of the towns people at least, she did not mean to speak big of herself.

She allowed the silence to settle between them as they journeyed along the street, gagging as the smell of human waste flowing in the gutters wafted up. Her opa had been right about her boots - she did not have to walk near this much animal waste on the farm! How could respectable people of a city tolerate being exposed to this every day? "Should we be getting back to prepare for Frau Schulz's birthday?" She was standing beneath the arch of the clock tower, hopeful he would have them return to the manor soon.

"Come, let's explore the market first." He clutched her elbow and led her back toward their waiting transport. She dared not shake it loose for the time being, but he dropped it readily when he arrived at the carriage and climbed in before her.

The coachman assisted her as she mounted the steps. "Best keep your coat on Frau Baumann," he advised. "Only a short trip back." He smiled at her kindly, warming her thoughts a little.

She sat in the carriage gazing out at the various coloured shops and houses as they passed by, pretending she was keenly interested in the town to avoid making eye contact with Conrad.

The town square was now a hive of activity, a maze of market stalls set alive under many different shaped and coloured canopies.

"Careful where you step, Frau Baumann," the coachman whispered in Ella's ear as he helped her dismount. Was he giving her a literal warning about the marketplace, or a philosophical one about conversing with her companion?

Conrad strode through the marketplace boldly as if he owned it, she almost had to trot to keep up. He paused occasionally at different stalls to inspect the goods, nodding to the owners of those he approved and using hand gestures to shoo the vendors of ones that he did not. The marketplace was loud from locals bartering and the smell of mouldy hay was heavy in the air, while well-fed cats lurked in corners near grain sacks, licking their fur, on the lookout for rats. A woman with a heavy wooden frill chained around her neck roamed amongst the stalls as if it were perfectly normal to wear that sort of thing while selecting fruit and cheese.

"Good heavens, what is that around her neck?" asked Ella, staring. She raised her hand as if to point, then brought it down hastily. She did not want to make a scene.

"Oh that," Conrad paused for a moment to explain. "She is a seamstress, and there are rules determining the size of collars and frills based on the class system in our society." He pointed to the wide wooden frill. "That is a way of controlling dressmakers who make the frill of a dress, or collar on a jacket, larger than it should be, for the station of the person who will wear it."

Ella furrowed her brows. "I am afraid I do not understand."

"She made someone's frill too big for their position in town." He motioned toward the dress she was wearing. "Take your own garment, for example. You have not noticed how your dress has hardly any collar at all? It is short, and the trim is narrow. It tells everyone that you are of low standing. Anyone here with a collar wider than yours is of a higher position, and worthy of greater respect."

Ella brought her hand to her neck and rubbed the edge of her dress between her fingertips. She had not noticed anything other than how pretty it was, and certainly did not know, or had not put any thought into, what it had meant. She regarded the ridiculously large ruff that sat around Conrad's neck and the size of the feather in his hat. It was all starting to make sense. "So, she has to wear that wooden… thing, because she made a collar too large?"

"Yes," Conrad replied, nodding all-knowingly. "She needs to learn society's rules are to be followed so that everyone knows their place."

How odd, to make such a public display of what may have been a simple mistake, or simply a bad call in the name of fashion.

"Oh, don't feel sorry for the wench," continued Conrad, as if reading her mind. "She would have known very well what she was doing, and that simply cannot be tolerated. Imagine if everyone went around doing whatever they liked at any given moment without being reminded there are rules for a reason. Now come along, it is getting cold and windy, and I have had just about enough of this town for the day." He clasped his hands behind his back and strode quickly through the marketplace.

They weaved their way through the many stalls until they arrived at the foot of the steps leading up to the town hall. Ella noticed a square wooden stage near the corner that led into the street with the tavern. It had been there yesterday when she had arrived, but was empty at that time save for a lone wooden post in the centre. Today, there were two people chained to that post. On the right was a man, dressed in an elegant deep green jacket with embroidered filagree pattern and matching breeches. His face was dirty and downcast, his shoes were made of leather with a shiny brass buckle. At his feet were scraps of food thrown at him by the passing crowd. On the left was a woman standing with her hands tied behind her back in a worn brown dress and apron. She was wearing an outrageous mask over her face that had tall, spikey ears and long red tongue. Bells hung from the ears, ringing each time she moved her head, slow and regular, indicating the pain of wearing such a weight. A wooden sign around her neck told all she spoke too freely about other people's affairs.

Ella's jaw dropped and her heart skipped a beat. She had never seen anything like this. "What have they done?"

"Have you really not seen this kind of thing before?" asked Conrad, appearing genuinely intrigued by her horror. "What do you do in your village when someone behaves poorly? Have you never needed to publicly decry other peoples' behaviours when they get out of hand?"

Ella thought of her village, so inviting and friendly. They had rolled the town drunk down the main street in a barrel once because he drank too much and got abnormally rowdy at a birthday celebration, but they had all had a good laugh about it later. Even he had seen the funny side of it at the time, but perhaps not so much the next day when he was covered in bruises. "Not really, no," she replied.

He pointed to the man first. "That man has cheated on his wife and been found guilty." He then motioned toward the woman wearing the mask. "While she has gossiped too much about others in town." He caught her eyes, shaking his head. "Honestly, Ella, how do you expect to keep so many people under control if they aren't reminded of the rules that should be followed?"

She brought her hand to her mouth, unsure of what to say lest she break a rule she was unaware of. She was becoming increasingly unsettled by Conrad's heartless explanations and how the prettiness of this town was overshadowed by its inhabitants' behaviours. How could people treat others this way for breaking unimportant rules to begin with? Even more bewildering, how could people live with so many rules governing every aspect of their daily lives? Perhaps they did not know any better, and perhaps they did not mind the punishments inflicted so publicly on others. Her heart grew heavy and her mood melancholy as the temperature dropped and a fine mist started to fall.

Conrad mounted the town steps quickly, beckoning her to follow. "Come Ella, before you get wet and end up with a fever." He opened his hand to catch some of the rain as his mouth twisted into a sardonic smile. "It seems you can talk to these clouds after all."

Chapter 10

The mad mob does not ask how it could be better, only that it be different.
And when it then becomes worse, it must change again.
Thus they get bees for flies, and at last hornets for bees. – Martin Luther

Ella rushed to the warmth and safety of her room, surprised to see an older woman sitting next to her bed with a gorgeous blue gown spread across her lap. "Carol, what are you doing here?"

"Hello dear." Carol stuck the needle she was holding through a seam and waddled over to hug her closely. "Let me take a good look at you." She patted down the seams around her waist. "Ah, yes, it fits you perfectly. What do you think?"

"I love this dress so much." Ella span around, admiring how the skirt floated, as if it were dancing on its own. "Thank you."

She winked at Ella, her eyes crinkling as she smiled. "How are you enjoying the town?"

Ella stopped spinning and fiddled with her thumbs. "Can I speak openly with you?"

"It's all right love." She cupped Ella's face in her hand. "It's probably very different to what you are used to. Anything you want to talk about?"

Ella sighed heavily and shot a glance to the side. "I'm not enjoying the town much at all." She breathed in deeply and brought her eyes to meet Carols. "Actually, if I am to be honest, the town is very pretty, but the company has not been the best. I was just in the town square where I saw a lady with a wooden mask, and another with a wooden frill, and a man was chained to a post." Her words were spilling out of her. Before she realised, she was sobbing.

"There, there dear." Carol rummaged through her basket for a handkerchief and passed it over. "Where there are more people, there need to be more rules."

Ella sat on the edge of the bed, unpinned her cap and shook out her hair. "Are you saying you agree with that sort of treatment?"

Carol resumed her position in the seat next to the bed, picking up the dress and her needle. "Agree would not be the word I would choose." She stitched as she spoke. "More that I understand why these rules have been put in place. We must abide by them to keep in line with the morality and structure of a decent society."

"I can see nothing decent or moral about the punishments I witnessed," she sniffed and wiped a tear from her cheek. "Would I sound ungrateful if I was to say that I can't wait to get dinner over with tonight and head back home to my village tomorrow?" She wiggled over closer to Carol. "How are your hands, by the way? Is the pain gone?"

"Oh, yes, thank you dear, my joints are so much better, especially in this cold. They usually get very sore at this time of year, but so far, no problems at all!" She paused mid-stitch to open and close her hands a few times, then pressed her thumbs for good luck. "I must come and see you to get more herbs before winter sets in properly. I've heard chatter that it's going to be a cold one this year."

"You're always welcome. Yes, do come sooner rather than later, I think we will get snow early, and more of it. We will be starting to prune the trees as soon as I have done the preserving. Opa may have already started while I've been gone." She nodded toward the dress Carol was working on. It was a beautiful, midnight blue satin that shimmered even in the dull afternoon light coming through Ella's bedroom window. "So, what are you doing in my room? That dress is exquisite." She leant forward to rub the fabric between her thumb and fingers.

"It's for you to wear tonight," she beamed with her chin raised. "I made this one too. I'm adjusting it for you." Carol held it up. It was without a doubt the most gorgeous garment Ella had ever seen – far more elegant than the purple one she was already so enamoured with. It had small puffs at the shoulders before the sleeves ran in tight down to the cuffs with a short, stiff collar atop a low sweetheart neckline. It would have been quite a revealing dress, except it had a fine translucent blue fabric that buttoned up from the centre front to the neck. It both attracted attention to the decolletage yet protected the virtue of the wearer. There were neat, flattened pleats stitched into the bodice, and a full skirt flowed out from the waistline.

"Oh, my goodness." Ella reached out to play with the skirt. "I have never seen a dress with so many layers. Are you sure I'm allowed to wear that?"

"I had to shorten the collar and bring the bodice in a bit, but yes, you are to wear it tonight. I really must make you another dress, lovey, if you are to visit court again. You simply cannot wear the same dress during the day as well as at night. Wait until you see what Frau Schulz is wearing for her birthday celebrations!"

"Did you make it?"

"Yes, and it's superb." Her eyes fluttered and she waved her fingers. "Tell me dear, what colour would you like next time?"

Ella smiled coyly. "Well, if you are able, there is something I would very much like for you to make."

"Go on love." Carol leaned in closer.

"A wedding dress, if you wouldn't mind?"

Carols mouth formed an 'o' and her eyes widened.

"I don't expect anything like that." Ella motioned toward the blue gown. "Maybe something like what I am wearing, just white or off white if you can?"

Carol dropped the dress on her lap and clapped her hands together. "Of course, dear. Tell me, who is the lucky man?"

"Well, it is not official yet, so please don't say anything."

"My lips are sealed." Carol drew her lips tight, pretending to lock them with a key and throw it away.

She flinched. Locks were not often used in her village, while it seemed even secrets must be stored away in this town. "Do you know Tomas Wolff? He is my neighbour back home. We grew up together, so it is no real surprise to the village, but we have not yet got the mayor's permission."

Carol shook her head. "No, I have not met him. I did see a lot of young men on that farm next door when I came to visit you." Her lips curved into a wry smile.

Ella giggled. "Yes, there are a lot of boys in that family. He is second eldest, with the cutest set of blonde curls. He is the biggest, even taller than his older brother."

Carol hummed her approval. "Next time I shall have to take more notice." She raised her eyebrows a few times. "I would be delighted to make your bridal dress. Have you got a date in mind?"

"We were hoping for late spring, or maybe early summer. The weather will be much nicer then."

"Ah, so there is no immediate rush to the altar then." She patted her belly low, where babies grow.

Ella flushed. "No, there is no hurry. We are going to wait until we are married to start trying for a baby."

"Very wise my dear, nothing good comes out of putting the cart before the horse, if you know what I mean." She nodded to herself. "Gives me plenty of time to get your dress made without having to, ah, reshape it." She chuckled lightly. "I know I've had to do that more than once or twice." She tapped the side of her nose.

Ella wondered briefly how well her secret might be kept after all.

"Well done, my dear, I hope he treats you well." She finished her stitch, snipped the thread, and put the needle and cushion in her basket. "There we go love, all fixed up and ready to wear. I'll fetch the maidservant to help you wash and get ready for this evening." She shook out the fullness of the skirts and rose from the chair, groaning quietly.

"Thank you so much for adjusting this extraordinary gown, and for my wedding dress in advance. I know it will be splendid."

"My pleasure, love." Carol squeezed her arm tenderly. "It's so nice to see you happy." She made her way slowly toward the door, hesitated, then swivelled back to face Ella. "Tonight, my dear, if I can give you a word of advice?"

"Yes?"

"Be seen and not heard. These people are not as welcoming as you would be used to." Her face became serious and she lowered her voice. "The less you say the better. Girls are to be nothing more than pretty flowers in the company of important men. Save your talk for when you get back home." She smiled encouragingly and left the room.

Ella was starting to understand the warnings she had been issued. Her opa always described these people as different, Ingrid had said the same, and now the tips from Carol. After what she had witnessed in the marketplace, Ella was finally making sense of their wise words. She was not too bothered about keeping to herself this evening if the male company included Conrad, or anyone even remotely like him. At least in a dress that beautiful, she would be a magnificent flower.

She unclipped her cape and waited for Ingrid to come help her prepare for the evening ahead. May as well enjoy the rest and get pampered while she could.

Now that Ella knew the 'collar' rule, she was finding the array of garments that night somewhat ridiculous and self-indulgent. Judging from appearances, she figured it must apply to feather plumes, the height of hairstyles, and size of jewellery as well. Katherine appeared almost regal in a gown of golden satin with the most delicate of snowflake inspired patterns swirling over the fabric. Her ruff was of course the second largest in the room, made ever so slightly smaller than her husband's. She had a golden feather plume that jutted out from her very tall hair and ran to well below her waistline. Where did they get all of these remarkable feathers, fabrics and trimmings from? Almost all of the men were dressed in brightly coloured satin or velvet vests and jackets, many with splits in the arms and white billowing sleeves beneath. Some wore wide ruffs, others grand stiff collars – everything was big, bold and bright. It reminded her of the mating displays of male birds in spring.

Ingrid and a few other servants were walking around with serving platters and pitchers, topping up drinks as they moved invisibly around the room. They were wearing nicer black dresses than their regular uniforms; Katherine's birthday party was evidently an important event. If the ladies in the room were to behave like flowers, the servants must be required to be shadows, making sure everyone's glasses were topped up and the noble company fed well on appetizers silently. There were no, 'please', 'thank you' or other pleasantries extended to the staff – it appeared they were to be neither seen nor heard whilst keeping the guests happy. She thanked one of them for refilling her glass only once; the look she received told her she was not supposed to acknowledge them lest that be considered poor service on the servants' behalf.

"Ella," she heard her name being called over the general hum. "Come meet the good councilmen of Rothenburg." It was Conrad, sounding like he had already had an ample serve of liquid cheer.

She headed over, moving slowly not just from reluctance, but also by the extra layers of her dress. She watched the other ladies in the room, appearing to sashay about so elegantly in their robes, while she found these gowns, as glamorous as they were, somewhat restrictive.

"Gentlemen, please allow me to introduce you to Ella Baumann." He presented her to the men gathered, each of them a little paunchy. They were all significantly older than her and Conrad, easily in their late thirties or even early forties. They clucked and tipped their heads to her like roosters around a new hen.

She curtsied politely then raised her head to nod as she was introduced to them in turn. It was as her eyes rested on the last man in the group that silence settled amongst them. The way his gaze fixed upon her made the hairs on her forearms raise, causing the men to pause mid-sentence.

It was of course Conrad that first found his voice. "My goodness Ulrich, you've gone white as a sheet." He chuckled loudly, apparently enjoying himself. "Are you not impressed by Ella's beauty? It seems as if you've seen a ghost."

The man he had called Ulrich did indeed look shocked. He was dressed in a bright maroon vest with black swirls that matched the curls of his moustache. His hair was set in long spiral curls which rested on his collar. His blue-green eyes were locked on hers. He stood there, mute, making her feel uncomfortable. She wiped at her mouth and patted down her bodice as discreetly as possible, wondering if she had crumbs on her face or a spill on her dress.

"Uh, yes. I mean, no." Ulrich cleared his throat and wiped at his brow. "You just remind me of someone. A familiar face perhaps." His smile was forced as he extended his hand out to Ella, who took it timidly and curtsied again.

"Ella is from Detwang. This is her first trip to the town. Can you imagine that?" Conrad informed the group, chuckling. "Unless you go milk the cows yourself, you could not possibly know her."

"No, I guess not," Ulrich muttered, absently.

"She tends to the mayor's land, grows apples, amongst other things." Conrad appeared to be in his element as the oracle of the group. "Her grandfather and her alone take care of an entire orchard." He bobbed his head, his eyebrows raised.

Mutterings of 'quite' and 'well I never' came from the men.

Their talk about the town resumed. Ella tried to appear interested, it was about planning or some such. She gazed around the room, smiling politely every now and again as she sipped at her wine. It was constantly refilled, so she had no idea how much she'd had, but could feel the buzz of it already. At least it was getting her through this ordeal. She had to force herself not to bounce on the spot and managed to hold back a sigh, wondering desperately how she could leave the small gathering without causing offence. Ulrich occasionally stole glances in her direction, an unsettling gaze of longing on his face, making her skin crawl.

"Ah, Doctor Voigt, won't you come join us?" Conrad called over to a tall man who had just entered the room. *Oh my, wasn't he just the entertainer?* But of course, she saw earlier that day how much he revelled in being the centre of attention.

The man he'd called Voigt was dressed entirely in black, an ominous ship afloat a sea of bright colours. His face was long and drawn, his hair silver. He wore gold rimmed spectacles that sat like a bridge across the top of his nose, positioned such as to make him carry his head high and peer down at others. He did not seem the type with whom you could enjoy a warm conversation, if only she had managed to find an excuse earlier to go pass time in some corner.

"Fellow councilmen," the doctor addressed the group. "I see you are ahead of me." He motioned to their drinks as he signalled to a maidservant carrying a tray. "And who do we have here?" He pivoted to face Ella, his eyes running up and down.

Her wine bubbled in her belly, but she curtsied dutifully while Conrad gave her introduction.

"A big trip to the city for a little farm girl," he remarked, much to the amusement of the others present.

Ella forced a gracious smile. What town women saw in these men she would never understand. If she had her way, she would be in her room giggling with Ingrid about their collars and feathers.

"So, Doctor Voigt, you have just returned from a seminar in Heidelberg. Is that where you studied?" Conrad shared more information with the group. By golly, he gossiped more than their worst busybody back home. "Please enlighten us, dear doctor, how was your trip?"

"Yes, it was the university I attended when I was much younger." He faced Ella, his chin raised. "I actually presented at the seminar." He gave her a wink then addressed the men. "There is rising opposition to the duality of medicine I have been practicing for many years, so I questioned their premise at abandoning these techniques. They have always worked so well."

Doctor Voigt had due attention of his audience now, he was indeed an influential speaker. She watched as Conrad shrank back in the presence of such self-assurance; she had not thought that possible. She was enthralled by what he had to say, since he had attended university, he would doubtless have so much more knowledge than her. Could this be the same physician the mayor had avoided taking his baby to? This man appeared so confident and authoritative, he did not sound at all like the man she had heard about.

"The body is composed of liquids, or humours: blood, phlegm, yellow and black bile. Our health is not only influenced by the balance of these humours but also reflected in our disposition, our temperament. One cannot hope to maintain the balance without good food and good thoughts, and without purging the body by the required means when one or another is in excess."

The group mumbled in agreeance although it made no sense to Ella. He droned on for some time, talking about new methods to drain blood or cause sweat, as well as new emetics and laxatives. She listened quietly, beginning to see how his methods were indeed extreme compared to hers. She preferred to use a Hippocratic approach, as her Opa had taught her: *first do no harm*. When she chose herbs to treat a condition, she always focused on what she needed them to do, to restore balance within the body rather than disrupt it further. If she was ever in any doubt over what to prescribe, she would consider her selections carefully to make sure they would at least not make the patient worse. This physician appeared to use something he referred to as the Galenic approach. She had never heard of it before, but it sounded like it relied on what appeared to be severe draining of one form or another.

Several times she wanted to comment or challenge his theories, but remembered Carol's words and remained silent, listening politely, nodding occasionally as if her opinions could not possibly matter. He spoke to the group, especially her, as if their experience in the subject was somewhat lacking. He obviously had no idea she was the one that treated the mayor's baby, so she preferred to show mock agreeance rather than disrupt the peace, hiding her boredom by sipping on her wine. Luckily, refills were in plentiful supply.

She was almost glad to see Louise saunter into the room, wine glass in hand, sizeable ruff around her neck and wide, flowing dress. Her pearls glistened low on her chest, her skin exposed, no doubt trying to attract a man or two. Tonight, she was wearing a dark red velvet gown that made its own entrance. Her raven hair was perched high atop her head, a long red feather was poking out and flowing down, following her around the room like a bustle for her bun. She was chatting with two other young ladies, both well dressed with tall, stiff collars, but they were nowhere near as striking, or as commanding, as Louise.

"Excuse me gentlemen." Ella curtsied and shuffled her way over to the women. "Louise, how nice to see you." She bowed her head to the ladies in turn.

"Why, Ella." Louise's eyes grew wide. "I did not know you would be here." She observed Louise admiring her gown momentarily, clearly surprised to see her dressed in such a sophisticated manner. Louise quickly averted her gaze and began prattling away to one of the other ladies she had come in with. Their eyes darted from Louise to Ella, as if waiting for an introduction.

Ella sipped at her drink and glanced around the room, wondering where else she could go. She was certainly not going to return to the group of men she had tried politely to leave for some time.

It was a few moments before Louise paused her conversation and glared directly at Ella, her stare as cold as ice. "I'm sorry, don't you have an apple to go stew or something?" She scoffed, then turned to her companions. "Please give me a moment." She grabbed Ella firmly by the elbow and led her a few steps away, where they could speak privately. "What exactly do you want?" she spat out in hushed tones, close and vicious like a viper striking.

"I was just saying hello," replied Ella. Surely, to not do so would have been rude? "I don't really know anyone else here." She fiddled with her wine glass. "Katherine is so busy with her other guests."

"As am I, did you not notice?"

Ella inhaled sharply and shook her head tightly.

Louise continued staring at her. "Well?"

"Ah…" Ella let out the breath she was holding and tapped at her glass. She leaned in and spoke quietly, "so, how have you been, have things settled down for you, with your cycle?"

"Everything is like clockwork, thank you very much, and I would ask you not to bring up my health here. I've finished with the tea, but I've still got plenty of herbs. The pain is all gone, and the flow has settled too. I will come find you if I need health advice. You have done your service and I paid my dues." She straightened up, patted down her bodice and jutted out her chin. "Now, do not come near me for the rest of the evening, I have nothing more to say to you." She trotted off like a bright red peacock toward Conrad and the men on the other side of the room.

Ella tried to melt into the drapes, wishing she was one of the flowers in the nearby vase right now. She sipped again at her wine, rather graciously refilled by the servants in attendance. Thankfully, it was not long before they were called to the table for supper, Ingrid fetching her and giving her arm a gentle but supportive squeeze. She led Ella to the table in her beautiful but difficult dress, helping her by tucking in the chair as she sat. Ella noticed the other women needed assistance with their chairs too, relieved that it was not just her struggling with the fullness of her skirts.

The table was covered with plates and platters of all shapes and sizes, loaded with roast meats of all kinds, pickled and roasted vegetables, cheeses, fruits, breads – there was so much food, it would have fed her village for a month. The guests sat around the long table, just twenty in all, and filled their plates from the array set out before them. Every setting was fine ceramic with silver cutlery and soft linen napkins. There was barely room for their glasses, so the servants stood back, lining the walls with their pitchers of beer and wine, ready to top up any drinks as they ran dry.

Ella was seated across from Conrad, and sadly not far enough away from Louise, who was just three chairs down from her on the opposite side of the table. Next to her sat the physician, still gloating about his presentation and knowledge. She hardly felt like eating but smiled at Katherine who appeared to be having a fabulous evening of it all. She drank more of her wine to keep in good spirits and put some smoked fish and roast venison on her plate.

Discussion focused on Katherine, her birthday celebrations, and questions about Clare. "She celebrated her first birthday just two weeks ago. She's starting to babble and trying hard to walk," Katherine declared proudly. "I swear she said Mama today, which was the greatest present of all." A loud round of 'hear, hear' and 'prost' was given in acknowledgment.

"So, she recovered from that terrible cough?" asked one of the ladies, as she piled a heap of food into her mouth.

"Oh yes, thanks to Ella over there." Katherine raised her glass. "To Ella."

'To Ella,' was repeated around the table as they rose their glasses and clinked them together. Ella's cheeks warmed as she gazed around at the guests, noticing Louise did not raise her glass or repeat the phrase. She caught Ulrich's eyes again and hastily glanced away.

Doctor Voigt, next to Ella, swivelled in his seat, his back as straight as a rod. "I believe we met earlier, but you did not tell me your profession." He held out his hand. "I thought they said you worked on a farm?"

She shook his hand gingerly. "Apple orchard," she mumbled, noticing the chatter around her hush. Some reached for their glasses while others cut at their food, the scraping of knives on plates the only sound.

"I've never heard of a woman at a university before. A girl, so young, to have graduated, and then to go work on a farm?" He made eye contact with those around the table as he spoke. A few of them leant over to whisper to their neighbour. "Tell me, where did you study?"

Everyone was staring at Ella. She gulped nervously. "I have not been to university, Herr Voigt." She spoke softly as she dabbed at the corners of her mouth with her napkin, her eyes flitting around.

"Well then, where did you learn your medical skills?"

He would have known her answer. He was setting her up for a grand fall in front of everyone. Silence reigned.

"I believe you would call it the school of life," laughed Conrad, raising his glass, a feeble attempt to bring humour back to the gathering. Everyone else remained mute, watching the exchange.

"So, without any formal medical training, you took it upon yourself to treat a baby with a deadly cough?" Voigt chortled, his eyes catching each of the nobles gathered. "Tell me girl, what treatment did you use to cure this deadly cough?"

Emboldened by far more wine than she was used to, Ella cleared her throat and raised her head, speaking clearly this time. "I gave her some sundew and thyme extracts to loosen the mucus, and a balm infused with ginger to warm the damp from her chest."

Voigt laughed. "Flowers!" he broadcast to the table, "and spices." He chuckled, waving his hands animatedly to encourage others to join in at the joke. "You risked a baby's life with flowers and spices?"

This was too much. She had needed to endure his bragging earlier about strange medical methods that were clearly not effective, but at least he had not been attacking her directly like this in front of everyone. Her blood boiled with an anger she never knew she possessed. "Well, my *'flowers and spices'* as you put it, did more good than your university degree. That baby is alive today because of what I gave her."

Cutlery clinked as glasses and knives were put down. There were some gasps from around the table, a few of the ladies put their hands to their mouths. The men leaned in, seemingly amused that a woman should attempt to speak up like this in the company of others. She could see the servants exchange wary glances; Ingrid edged closer to where she was sitting.

"Why you're barely more than a peasant, with no idea of who you are talking to and no right to be seated at this table." He sputtered. "I spent years studying the latest medical techniques at university, and you sit here, with your flowers and spices, pretending to know more than me about the workings of the human body. There would be more flavour in this food than good in your remedies. I bet the gulden clinked as loudly as your promises."

She fought to hold back the tears welling in her eyes. She had never been so openly ridiculed, nor felt so desperately alone. She noticed Katherine place her hand on her husband's arm and lean over to whisper something to him.

"I will not sit here and take this from you." Ella tried to push her seat back from the table in a feeble attempt to stand. The weight of all the layers of the dress, as pretty as it was, made her effort to exit elegantly completely impossible. Despite her struggle, she could not manage to move back. The layers of her dress were twisting up around her ankles as she swivelled, trying to get out of her chair.

"My word, girl, whatever do you have on your feet?" Voigt was looking down as her skirts had ridden up just enough to expose her boots. "Are they... *farm boots*?" He let out a haughty laugh. Louise joined in all too rapidly, setting most of the guests off into wild cackles.

'Farm boots' reverberated around the table. Ulrich rose to his feet but said nothing, compassion written on his face. Neither he nor Katherine were finding Ella's embarrassment amusing.

Ingrid handed her pitcher to one of the other servants and rushed forward to pull the chair back, allowing Ella the freedom she needed to move. Ella's face burnt with rage and humiliation as she finally managed to stand.

"Haha, dear Conrad," chuckled the mayor. "You'll be doing well to control that one." He laughed with the rest of the party, slapping the table for good measure.

Louise threw a sharp glare at Conrad as he managed to leave the table far quicker than Ella, nearly catching her as she dashed out of the room. Ingrid trailed closely behind, staying in the background.

"Ella," called Conrad, racing after her in the hall. He caught up to her rapidly, not inhibited as she was in her gown. He grabbed her hard by the arm and span her around to face him. "Do you realise who you insulted in there? He is the town physician, a respected and learned man who has spent many years at university, and many more years since, studying the human body. He is the finest physician in these parts and has earnt his place at that table."

"What am I then, just some farm girl that managed to save a baby when he could not?" Tears ran down her face. How she longed to be home with Tomas and her opa. "If he is so great, then how come your townspeople come to visit me instead of him?"

"You will keep your voice down. You have dishonoured yourself enough already." He glanced around to see if anyone else was listening, ignoring Ingrid's presence. "You would do well to earn a place at that table, beside me as your husband, but if that were to happen, you need to learn when to keep your mouth shut first."

Ella gasped, putting one hand to her chest and the other on her waist. "I don't want a place at that table," she spat out, "or by your side." She was shaking now, unable to control it. "And there is no way I would ever want to call you husband."

Conrad squeezed her arm tighter before pushing her away with a low growl. "Go then, you silly farm girl, run back to your apples and your garden. You don't belong here." He stormed back to the dinner party, grumbling at Ingrid as he passed, "make sure Frau Schulz's dress is cleaned of that farm girls' stench before it is returned."

Ingrid curtsied, bowed her head low and waited till he left the hall before running after Ella. She led her back to her room, soothing her as she helped her undress, then fetched her a cup of warm milk and honey. "You only need get through the church service tomorrow, then you can head back home," she reminded Ella, as she stroked her hair tenderly.

Ella closed her eyes and hoped sleep would come fast.

Conrad, enraged by Ella's refusal, was quick to whisk an all too willing Louise from the party to his bed chambers, as he had many a night before. He was rougher with her than usual, but Louise always opened her legs to him gladly. And so she should. Here was a girl that recognised the power and privilege a life with the mayor's nephew could provide.

Just a pity I could not endure her for more than a year. He smiled to himself smugly as he pounded away at the flesh he wished was Ella instead.

Chapter 11

Reason is the greatest enemy that faith has;
it never comes to the aid of spiritual things. – Martin Luther

Sunday morning began early with a knock on the door at seven.

"How did you sleep Frau Baumann?" Ingrid pulled back the curtains from around the bed while the other maid servant busied herself setting up breakfast and removing the night's chamber pot.

"Terribly." Ella opened her eyes bleakly, unmoving on the bed, not wanting to rise.

"Come now Ella," encouraged Ingrid. "Let us get you to church, and then you can go back to Tomas."

Ella hauled herself up wearily. Sitting through a service with the town's spiteful old pastor was a sadly fitting way to end such a dreadful trip. She'd woken in the middle of the night, her mind whirling with the events of the evening. Her eyes were puffed and swollen from crying herself back to sleep, and she had a terribly foreboding feeling about the day ahead. She glanced outside the window sadly then focused on the flickering flames of the fire. Ingrid was adding some logs and stoking it up to get it going again. She came back over to Ella with a brush, placing it next to her on the bed before unplaiting her braid and running it through her hair. It was such a kind act of caring after the humiliation of the night before that she began to sob quietly.

"Hey now, please don't cry. You need to go to church with these people, and they think nothing of putting us working class back in our places." She parted Ella's hair and continued brushing. "Remember, *you* saved Katherine's baby. That Doctor Voigt, for all his big words and fancy degrees, did nothing to help her. If it were not for you, Clare would not be here today. He put down your healing abilities simply because you did what he could not. You showed him up – not only are you young, but you are also a woman, and from the country without a degree. Did you learn nothing from being in that room with them last night? They all want the biggest collar, the best title, and to boast the loudest. You didn't need to say a thing to draw his abilities into question, your actions did the talking for you. Well, regardless of your education, or where you were born, you were better with Clare than he could ever be, and what he really cannot face is there is no way of denying that. All he could do was put you down for what you do not have; a piece of paper that he thinks proves he is best. That baby lives today without that piece of paper, and don't you forget that. Of course he wants you to feel bad, Ella." She bent down before Ella to meet her eyes as she spoke. "You made him feel inferior. Simply by doing your best, and saving that baby, you became better than him."

Ella stopped crying, wiped away her tears and forced her lips into a smile.

"Ah, that's better. A man is not judged by what he says." Ingrid moved to Ella's side and crafted two long braids as she talked. "A man is judged by what he does. Or in his case, does not." She smirked to herself, wrapping the tails of Ella's plaits neatly into a bun at the base of her neck. "The fact that you are a woman – no – a *girl*, would have been doubly demeaning for him." She used hair pins to hold the bun in place then affixed Ella's cap over the top. "Let alone a farm girl with no education."

"Thank you, Ingrid." Ella rose to embrace her friend tightly, thank goodness she was there. She walked over to her purple dress and fell in love with it all over again. It symbolised gratitude from someone who appreciated the care she had provided and proved what she did for others helped, even without a degree and regardless of what was said to her last night. She hesitated, "I just don't know how I am going to sit through church today, with everyone knowing what happened last night. I am sure it will be spread halfway around town before the sermon is over." She cringed.

"Their version may be spread part way through town," said Ingrid, coming over to assist her with the buttons. "But the far larger population of this town is not nobility. Every one of the staff in this building has already heard the servants' version of what happened, and trust me, it draws you in the best possible light. If word is to spread, it is our version that will spread furthest, fastest, and in your favour." She came around to face Ella, pulling the bodice down and straightening out the skirt before helping her fasten the cape. "We will all be at church too. So, for every one of those nobles that wants to look down their nose and over their collars at you, just remember there are many more of us admiring how you stood up for yourself, and what you have done for those who need your help, including baby Clare." She gave Ella's shoulders a squeeze. "There now, make sure you have breakfast and have some of that hot water with lemon and honey. The pastor's sermons here are so dull you will otherwise surely fall asleep."

⚘ ⚘ ⚘

Ella ate quickly and went downstairs to wait for the mayor and Katherine. She was in the sitting area of the grand foyer, and despite everything she had been through, could not help but be impressed by the size and elegance of the council's chambers. Conrad came down first. She stiffened when she saw him, her breath catching in her throat. He was dressed in yet another pompous outfit, the feather plumes reflections of his ego.

"Same old dress again I see," he remarked rudely, marching past. "Why don't you go get some mud on those boots, farmgirl."

She exhaled loudly once he'd gone. After Ingrid's talk that morning, her resilience had grown, his words deflecting off some invisible armour. She grinned, at least he would stop pursuing her now. Shortly after, the mayor and Katherine descended the stairs. Katherine was as graceful as always in a pale pink dress much like the one she wore, but with a much longer cape, and those ridiculous ruffs they insisted on wearing. Ella curtsied deeply. "Good morning, Herr Schulz, Frau Schulz." She bowed her head low then faced Katherine directly. "I am so sorry about my exit last night, Frau Schulz, I did not mean to cause you any embarrassment. I wanted to thank you for your kind hospitality and letting me borrow your dress."

"It's alright Ella." Katherine reached out for her hand. "I had a lovely time, and everyone forgot about what happened shortly after you left."

That could not possibly be true, but at least Katherine was letting her off easily.

"I did not realise you do not have formal shoes," said Katherine. "But of course you don't, you've never needed them. I am so sorry, I should have thought of that. Next time, if you ever want to return to the city, please ask me for some more appropriate footwear before dinner." She smiled kindly.

"I never did mind a good pair of boots," said Carl with good humour. "Much more practical than those ridiculous pattens some women insist on wearing. You certainly added some colour to the evening." He cleared his throat. "I do hope you are done for the moment though, as our pastor would not take so kindly to such a performance in his church." He grinned at her.

"We really are grateful you saved our Clare, regardless of what Doctor Voigt had to say. What you did to save her life cannot be undone, nor forgotten."

"Thank you." Ella curtsied deeply again. "For being so kind and understanding."

"Now, let's to church shall we, before the best part of the day passes before us." The mayor led them out of the building and on the short walk over to the St Jakob church.

Ella had been impressed by the council's chambers, and always thought her church in Detwang was beautiful, but both were cosy by comparison to this amazing structure. It appeared daunting enough from the outside, but with its soaring ceilings and white stone finish, it was simply enormous on the inside. Behind the alter were arched, stained glass windows that soared six or more stories high. Dotted around the church were the most elaborate wooden carvings depicting different stations of the cross. The pews were long and so numerous, that as much as she tried, she lost count. Inside already were hundreds, if not at least a thousand of the town's inhabitants. Ella followed Carl and Katherine to the front pew, where she settled beside Katherine. Conrad sat with his chin raised high on the other side of the mayor.

The singing and ritual of the mass commenced shortly after they arrived, but was distinctly less joyful than the service in Detwang. Although the congregation sang together, it was more of a chore than a joyful joining of voices. Ella did not know the words to these hymns and did not want to let on that she could not read the booklet of verses, so moved her lips in time and hummed. After reading the bible from the front of the church, the pastor sauntered down the side of the pews to ascend a spiralling staircase to the pulpit. It was encased in gothic wooden carvings with a large sounding board above, appearing even more like a crown floating above his head than the one in her familiar church. She avoided eye contact with this pastor as he had always been so rude to her, she just could not take another personal attack on this visit. As he droned on, she realised his voice was oddly unsettling; it seemed to echo from some dark recess in her memory.

"For today's sermon, I will be taking a reading from the good man himself. Our leader for these modern times, Martin Luther, may the good Lord bless his resting soul." He made the sign of the cross and bowed his head for a short moment before continuing. "On his views from Exodus 22:18: Thou shalt not suffer a sorceress to live, and I quote: *"let them be killed. The law that sorceresses should be killed is most just, since they do many cursed things. Let sorceresses be killed since they are thieves, adulterers, robbers, murderers. Go against them with the sword or strong faith. They do manifold damage therefore let them be killed, not only because they cause damage but also because they consort with Satan."*

Ella gasped, placing a hand over her mouth. She had never heard a sermon so full of hate with decrees of killing in a church. She gazed around, observing others in the congregation to see if they were as distressed by this sermon as her, but it became apparent that this type of speech was normal for the towns people. While the pastor droned on at length about the evils of sorcery, no one else seemed in the least bit upset by his preaching. She had heard her pastor talk of the need to avoid evil in all its forms, but never in these terms or with such malice. Ella watched Katherine discreetly, who seemed ignorant of the message, busy fiddling with the lace trim on her gloves. She leaned back to gauge the mayor's reaction, but he was sleeping quietly, some dribble forming at the corner of his mouth. She averted her eyes quickly when they fell on Conrad, who stared back at her with cold anger.

After what seemed a short eternity, the service was over, and Katherine was nudging Carl awake. Conrad bolted from his seat. "Dear, we must go and bid our pleasantries," she said to Carl. They rose and Katherine reached out to Ella, taking her by surprise and embracing her briefly. "I have arranged for our carriage to take you back home. The coachman will have already loaded your belongings and should be waiting at the front of the town hall for you. I do hope you will visit us again sometime."

"Thank you again, Herr Schulz, Frau Schulz." She curtsied. "Before I take leave, may I ask a favour?"

Carl, fully awake now, tipped his head from side to side. "Well, it depends on what it is young lady." He grinned and winked, to show he was only teasing.

She paused briefly then smiled. "Well, it's about my impending nuptials." Ella blushed, "I was wondering…"

"You mean you want to go ahead with that after last night?" Carl wobbled his head, flabbergasted. "I must say, after what Conrad told me you said to him last night, I thought that was no longer an option. Why the change of heart, and what is to happen to the orchard?"

Ella's brow creased. "I was hoping Tomas could move in with us, and we would take over the lease?" She spoke slowly, confused.

"Who is Tomas and what does he have to do with your marriage to Conrad?"

Katherine watched the exchange between her husband and Ella, a bewildered expression on her face.

It took Ella just a short moment to catch up. "Oh!" She clapped her hands together and let out a chuckle. "I'm sorry Herr Schulz, there seems to be a misunderstanding. Tomas is my neighbour, back in Detwang. Our pastor has been writing to you for a couple of months now, seeking a time for Tomas to meet with you and ask your permission to approve our marriage. He was also going to ask if he could become the new lessee of your orchard with me, and we will tend your land."

"So, you are not going to marry Conrad?" asked Katherine.

"No, I have no interest in Conrad," assured Ella.

"Ah, this is making much more sense now! And you will stay on as lessees?"

"Yes, Herr, Schulz, with your permission of course."

"Well, I must meet this Tomas." He folded his arms, his eyes narrowed. He rocked on the balls of his feet. "You say your pastor wrote to me about this before?"

"Yes, Herr Schulz, several times, over many weeks."

Carl's eyes widened, resolution settling on his face. "What did my office have to say in reply?"

"That you were very busy, and we should wait until you had time."

Carl nodded, stroking his short beard. "Yes, of course it did." He chewed at his top lip for a moment then replied. "I tell you what, you have that man of yours come and see me at ten in the morning on the first day of spring. If the two of you still feel the same way, and he can assure me he will care for you and my land, you will have my blessing."

"Oh, thank you, Herr Schulz." Ella had to hold herself back from jumping up and down or hugging him. "He will be there."

"Now off you go, I have pleasantries to attend to and a nephew to demote. Safe travels, Ella, and take care of those apples."

"Oh, I will, Herr Schulz, Frau Schulz." She curtsied again, a few times, so happy was she with the news, she had to contain herself as she all but skipped out of the church.

She was only vaguely aware of Ulrich standing a few pews back. His mouth opened, as if he was about to say something, but Ella just wanted to get home. She smiled politely and raised her hand in a wave as she scooted past.

🐚 🐚 🐚

Even though the sky was grey, and the trees of the town were now bare, Detwang had never appeared so inviting. As the carriage rolled to a halt outside her welcoming cottage, both Ernest and Tomas came running to see Ella and hear of her adventures in town. She exited as fast as she could with the help of the coachman, racing over to hug both Tomas and her opa at once. Kissing them both firmly on the cheek, she turned her attention to Tomas, hugging him tightly while he lifted her off the ground.

"My beautiful girl, I missed you," he said, covering her face with kisses. "I was worried some nobleman may have swept you off your feet and you would not return."

She laughed. "Oh Tomas, nothing could be further from the truth. Have you met the noblemen of that city? Trust me, you have nothing to worry about." She cuddled into him again. "I have great news. The mayor has asked you to meet with him at ten in the morning, on the first day of spring, and ask for his approval for our union."

Tomas put her back on the ground, locking eyes with her. "He said what? You're not playing with me, are you?"

"No, Tomas, I am not!" Ella was beaming. "He wants to know we are certain about a future together and have you confirm that you will take over the orchard here, and he will give us his blessing."

"Oh beautiful, this is the best news yet." Tomas picked her up and twirled her around. "So, we can start to make our future arrangements? Mama and Sarah have been keen to make all sorts of plans about our wedding day, with your approval, of course."

"Tell them to organise whatever they want, I just want to marry you." She unlocked herself from his embrace and stepped over to her grandfather. "Opa, I understand now what you meant. The people of that town, well there are some nice ones, like Hans and Magda and Carol, and I saw Ingrid…"

"You saw Ingrid?" Tomas cut in. "Did you see Otto as well? How are they?"

Ella giggled and faced Tomas, "I did not see Otto, but I got to taste his cooking. They are both doing well." She turned back toward her grandfather and clasped his hand. "I know what you mean now, by those people being so different. The cruelties I saw them inflicting on their own people… I went to market yesterday and there was a man and woman chained to a post for petty indiscretions. A seamstress was forced to wear a block around her neck for making a collar too wide. It was horrible, Opa, simply horrible. And then the sermon I had to sit through today…" She shook her head, trying to clear it from her mind. "It was full of hate for an unbelievable evil. They're such a superstitious, jealous and controlling bunch of nobles, I never want to go back there again!"

"Woah, Ella, surely it was not all bad?" asked Tomas.

"Well, I got to wear the most amazing gown on Saturday night, and the food was delicious and there was just so much of it." She gazed from her opa to Tomas and back again. "But all of it was just a front for some of the meanest people I have ever met."

"Well, you are back here now, safe, and where you belong," said Ernest. "That is all that matters." He picked up her basket and ambled toward the cottage. "Now, I think you should unpack and get some rest. You have a lot of apples to preserve, and winter is fast approaching."

"It's always work with you, isn't it Opa?" she sighed, exhausted at the thought.

"The winter does not wait for the idle man, my dear, and it will be a cold one this year," he called over his shoulder. "Come inside, I've made some bread."

"Do you mind if I stay with you today?" asked Tomas, taking her hand firmly in his. "I have missed you so much, and I want to hear all about your big trip."

"If you don't mind, Tomas, there are parts of what I saw that I would rather not retell. But did you know, they don't use chamber pots?"

"Do they not need to go?" he asked, aghast.

"That's exactly what I first said." She laughed as she explained about the garderobes and described the beautiful furniture. She told him about the soaring stained-glass windows in the church, and that she saw Hans and Magda's bakery. She pushed the repulsive thoughts of time with Conrad, and that dinner party, to the furthest corners of her mind, hoping never to relive them again.

It was a particularly cold and brutal winter that year. Snow fell almost twice as heavy as usual, the pruning chores made harder by darker days and chilly winds. The inclement weather had prevented Ella from going on all but very short trips to the nearest cottages to check on the wellbeing of the locals. There were several weeks where the church bells rang, notifying the villagers that the service was cancelled, and they should instead gather with their families and stay in their cottages where they could keep safe and warm. Luckily, illness had not impacted the village people much considering the weather. Many had been taking preventative herbs from Ella or kept tinctures for coughs and sniffles handy, to tackle them at the first sign of sickness. At the few church services that ran, the pastor informed his parish of colds and disease that had spread through Rothenburg, claiming many lives, warning them to avoid trips to the town where possible lest they find themselves affected also. Avoiding the town went without saying, as the snow and slush that covered the short trek made it all but impassable anyway. Carol never made it back to see Ella in time before winter set in. There had been no visitors from the town seeking her help for several months because the weather had made it too dangerous to travel. It was unreasonable to make the trip, even with horse, cart, or especially by carriage.

On Tomas' farm they moved their pigs to the barn and chickens inside their house; they were not alone in doing so. Many of the villagers moved their animals inside if they did not have the barns or sheds to shelter them, as they simply would not have survived the winter if they were left outside. The animals inside the houses tended to bring fleas or lice, but also much needed warmth. Ernest had constructed a special area for their chickens and goats in the packing shed, as it was empty of apples during the winter months. They kept the stove burning for their animals and let the goats out to wander on the better days, their coats thick and resistant to some of the cold.

While a winter like that would have been avoided by all if they had a choice, for Ella it was a welcome respite. She warmed herself by the fire in the company of those she loved, working on knitting or other projects, sometimes in the company of Julia and Sarah. Other times she sat with Tomas and Ernest while they whittled or carved to keep their minds busy.

She had all but wiped away the dreadful memories of her town visit and restored her faith in other people.

At least, until spring arrived.

Chapter 12

The reproduction of mankind is a great marvel and mystery.
Had God consulted me in the matter, I should have advised him to continue
the generation of the species by fashioning them of clay,
in the way Adam was fashioned. – Martin Luther

March, 1605

It was only as the first days of spring approached that planning a trip to Rothenburg became possible. Tomas made sure he was at the town hall, ten in the morning on March the first, to meet with the mayor.

They talked about the weather, and his promise to tend the orchard. The mayor, being satisfied, granted joy to their marriage. He fetched for Carol, who gave Tomas a large box with Ella's wedding dress inside. Tomas in turn gave Carol some herbs and balm from Ella, who was ever so grateful to finally have them since she had not made it in time to restock before winter, the pain in her fingers having returned worse than ever.

Tomas took his leave shortly after with the box in hand, a contented smile on his face. He had not even noticed the smug overdressed clerk attending the front office scowl at him as he left.

🌸 🌸 🌸

It was growing late in the day as a distressed Louise arrived at the town hall to speak with that clerk. When the mayor had realised Conrad had stopped the letters requesting an audience with Tomas, even refused the audience on his behalf, he was outraged. Carl investigated what other actions Conrad had made under his good name, only to find frivolous tavern spending, the purchase of several expensive garments, and even some feminine gifts being paid for with the town's taxes, none of which he had approved. There had been multiple appointments that had not been made, some of significant importance, like issues of town waste and stocks to be made before their coming winter. Conrad was quickly demoted but still chose not to return to Munich. The anger of his uncle was pale by comparison to the wrath of his parents, so he had chosen to stay in Rothenburg, albeit demoted to the position of clerk.

Seeing Louise was the last thing he felt like that day, but he was the only one tending the desk that afternoon so could not dash out; he did not dare deceive his uncle again. He was intent on earning his favour and place back, even if it took some time.

"Conrad, I must talk with you," pleaded Louise. "Privately. Now."

He raised his head, glancing around at the empty hall. "I see no one around."

"This is of a very personal matter," urged Louise. "We really should go somewhere else to discuss it."

This girl was starting to get on his nerves. Even with his demotion, his strong family connection still made him a favourite for the next position of mayor, although it could be some ten or so years away. It was probably the main reason Louise kept hanging around, it certainly could not be for the way he treated her. Since Ella's rebuttal, he had shown less and less interest in Louise unless she was in a position to give him something in return. "Hurry up, girl, out with it. There is no one here." He was tired, cold and grumpy, and really not in the mood for her at that moment, or ever, if it came to that.

"Very well then." Her lips curled nervously. "We are going to have a baby."

He dropped the files he had been sorting. Could his life get any worse? "I am sorry, I think I misheard you. What did you just say?"

"I am with child. We are going to have a baby." Her smile faltered. "We need to marry soon though, before I start to show."

"What exactly makes you think it is mine?" he asked, sighing loudly.

She glared at him sharply. "Excuse me?"

"You heard me. I cannot be the only man a girl like you takes up with. How do you know it is mine?"

"Because," she grunted, "you *are* the only man I have taken up with. How dare you say that to me. You know very well how often we have laid together."

He watched her fiddle with those damned pearls around her neck. How he would like to pull them tight until her face became blue. "Keep your voice down woman. I do not want other people hearing of this." He checked around again, wishing he'd had this conversation in a more private place after all.

"Well, what are we going to do about it?" she asked, her voice trembling.

He ran his hands through his hair, in truth, not wanting anything to do with her. There was no bigger shame a girl could bring on her family than to find herself unwed and in a delicate position. "How did this happen? Are you sure it is mine?"

"Do you need me to explain how it works?" she barked at him, panic rising in her voice. "If you are not going to take responsibility, my father will take this up directly with your uncle!" She stared icily at him. "You are to ask for my hand in marriage at once, or else I will have him come visit your uncle this evening."

"Your father knows?" he almost shouted. His head pounded, he felt dizzy. This was not good. If that were the case, it would get back to his uncle quicker than he could tell him himself.

"No, not yet." Her face crumbled and she started to sob. "I was hoping this would have been joyful news, and that you would have been happy to marry me."

His legs were shaking. He could not go back to Munich, he had left a similar situation there, but with hired help. At least Louise was of good standing in the community, until her condition became known that is, and her father was a trusted advisor to the mayor. If he wanted to win favour back, he had only one option: marry Louise and live a life of misery. He put his head in his hands, massaging his temples. "Are you absolutely sure? How long have you known?"

"I have only just become certain. I am two weeks late today."

"Can't that be normal though? I mean, can't that happen anyway, being late?"

"Several months ago, perhaps. But then I saw Ella at the end of summer, and she gave me some herbs. They made my cycle as regular as clockwork. Since then, I have been on time, to the day, for five cycles. Until this one. Now I am late, and my breasts are tender." She went quiet, almost muttering to herself. "Ella said this would happen."

His head snapped up and his brow furrowed. "Ella said what would happen?"

Louise explained, "Ella said a healthy cycle makes things ready for babies. In other words…"

He finished her sentence, "she gave you herbs that helped form a child." His voice trailed off as he voiced his thoughts out loud. "That witch has conjured us up a baby." He muttered it under his breath, not caring if Louise heard him or not. He was thinking fast, talking out loud as his mind raced. "If she can give you herbs to make a baby, she can give you herbs to take it away."

Louise shook her head, her face aghast. "A baby is a gift from God, I don't want it taken away." Tears rolled down her cheeks.

"Louise, I do not want a baby at this point in my life. Think about it." He rose and paced around his desk, preparing his lie before he spoke. "We are young, and I have not yet improved my position. We do not have the money to start a family. I doubt the mayor will have us live here as husband and wife, so what are we to do?" He was rambling now. "I will go and see Ella, explain what has occurred, and she will give us some herbs that will alleviate the problem." He nodded. "Yes, that is what has to happen. She has to make this right, you will see." He checked the town clock, noting it would be dark soon. "I will go, first thing tomorrow, and get some herbs that will remedy the situation."

Louise nodded as she bit her lip and dried her tears with her handkerchief. "If that is what you think best."

"Oh, it is," he assured her. "It is for the best, my darling." He was acting more tenderly with her now than he had in the past, placating her so she would not be tempted to tell her father. He needed to make sure she would follow through and take whatever herbs he could get. "I must close the office now and organise the carriage for the morning. Please go home, put your feet up, and by tomorrow afternoon this will all be taken care of." He kissed her on the forehead and led her out of the town hall, locking up for the evening and racing upstairs to see his uncle.

He rapped on Carl's office door. A stirring could be heard from inside. "Come in." The room was soporifically warm. Carl's cheeks were red, his eyes drowsy. He appeared as if he was either about to fall asleep or had just woken.

"Uncle, it has been a harsh winter. I would like your permission to book the carriage and visit Detwang and the hinterland, to check on your land and the villagers. I know there has been a significant loss of life here in Rothenburg, I wanted to see if the villagers have been as severely affected."

Carl nodded. "That is most considerate of you. Very well." He leaned forward on his desk. "Please check on the orchard too."

He bobbed his head and bowed as he swivelled on the spot to leave. That was all too easy.

"Oh, and Conrad," his uncle called after him.

He pivoted back hesitantly. "Yes?"

"Stay away from Ella. I have just today given my permission for her to marry another man. I do not want to hear that you have interfered in any way."

"Of course, Uncle, she is the last person I would want to see." He feigned disinterest at visiting Ella, although she was in truth the only reason he was going. He had no intention of taking stock of the villagers' health and wellbeing.

🌸 🌸 🌸

Ella opened the package from Carol eagerly, holding her wedding dress up against her body. She extended a sleeve and danced around the small living room of the cottage, the fabric moving in time as she twirled in circles. It was all going ahead now, they had the mayor's permission, and Tomas was in the bedroom measuring up to make them a more comfortable, wider bed. Julia and Sarah were taking care of all the arrangements and planning the food for their special day. It was to be a celebration for most of the village, Ella being such an important part of their everyday life. The local pastor would be overseeing their nuptials and the celebration was to be the first Saturday of July.

She folded the dress carefully and fetched the lace collar and cuffs she had been working on. They would suit it perfectly, since Carol had made barely any collar at all, Ella could attach the lace she had crafted with great effect. In Detwang, the size of collars was never measured, it was purely at the whim or fancy of the wearer. She squashed the horrible memories of what she saw in the town square a few months ago.

I shall have the grandest collar in the village on my wedding day, she thought, smirking to herself as she pinned them in place.

The next day was still chilly. Even though it was spring, the severe winter they'd had meant a lot of warming of the ground was needed before the trees and plants would be woken from their winter slumber. Ella had the fire burning brightly in the stove of the packing shed to warm the building. Today she was making more of her balm base and needed to purify the beeswax. It came to her as hard, solid blocks with some residue of the hive left behind. She heated it until it was all melted, then gave it a stir and removed it from the stove to set semi-hard again. She then scraped the lighter fragments of the beehive that had floated from the top, and heavier debris that had settled from the bottom, leaving an almost pure block of beeswax to work with. After preparing it in this way, she could just chip off smaller

BELINDA CARLI

portions, then melt and combine it with sunflower or flaxseed oil to make her salve base.

Some of the balm she would leave plain, so that it could be mixed with other herbs in a hurry as needed. With the rest, she was going to make infusions, by placing different crushed flowers or herbs in the ointment and allowing them to rest for a month. After that, she would heat it gently and strain the flowers out before replacing with more fresh, crushed flowers and repeating the process one more time. In this way, it made a concentrated balm that was rich in the properties of the herbs or flowers she had used. She always knew these balms were needed, so preparing them in this way made them stronger than mixing them on the spot. She most commonly used comfrey for sore joints, or a combination of calendula and arnica for cuts and wounds. This was also how she made her perfumes, by infusing the balm with rose petals, geranium flowers and lavender – sometimes as a combination, other times on their own. While the flowers had not yet blossomed, she could prepare the base now, then collect, crush and infuse it with flowers once they were in full bloom.

A knock on the door brought her rapidly back to reality. She jumped and turned, snarling when she saw Conrad. He was leaning against the door frame, his arms folded, a smug grin on his face. How long had he been watching her? "What do you want?" she huffed.

"I guess congratulations are in order," he said sarcastically. He swaggered over to her slowly, his smirk broadening as he watched her squirm in his presence.

She stepped back toward the bench. "If you have come to say congratulations, you've said your bit, now leave." She did not take her eyes off him, did not trust him for a second. She hoped her grandfather or Tomas had seen his carriage arrive and would be on their way to help her. The hairs on her arms rose, goosebumps prickled her flesh.

"Silly. Little. Farmgirl." He stepped forward as he spat out each word bitterly. He slapped his gloves on his palm, his eyes fixed on her like a wolf stalking his prey. It did not take long for him to cross the room and stand before her.

She leaned back. He had trapped her in position, an arm either side of her, pressing her against the bench. His nostrils were flaring, hatred flamed in his eyes. "It seems you have got Louise into a fragile position."

His breath was warm on her face, but her blood ran cold. "I beg your pardon? Whatever do you mean?"

He exhaled loudly as he ran his hand on the bench to collect some herbs between his fingertips, then picked them up and flicked them in her face. "Louise is with child because of you."

She blinked away what he'd just thrown at her. Her pulse quickened. "I can assure you, Conrad, I do not have the ability to give her a child. Only you or some other man can lay claim to that."

"Oh Ella, why are you making this harder than it needs to be?" He tipped his head back as if to chuckle, but the sound came out choked, like an evil gargle. He glared directly into her eyes. "Everything with you is such a fight. Why can't you just cooperate?" He raised his voice, slamming his hand on the bench next to her. "You gave her herbs. They gave her a baby."

She started to shake, struggling to find her voice. "I gave her herbs to help with her monthlies. The herbs did not give her a child. You planted that seed inside her."

"If you had not given her the herbs, she would not have grown a baby."

Her eyes grew wide. How could he possibly be blaming her for this? "If you had not cavorted with her, she would not have grown a baby."

Conrad removed his hat and set it down beside her. He ran his fingers through his hair and thumped his fist on the bench. She jumped. "Listen Ella, whether you want to take responsibility for your part in all of this is up to you. The point is, you helped her make a baby, now you need to help her unmake it."

Her mouth dropped open. "Surely you are not asking me what I think you are? I will not have any part in this."

"I am not asking you. I am telling you. You will unmake what you have made."

She swallowed. She simply would not comply with the ridiculousness of what he was suggesting. "I am telling you, I did not make the baby. So, I will not unmake it."

He stepped over to the part of the bench where she had been slicing the setting beeswax with a small axe. He picked it up and ran his thumb along its edge. "This is really blunt, farm girl. What are you hoping to chop with this?"

"It is for the beeswax. It does not need to cut it, it only needs to shave the top before it sets hard."

"No matter." His mouth twisted into an evil smirk. "It is still useful to break a few fingers if you are unwilling to fix your mess." He slammed the spine of it against the bench, his face menacing.

Before that moment, she would have considered him far too soft to act in such a violent manner. Now, however, she believed he would be capable of carrying through with his threat. She gasped and formed tight fists with her hands, bringing them to her chest.

He stepped back to her and pulled at her hands viscously.

"You need to leave." Tomas' voice boomed from the doorway of the packing shed.

Conrad spun around quickly. Ella finally let out the breath that she'd been holding.

"Ah, the pig farmer." He spoke first to Tomas, then to Ella, his words full of spite, "I cannot believe you would marry a pig farmer with barely a gulden to his name, over me, an important councilman in the city. As for your tattletales with my uncle on the day you left Rothenburg... do you know he demoted me to the clerk's office, where I have to deal with the townspeople's petty problems?"

"Better to marry a pig farmer than to marry a pig," she said, spitting in his face.

Conrad dropped the axe on the bench and slapped her hard, forcing her to the ground. Within seconds, Tomas was on top of him, landing several punches before Ernest appeared as if from nowhere and pulled him away.

"Tomas, he's not worth it," Ella shouted as she ran to hold him back. Tomas was breathing hard, a growl reverberating from within his chest like a bear.

"Get out of here, you animal." Ernest pulled Conrad roughly to his feet and threw him toward the door.

Conrad stumbled and straightened out his vest and jacket. He smoothed his hair back and wiped some blood from his face. "Old man, you had better watch who you are calling an animal. Why, you've raised nothing more here than a common witch." He spat out blood and wiped his face again. "Give me the herbs to fix this situation Ella, or I'll have you burn at the stake for your part in all of this."

The colour drained from Ernests' face. He leaned back on some crates to steady himself and clasped at his chest. His breathing became broken and shaky.

"Opa?" Ella let go of Tomas to tend to her grandfather.

Ernest nodded, as if to reassure her he would be alright. "Get. Out." He managed to point to the door, each word an effort.

Tomas raised his chin and clenched his hands into fists. He was only a thumbs width taller than Conrad, but farm work meant he was significantly bigger and stronger.

Conrad was covered in dirt, and blood ran from his nose, yet he persisted. "Give me the herbs."

"I will not." Ella spoke fiercely now. "Do not ask me again. You got her into this situation, now do the right thing and marry her." She reached for his hat, still on the bench, and threw it across the room toward him. The feather appeared broken, much like his ego.

He picked it up, dusted it off and placed it back on his head arrogantly. "You got her in this situation," Conrad yelled at her. "There will be others that will see it that way, I will make sure they do." He limped back toward the door, his eyes on Tomas, wary. "You will burn for this, witch." He hobbled out of the packing shed and fled toward the carriage.

"This is not good, my dear girl," said Ernest, resting on a pile of crates. His face was pale, his breathing short. His hand was still on his chest, massaging the area over his heart. "Who knows what lies he will concoct for the councilmen in Rothenburg to save his own skin."

Ella came back to her grandfather, hugging him gently. "Opa, are you alright?"

He bobbed his head shallowly. "Yes, are you?"

She nodded. "He is just an evil man with a twisted tongue."

"All my life I've tried to protect you from this exact situation. No good will come of this," said Ernest as he rubbed at his temples, his breathing slowly returning to normal. "That town and its people are so blinded by superstitions, their minds are muddled. If he suggests your herbs could brew a baby…"

"Opa, the truth is still the truth even if someone tries to cover it with lies." Ella scoffed as she cut him off. The idea that a tincture in a bottle could produce a baby was almost laughable. "How silly will he sound if he tries to make these claims before his uncle? The mayor is not stupid."

"Perhaps you are right. Perhaps time has brought with it some reason." He ambled toward the door, then pivoted back to Ella and Tomas. "I am going to visit our pastor, let him know what has happened. He is a wise and moral man, he will know what we should do."

"Yes," she agreed, then thought better of it. "Are you sure you should be going that far?" He had not seemed this weak before, surely he should be resting.

"Yes, my dear, the trek will calm me down. I will take it slow, the fresh air will do me good." He was moving more steadily now, his colour had returned a little.

Ella hugged Tomas, relief washing through her. "Thank you for coming in to help. That animal is gone, so let's get back to our chores, so that we may find the funny side of this later."

"Alright beautiful, but I'll be watching from the field, in case he returns." He kissed her tenderly on each cheek then headed out the door.

Ella watched him leave reluctantly before returning to her balms, hoping that would be the last visit from Conrad to their orchard.

Unbeknownst to her, he was able to do far more damage from town.

Chapter 13

But since the Devil's bride, Reason, that pretty whore,
comes in and thinks she's wise…
who can help us, then? Not Judges, not doctors, not king or emperor,
because Reason is the Devil's greatest whore. – Martin Luther

Conrad's mind raced faster than the carriage as they sped back to town. He could not return to Munich, his father had banished him in shame already. Life in Rothenburg had been pretty sweet until Ella had entered his world and turned it upside down, damn that farm girl. He watched the passing countryside roll by his window, the ground still hard and barren from their unseasonably cold winter. He thumped his fist on the windowsill, causing the driver to call out to check if he was alright.

He waved his hand forward in a gesture to keep going. He would have to tell his uncle, who would make him marry Louise, and then he would be stuck in an unhappy union with a baby on the way. Neither of these things he wanted. If he left it too long, however, the townspeople would find out before he would have a chance to marry her and make it look like the baby was intended. If they were to start talking, it would cause his uncle untold embarrassment, and that would ruin his chances at ever becoming mayor, not to mention destroy his standing in the community - he would even be at risk of being sent back to Munich. There was only one plausible option: he would have to take responsibility. Louise's father was a high-standing member of the council and a wealthy landowner. If he did not ask Louise to marry him, she would make good on her threat and tell her father, and that would end badly for him. If he acted fast, they could make it sound like it was a happy accident, and it would be celebrated as a joyous occasion. His uncle and her father would make sure the wedding was prompt and any gossip of a baby before marriage hushed – they had punishments to ensure the locals did not speak out of turn. He grinned as he thought of those hideous masks they forced people to wear when they spread rumours too readily.

He knocked on the roof of the carriage and the coachman slowed. "Driver, do you know where to find Hugo Meier?"

"Yes sir," he replied promptly. "I have taken the mayor to his house several times for dinner."

"Please take me there," he said as he fished out his handkerchief, moistening it with saliva to clean the blood from his face. "When we arrive, I'd like you to ask for Frau Meier, Louise, to come join me in the carriage. I do not want to get out in my present, ah, condition."

"Yes sir," replied the coachman, whipping the horses into action.

They soon arrived at a buttercup yellow building with criss-cross timber beams and framed windows. Boxes were perched from the first story windows, still empty from the season past; the winter they'd had was devastating to more than just the farming lands. The roof was pitched high like all the others, but it was quite a sizeable house in excellent condition, indicative of the owners' standing within the community. The coachman did as he was asked, and Louise hastily joined Conrad in the carriage.

"Oh, my word, what happened to your face?" Louise leaned forward. She reached out to touch him, but he drew away fast as if her fingers were burning coals. She sat back in her seat opposite him, resting her hands in her lap instead.

"Leave it woman." He waved her away, he did not want her sympathy or compassion. He knocked on the roof again and the carriage took off toward the town hall. "I went to see that witch out there in the countryside." He dabbed at his nose. It was no longer flowing but instead crusted with blood. "There was an altercation of sorts with the pig farmer next door." He glanced at her sideways as he tended to his wounds, trying not to face her directly.

Louise smirked briefly, seemingly satisfied that he now showed so much contempt toward Ella. He could not believe that silly farm girl had once been such an object of his affection, when he should instead be happy with the easy conquest that sat before him.

"And?" she asked.

"She said she will not give me herbs to fix your condition." He faced Louise squarely.

She pulled back as her eyes rested on the full extent of his cuts and marks. "So now what are we going to do?"

He drew in a deep breath and changed his demeanour, etching a convincing smile on his face. He had to get her to agree to his plan, so that would take making her believe marriage would be a good thing when only yesterday he had made it sound like it was not. It's not like she had much choice, a girl in her predicament would be stupid to refuse a proposal, especially his. "I'm sorry, I have a lot on my mind." He reached forward, taking her hands. "Louise, I believe the best course of action is for us to get married, as soon as our families can arrange it, and we will celebrate this baby as a happy event in the start of our lives together. Did you not say yourself, if we marry fast, it is still too early for anyone to know this wasn't planned, or conceived on the wedding night?"

"Yes." She squeezed his hands tightly, smiling broadly. "When do we tell my father?"

This was working better than he had hoped, she had accepted him eagerly. "We're on our way to see my Uncle Carl for his permission now." He patted her hands to release his from her grip, leaning back in the chair, one arm on the windowsill, the other on his knee. "Once he agrees, I can take you back to your father and we can set a date."

"Oh, darling this is such wonderful news, thank you." Her knees jiggled up and down, her fingers fiddled childishly with those damned pearls she insisted on wearing. He tried to appear pleased for her sake, when inside, his stomach churned.

They pulled up at the town hall. He got out first and waited next to the carriage door as she stepped out with the help of the coachman. She almost danced up the steps ahead of him, while he ascended slowly, trudging like a man being led to slaughter.

It was still early in the day and Mayor Schulz had no pressing appointments, so they were permitted straight in to see him.

"Goodness me lad, what happened to your face?" asked Carl as he took in Conrad's appearance.

"It's nothing, a silly misunderstanding with a farmer." He waved it away and reached for Louise's hand. "Uncle, I come to you with some joyful news today. You have met Louise Meier before, have you not?"

"Yes, of course, her father is one of my closest advisors." He bobbed his head as she curtsied.

"I would like to ask for your blessing on our marriage."

"Ah." Carl slapped his chair in delight. "I knew you'd find a good town girl. Absolutely! Frau Meier is a good match. Perhaps you can make some suitable decisions after all. Well done boy, you both have my blessing indeed."

Conrad bowed, Louise curtsied.

"When shall we look forward to this celebration?"

"I am off to see Louise's father next," informed Conrad. "We were hoping now that it is spring to get married straight away. We have seen the joy Clare has brought to you and Aunt Katherine, and we would like to start trying for our own little one as soon as possible."

The mayor stroked his beard and raised an eyebrow. "Yes, of course," he said quietly.

He could tell his uncle had heard that story before.

"We will need to quieten the gossips early if this is to be a hasty wedding. You know how much the town will talk at that sort of news." Carl rapped his fingers on his desk, his expression stern. "Is there a need to have your nuptials this fast?"

There was no point in trying to deceive his uncle, he was not a fool. He glanced down at his feet and cleared his throat. "Yes, Uncle, I'm afraid there is." He could see Louise out of the corner of his eye. She had dropped into a low curtsy and was staring at the floor in shame too.

"Well, off you go then boy, and speak with her father. Make it sound like joy has been brought into your lives and you are just making right of the situation. He is not stupid and will know, as do I, what has really happened here. When you present it with happiness in your voice, I am sure he will be pleased to hear of this exciting news and your willingness to accept responsibility." He flicked his hands at them, ushering them out, the conversation over.

He bowed and Louise curtsied again. They headed toward the door.

"Oh, Conrad," called Carl.

He turned, his voice shaking. "Yes, Uncle?"

"Go wash your face and change your clothes. You don't want an audience with Herr Meier like that." He gestured at his face and clothing, still covered with dirt and blood.

"Yes Uncle." He bowed again, leading Louise back to his room where he hurried to clean himself up. He dressed smartly in a brown jacket and olive-green breeches with brown hose, then placed an olive capotain hat complete with white feather plume on his head. He rolled his shoulders back and puffed his chest out proudly, combing his moustache and beard in place with his fingers, reminding himself of who he was and how bright his future lay ahead. He took Louise by the hand and headed down toward the carriage to escort her back home.

Herr Meier had of course agreed straight away. This union would bring him closer to the Schulz family and secure his position in the council, not that he ever had cause to worry. Conrad had delivered Louise back to her house and asked her father swiftly, then made his exit even faster once Louise and her mother began with their plans. The wedding was to be in two weeks, the dowry would be resolved between Herr Meier and his uncle in exchange for a room or two at the mayor's manor once they were married.

Back at the town hall, Conrad sat at his wide oak desk and prepared to write a letter to his father. His first attempt aimed for jubilation, but he knew his father would see straight through his current predicament, especially since he had left a very similar circumstance behind him in Munich. He re-read what he had written, then screwed it up into a ball and threw it across the room. He ran his hands through his hair, ruffling it, hoping to free up words that would break this news to his father in a way that would not anger him further.

Irritation stewed inside, gathering pace, a boiling pot that would soon overflow. The person who should be made responsible for his situation was out in the country, enjoying her life, planning a marriage with someone she actually loved, someone she had chosen over him. A pig farmer, with mud on his britches and barely a gulden to his name. How infuriating! She should have been his, swooned over him, seen everything he had to offer and been absolutely flattered that he would even consider her. *Farm boots under a formal gown indeed.* The girl had no class, no education, and yet she had refused him. Exactly who did she think she was? To add insult to injury, she had caused this current predicament. Without those herbs, she would not have come into his life. Without those herbs, she would not have been invited to Aunt Katherine's party and made a fool of him, denying him in front of the other councilmen. Without those herbs, Louise would not be with child.

She was such a silly, naïve farm girl. Why, she could not even read! What was it about her that he found so captivating, so intoxicating? Why did he find himself drawn to her, obsessed with her, thinking of her constantly? He was without a doubt the last thing on her mind. As much as he wanted to despise her, she held some sort of power over him. It was like he was possessed.

He sat up straight in a moment of clarity. That was it. A calmness washed over him as he saw her for what she truly was. He just had to make sure others could see it too.

She had cast a spell on him – he was bewitched! That was the only possible explanation for his inane infatuation. She had cursed him, damned him, trapped him in what would be a miserable life. That *witch.*

He had called her that earlier out of anger, but now it was as clear to him as the nose on his face. She was nothing but a common witch, making potions in the country from plants, thinking she could play God with people's lives. How many other's futures had she twisted out of control with her sorcery and herbs? How many other babies had she made that would not have existed, or perhaps others had died at her hands? How many other men were intoxicated by her devil's spells like him? Why, he had even seen her control the clouds that day she was in Rothenburg, how quickly the weather worsened at the market once she had shown her dismay at the treatment of others. He thought about the many dreams he'd had where she had danced for him, plagued him; of the times he woke in a cold sweat only to find she was not in his room or his bed after all.

He wrote a new letter.

Dear Father,

I have fallen victim to a most hideous crime, and for this I need your help and understanding.

A witch from a nearby village has captured my mind and my soul, to the point that she was all I could think about. To torture me, she made potions that have made a town girl of high standing carry my child without my permission.

Please know that I have learnt from my past mistakes and am doing the right thing by this fine woman who now finds herself in a delicate situation. I do however need your help, as Mayor Schulz has also been cursed by this witch and will not see her wrong-doings or pact with the devil for what it really is.

I ask if you can please work with the members of your council in recommending someone knowledgeable in holding a trial, so that this sorceress of evil may be judged and found guilty of her crimes.

I am to be married in two weeks, to protect the innocent woman's virtue and her future. I seek your help to not only free my tortured soul, but also to ensure other men do not fall victim to the same fate. Should you find yourself available, your attendance at my wedding would be most appreciated.

Your son in hope,
Conrad Sauer

He sealed the letter and sent it with the next delivery to Munich. With any luck, his father would come to the wedding, bestow his blessing, and bring with him someone able to hold Ella accountable.

🌸 🌸 🌸

Since the winter had been extraordinarily harsh and cold, despite their prayers and the turning of the season, the frost still hung in the air. Many cattle and animals had died over the winter months, and the blossoms much needed on trees and plants, so late already, had only just started to appear. The country folk knew crops would be scarce that year, so they had to conserve their stocks. A second winter like the last would cause untold devastation and deplete their resources completely.

Ella's orchard had not been unscathed. The trees had not budded well over the spring so it would be a low yield in summer. Tomas had been spending the last couple of months working between his family's farm and

Ella's orchard. The ground was unusually hard, his family were having a difficult time ploughing and even more trouble planting their various grains.

It was not until well into spring that a slow but steady stream of townspeople returned to see Ella. Many of these were the familiar faces of those who had come to see her before, while a few were new, seeking her help for the coughs and colds that still lingered from winter. The idle threats issued by Conrad that second day of spring were fading as the weather started to warm and life settled back into its normal rhythm, albeit far less busy for the first time in years, with a much smaller crop to attend to and the extra pair of hands provided by Tomas. Plans for their wedding were progressing well.

They had no idea of the darker evil that was brewing in the town and far beyond.

Chapter 14

*If Satan can turn God's word upside down and pervert the Scriptures,
what will he do with my words - or the words of others? – Martin Luther*

The wedding to join Conrad and Louise came and went, and still he had
not heard from his father. Louise, of greater height than most women in the
town and with access to a skilled dressmaker, did not show her condition
early, so her move into the town hall chambers was taken well. News of their
delightful surprise, a month after the wedding, was believed by all to be a
fortunate blessing.

It was only when things had settled down for Conrad and he was starting
to accept the imprisonment of his new life, that a letter finally arrived.

Dear Son,

*I was pleased to hear of your most fortunate union and hope you have
found much happiness with your new wife. I am sorry I could not make
it to share in your happy day, but the other news in your letter was very
distressing. The urgency of finding the right people to deal with your
predicament took precedence over my trip.*

*I made some enquiries around town, and we are not able to assist you
with the appropriate men of legal standing or knowledge to help with
your current situation.*

Conrad's heart sank. He would be stuck in this interminable marriage forever without being able to enjoy any sort of retribution over that witch in the countryside. He inhaled deeply, his hands shaking, and read on.

There is, however, a legal team I have heard of in Fulda. Perhaps you could write to the Prince-Bishop of that municipality for assistance; I am led to believe they are most active in controlling the spread of witchcraft throughout Franconia.

I wish you luck in finding justice in this matter, and that your soul be freed from this torment.

Your father,
Heinrich Sauer

Conrad reached immediately for another piece of paper and wrote to the Prince-Bishop of Fulda. This time, he embellished somewhat to make his dilemma sound even worse. He wrote about his suffering, the baby put there by potions and sorcery, the terrible winter that had killed many cattle and townspeople. He wrote about the hard soil, the late spring, and Ella's ability to speak with the clouds. He wrote about the many nights of suffering when she had flown to his room and tortured him in his dreams.

This time, he would get the support he needed.

Conrad had heard back from the Prince-Bishop of Fulda within two weeks of sending his letter. They were keen to act swiftly in bringing witches to trial, they had said, but needed evidence of the sorcery: two witnesses who could attest to the accused's actions, and a handsome upfront payment for their services.

He had gained some respect from his uncle when he married Louise but had not been granted his former position back on council just yet. Not wishing to risk his higher position, or good favour, Conrad worked diligently during the day, but on weekends and in the evenings, he plotted to gather the evidence he would need. While it would drain him of most of his savings, he had the funds required, he just needed another witness. He sought out as many of the townspeople who had seen Ella for treatment as he could, surprised at how many that was, and even more astonished when they all spoke so positively about her healing herbs. The only one that would testify against her was Louise, but he needed another man of position to stand behind him and provide evidence if he were to be taken seriously.

It was late in spring when fortune smiled on him in the most ironic way. Johann, a fellow councilman, came to work one day, his eyes red from crying, his vest unbuttoned. He explained his son had died during the night. A sickly boy, he had struggled throughout the winter, and finally, as spring had arrived and they hoped things would be better, he took a turn for the worse. It was only by chance that he mentioned he had taken the boy to see Ella once, and she had given him a tonic.

"But it did not make him better, did it?" This was the type of evidence he needed. "What other help did you seek?" he asked, sharing his condolences.

"We visited Doctor Voigt, the town physician last week. He said his blood was poisoned and that it needed to be drained of evil if he were to have any chance of surviving." Johann was distraught, he was barely making any sense. "He took great volumes of blood from him, saying that it would kill him faster to leave it there. If you ask me, I think his treatment was too much for Harvey, but I do not want to speak bad of Doctor Voigt, because my son was not well. It was like Ella said, there was not much anyone could do for a boy with his poor health. Now may I go? I need to be with my family at this difficult time."

"Yes, of course, I will record all that you have told me and let Mayor Schulz know. He is a father too, so I am sure he will understand." He reached for a ledger. "Please, take leave, come back in a month when you are feeling more up to work again."

Conrad had procedures to complete, events to document. He also made a note to visit the doctor that evening. He was sure that when the time came, the vote from Johann would be in their favour.

🦶 🦶 🦶

They met in the tavern, as was the case with most meetings between men. It was dimly lit, its walls considered a haven for what was discussed, and often decided, amongst drunken ramblings. The tavern girls wore loose fitting shirts, often buttoned low, to attract the men to linger longer. They were not averse to a bit of fondling or companionship if one could pay.

Voigt found Conrad already sitting at a table and strode over, knocking on its surface as he took his seat. Conrad signalled to the bar maid to bring them both a wine. They made small talk as they waited for their drinks to arrive.

Once served, Voigt wasted no more time in asking, "what have you called me here for, Herr Sauer?"

"Doctor Voigt," his voice was serious, "it has come to my attention that a certain patient of yours has recently passed."

"Which one?" he asked suspiciously. "Surely you are not accusing me of foul play?"

"Oh no, quite the contrary, actually." Conrad's tone softened and he spoke fast to avoid any defensiveness, he needed this man on side. "Do you remember a young boy named Harvey Engel?"

He nodded. "Sickly child that one. He was coming on nine, but very frail, about the size of a six-year-old. His blood was weak, he was not at all well." He took a generous swig of his wine, swirling it around in his mouth before swallowing. "What about him?"

"I have it on good account that before he saw you, he had gone to see that farm girl with the herbs in the country."

Voigt grinned, self-righteously. "That would explain why he was so sick then."

"Do you think she was poisoning him?"

Voigt sat back, one arm folded in front of him, the other stroking his beard. "That is a strong accusation to make. On purpose? No, she did not seem to be that type." He sat forward, leaning his elbows on the table. "But poisoning him with stupidity? That I would believe. She has no proper education, no formal training. She is brewing toxic mixtures she knows very little about. She pretends she is so clever with her tinctures and potions, but really, she knows nothing." He swilled on his wine and nodded. "Poisoning him with her cunning ways? Yes, that I could believe."

"I have heard of these cunning people, you are wise to have spotted it." Conrad nodded, one eyebrow raised. The best way to get a man like this to follow his line of thinking was to win his trust through flattery. "They make so many promises, but they are really just swindlers making people believe they can be cured to con them out of money."

"Those herbs she uses, they are the ways of the past... it is not 'science'. What I do is medicine. We take proper patient histories and use modern approaches. We are taught of their old ways so that we can do better. Fix the harm they cause."

"Would you go so far as to say that she is playing God with her herbs? Choosing who will live and who will die?"

Voigt chuckled heartily. "Well, that is a bit of a stretch. But I would say she is playing indeed - playing with people's health and good fortunes. They should be coming to see me. I have been trained properly, I am qualified to give advice, she is not."

"What if I told you there are people in this town that would like to see her stopped? People in this town that would like to hold her responsible for what she has done? To ensure she is prevented from wreaking additional pain and suffering and risking more lives. Would you support me in this cause?"

Voigt appeared to be considering this for a moment, then nodded. "What exactly do you have in mind?"

He leaned in close, lowering his voice. "Hear me out, for what I have to say is bold, but necessary. I need your support."

"Go on, you have my attention."

"This girl, she is giving people potions to drink. Liquids she has brewed, from plants she has picked. She 'tells' them what she is giving them, she promises it will work. But what if she is not giving them what she says it is, or what if she simply does not know any better, so tells them what they want to hear? Isn't that a crime too? Even worse, let's say for just a moment that she does know what she is giving them, but it is something else altogether. Like Harvey. What if she was giving him something to make him ill, pretending it would help him instead? Or what if she was testing out a

BELINDA CARLI

new potion for the devil, to see what results it would have, and if it would turn him to follow her." He tapped his fingers on the table, trying to reinforce the solemness of his words. "Several people of this town have seen her for her herbs. But what if those extracts were really just a potion that affected their mind? A concoction that would make them want to follow and believe in her? Like she is another deity, or devil. That made them think they were getting better, so they went back to see her, and get more of these potions. You yourself have said she is not qualified to help others with their health. What if she was instead conspiring with the devil, making his potions, poisoning people to believe in her magic and building a league of followers?" He sat back, raising his chin.

Voigt's expression suggested his story was a bit too hard to believe, so he had to find the right words, fast, to make sure he would agree.

He leaned back in. "If she is not qualified to treat people, then how are they 'magically' getting better with her flowers and spices?" He saw a flicker of jealousy pass across Voigt's face; this message was hitting its mark. "Is it not the work of the devil that they seek her out for more magic, instead of coming to see you, a man of science? Is it not making you out to be a fool for all your years of study, that people are finding more faith and healing in her herbal potions than your medical treatments?" He could read Voigt's exasperation. He sat back, appeased, sipping slowly on his wine to let his words sink in and take full effect. He signalled to the tavern girl to come refill their glasses.

It was several minutes before Voigt spoke. "You're right. This farm girl is making a mockery of everything I stand for, and these people have been tricked and lied to long enough." He fiddled with the stem of his glass. "But what are we to do about it? Are we to report it to the council? The mayor?"

Conrad flicked his hand to dismiss those suggestions. "No, Mayor Schulz is too blinded by her magic to see her for what she really is. No, I have a more important advocate in mind. The Prince-Bishop in Fulda has written to me, personally, to seek out acts of witchcraft in our land, and I believe Ella is acting for the devil." He sat back, crossing his legs, one arm slung over the back of the chair, confident he now had the ally he needed. "I am willing to testify to her acts, I just require another witness who is able to give the proof they need. Who better than a man of science? Will you join me, and testify against her crimes of magic?"

"What if Mayor Schulz opposes this?"

"He has no jurisdiction if the Prince-Bishop runs the trial. If anything, we will be honoured at the end of this by the people of the town, if we are the ones brave enough to speak up about her evil before it infects more of them."

"Are you sure this will go in our favour?"

"Did you not say yourself how sick that young boy was? I know for a fact he saw Ella before you. The Prince-Bishop needs people like us to report these incidents, lest the witches of this land poison more minds and bodies, and then what are we to do? You cannot possibly save them all, or save them at all, if she is allowed to keep testing out the devil's potions. How many more lives will you see her take away before you are encouraged to stand up? And then what are you going to say if asked, why did you not act sooner? A man of your education, I cannot see why you have not come to seek me out first, start the accusations for yourself! Your training is all the proof they need, the witch must be condemned. Why, I hear that when the devil is amongst us, all sorts of strange things can occur. This last winter – the snow was twice what it is normally is, and we lost many souls. Food is scarce, illness is everywhere. That is the evil spreading, just as the pastor warns us in church.

"The girl is a temptation in herself. How the devil picks his whores, to seduce us and trick us into believing they are naïve and stupid. Really, she has known what she has been doing this whole time." He smiled slyly, drinking his wine and ordering more again. "I'll see to it this is brought to a rapid close so that we may have fine weather return, and good health for our people."

The tavern girl refilled their glasses and Voigt raised his in a toast. "Down with the witch, prost."

"Prost." Conrad clinked his glass with Voigt's as they toasted their egos and drank to their agreement. He would not rest until he saw Ella burn for refusing him. *Silly little farmgirl. You'll see how foolish you were to not come willingly into my arms.*

The alcohol warmed his blood even though his heart had turned cold.

Chapter 15

Even if I knew that tomorrow the world would go to pieces,
I would still plant my apple tree. – Martin Luther

July, 1605

It was the first Saturday of the month when the bells rang out at the Church of St Peter and St Paul in Detwang, marking the wedding of Tomas and Ella. The village had come together for the celebration, sharing in the festivities and feast as there really was not the means for any one family to host it all. There had not been much mellow weather since winter, and even now, nearly the middle of summer, it was barely warmer than a normal spring day of previous years.

Ella's dress was beautiful, she appeared almost angelic. Julia and Sarah had fussed over her hair for hours that morning, braiding it on either side and twisting it into a low scroll at the base of her neck. Daisies had been delicately woven in on the sides and dotted through her bun. Tomas was dashing in a fine mustard vest over a shirt of pale yellow, with matching breeches and off-white stockings. He was also wearing a fine capotain hat with short brown feathers tucked in on the side.

As the pastor gave the wedding rites and the couple exchanged vows, there were whisperings throughout the church of, "it's about time," and, "they have always been such a lovely couple." Guests wished them well, plates were broken for good luck, and most of the villagers danced and drank with them until late that night. The couple were even given a ride home on

Friedrich's cart, until Tomas had to pull him over, the horse coming to blows over the rather drunk direction of the driver.

Ella could not have been happier, and their wedding gave the town some much needed joy and optimism after the rather dreadful weather they had experienced.

❦ ❦ ❦

It was growing late on the Monday just over a month after their wedding celebrations when the pastor came running up the hill of the orchard. Ella was

standing with Ernest and Tomas inspecting apples at varying stages of growth with some dismay.

"Ella, oh Ella, thank goodness I found you." He glanced up to the heavens in praise, his hands on his hips, catching his breath.

She observed the pastor, panting and red faced. "My good man, whatever could be the problem?"

"Dear child, I have just received word." He waved a paper in his hand. While she could not read the letter, she could understand the concern written on his face. "They are sending a trial party from Fulda, the Prince-Bishop himself is to attend. They are on their way now."

"A trial party… whatever for? Why are you here telling me this? What does it have to do with me?"

He waved the paper in his hand again. "It says I am to detain you, to prevent you from leaving the village."

She sniggered, incredulous. "Good heavens, why would I leave the village?"

"Because…" He appeared to be struggling to get the words out. "They are coming here to arrest you for witchcraft."

Ella turned to Ernest, her brow furrowed. His face drained of colour, his breath caught. He grabbed her by the shoulders. "Run. Go, now."

She shook her head, gazing from the pastor to her opa and back again. A wave of panic rose inside of her at the thought of having to leave and never return. "I cannot go. You are here. Tomas, Julia… you are my family. I cannot leave, it's all I've ever known."

Ernest repeated himself. "Ella, you must go now, pack what you can, and get far away from here."

"I will help you do whatever you ask of me," Tomas said, his eyes imploring Ella to consider her opa's advice.

"No, I will not be run out of my village. Our village." She faced the pastor. "On what grounds do they make these claims?"

"The letter does not go into that sort of detail, I'm afraid. It says only that I am to detain you." His face was one of sorrow, beseeching forgiveness for what was surely yet to come. "I came here to warn you."

"I will not leave!" she shouted. "What can they do? How can they accuse me of this? I have done nothing wrong."

"It does not matter," said Ernest, tears welling in his eyes. "Someone has taken a disliking to something you have said or done, and now you stand accused."

"But Opa, Pastor, you know I am not a witch! How can you demand me leave? How can I be made to defend myself against these charges if I stay?"

"Because," Ernest said, doubling over as if he'd just had the wind knocked out of him, "there is no such thing as an innocent witch."

The pastor nodded in sad agreement. The letter hung limply from his hand.

"But I am not guilty of witchcraft! I am not a witch!"

"Once you stand accused, it is almost impossible to prove otherwise. These men do not come here to host a trial only for you to make them look like fools." Ernest's voice was heavy. "Whatever they have been told, whatever 'evidence' that has been found, there is little reason you can hold that would succeed in contesting it. You will die trying to prove your innocence or be found guilty and die at the stake. The outcome is the same, either way." Ernest wiped at the tears forming in his eyes.

Ella's thoughts swam. "Opa, I will not leave you. I will not leave here. This makes no sense."

"You need to leave, NOW!" Ernest shouted this time, making Ella jump. He rarely raised his voice at her, he could be stern, but never yelled like this.

"Why would you tell me to leave when you know the accusations are not true?"

"Because I have seen it happen before, to other women who were also innocent. It did not matter then, it will not matter now."

"How can you know?" Ella remained indignant. "Perhaps those other women were guilty, whereas I am not."

"Because it happened to your mother!" He cried out, his voice strained.

The words hung in the air, heavy and potent. Ella gasped as her hand flew to her mouth.

Tears welled in his eyes, the burden of the truth written in every line of his face. "They will take you, torture you and trial you. If you make it through all of that without confessing, they will test you, and it is a test you cannot win."

"Opa?" Ella sank to the ground in a heap, her hand at her heart. "Mama was killed as a witch?" She raised her face toward him, her eyes moist, her voice barely a whisper. "You always told me she drowned."

He nodded. "She drowned, yes, she did. But not before she was pushed into the river as her final trial." He sat down opposite her and reached for her hands. Tomas sat down beside her, his hand on her shoulder. "You weren't born in this village. You were born in Rothenburg. Your mother, my aunt, we all lived in the town. My aunt was a seamstress and a healer. She taught me everything I know about the medicinal power of herbs, from when I was young. She never had children, she only had me to pass her knowledge onto. We both taught your mother. They were both seamstresses, too, before your mother realised there was better money to be made from treating people, and then she went too far. She started offering people blessings of hope and gave amulets for good luck. She meant well, but she was behaving recklessly. She found herself with child – you - and would not name the father. He worked in the council, of that I am certain, but she never said who it was. He must have been married, or engaged, and she must have loved him very much to protect him like that at the cost to her own reputation. Whispers started in the town, and they grew like a wildfire out of control. It soon worsened into gossiping and accusations.

"She refused to give you up, and when no man would step forward and take responsibility for her, or you, she was all but ostracised from the town. I think she was always a bit afraid that if she named the father, you would be taken from her. It was shortly after your second birthday when they came for her. They claimed it was witchcraft, that she was a seducer of men, and that the baby, you, were the devil's spawn. They claimed there was no father. She was blamed for all sorts of events, none of which made sense. We had a bad winter that year too – not cold like this one, but lots and lots of rain.

Our lands were flooded, crops were destroyed, many animals and lives were lost. There was famine and illness. They blamed her for all of it.

"They took her away and tortured her, it drove my aunt mad. She had been a widow for years, with no children of her own, so they were always sceptical of her. To be old, childless and unmarried has always been regarded with suspicion, so when she tried to defend your mother, they took her, labelled her a witch, and tortured her too. They did such horrible things to them. They crushed their thumbs in screws and pricked them, all over their bodies. They whipped them, starved them, deprived them of sleep. My aunt confessed quickly and named your mother as a witch.

"Your mother never gave in. She was a stubborn woman; you could not get her to do something she did not want to do. She would not confess, even after all of that. Eventually, they had to test her by throwing her in the water, by giving her a dunking. If she managed to swim or float to the top, she would be accused of having the devil save her. This would have confirmed she was a witch, and she would be pulled from the water and burnt at the stake. When she did not resurface, she was deemed innocent, and given a holy burial."

There was silence as the weight of Ernest's words settled amongst them.

It was Ella who spoke first, her face streaked with tears. "So, they pushed her into the water, and she drowned?"

Ernest nodded. Tears were rolling slowly down his face. He wiped them away before continuing. "It appeared as if she hit her head when they threw her in. She barely struggled. I like to think… to hope, that it was over quickly for her." He raised back up, helping her stand too. "We moved out here almost straight away, I could not look the people of town in the face anymore. They were all there, they all saw what happened. Many of them knew the events leading up to that awful day, but no-one said a word, no-one defended your mother. She helped so many of them, just like you help others now. But they could not speak up, nor could I. My aunt spoke out in her defence, and she was trialled and tortured. If I vouched for her, there was just as much chance they would have taken me as well. I had to stay quiet to protect you, to be here for you, and I have remained silent all these years.

"The ones with the power, they are the true devils. The mayor of the time has long since passed, but the pastor who presided over your mother's final trial still lives and preaches in the town today. That is the real reason he is always so rude to you. You stand as a reminder that he got it wrong and sent an innocent woman to the grave too soon. They are the ones that act like the devil. I'm sorry Pastor." He bowed his head to the religious man before them. "But He is not fit to wear your robes or hold a bible. He became mad with power and control, yet they never had to stand trial or take responsibility for their actions. They somehow twisted the truth of what happened until the lies became believable. Now, it appears they are doing the same again. Everything you know gets upended, so often are you told their lies that you even start to question yourself. Neighbours become distrustful of neighbours, husbands unsure of wives, siblings turn on each other. It spirals out of control, so you don't notice that those promising to bring truth and rid the land of the devil are actually the very source of evil itself.

"This is why you must go Ella. There is no sense trying to reason with these people. There is no logic. Their grounds for a trial, the basis on which they accuse you, has no rationale. Even though we know you are innocent," he reached out to hold her hand, stroking it before continuing, "there is no such thing as an innocent witch. Once you are accused, you are as good as dead either way. So, you must go. Leave now while you still can."

"Pastor?" Ella glanced up at him, yearningly. "Do you know all of this to be true?"

He nodded slowly. "I was not here to see the events mentioned, but I know that is how witch trials are run. Compared to the rest of Franconia, this town and our village have hardly been affected, it is one of the reasons I moved here. Where I came from, it has happened far more. I heard there was a woman pushed from the bridge of this town many years ago. She drowned and was therefore declared innocent. That must have been your mother."

Ernest sighed, his shoulders slumped. "I am sorry I have kept this from you all these years, but I did not want you to know that such evil people could exist. My Leyna..." his breath caught in his throat as he let out a sob, "your mother was a good person, I did not want you to ever think less of her. Her memory did not deserve to be tarnished with the truth of what happened." Ernest removed his hat and scratched his head. "You have grown more skilled and have always been more careful than her, but you now stand to share the same fate. You saw some of the wickedness of the townspeople last year when you went to the city, and that upset you enough. I would bet that snake Conrad is behind at least a part of this madness now. You cannot win against this type of immoral behaviour, or these people, my dear. You must leave, so that you can live."

Ella chewed on her lip for a moment. "Opa, things are different now. I helped save Mayor Schulz's baby last summer, they will not forget that. They will speak for me, they can turn the evil around." She leant over to hug him. "It will be alright, you will see."

"Oh, my dear girl, I hope that you are right." He put his hat back on. "But I fear that you will be wrong."

"Well, I guess we are about to find out," said Tomas as he stepped over and placed a protective arm around Ella. He pointed up the road, to where several horses and a carriage were fast approaching.

Chapter 16

Such sorceresses refuse absolutely to talk and are contemptuous of the
agony of torture – the devil does not allow them to talk.
Such deeds are sufficient witness that they should be severely punished so
that others are deterred from such devilish tricks. – Martin Luther

Ella could feel the agony written on Ernest's face as the guards led her away. They had cuffed her in heavy iron shackles, totally unnecessary as she had not raised any sort of opposition. The guards had read her charges out and she had complied with their orders. She had asked Tomas not to put up a fight, assuring him this would all be sorted quickly, and in her favour, once she had gotten to town and had a chance to speak with the mayor. Perhaps the shackles were merely for impressions, she hoped, to show the village that charges like these would be dealt with seriously, and rules were to be obeyed, even if only temporarily. She was not one to cause a fuss, preferring to sort out any issues calmly rather than cause a confrontation.

When they arrived in town, she did not get to see the mayor, and was instead led straight to the dungeons below the town hall. The steps were so narrow as to cause them to walk single file, with candles on the wall to light their way. It smelt damp and mouldy and there was a constant drip in the background, she could not see from where it came. When she reached the bottom of the staircase, she gasped at the room that lay out before her. It was arced, somewhat like the inside of a barrel, but made of stone. Along one wall ran a rack that was filled with what could only be considered as instruments of torture: pincers, prongs, even a branding iron in the shape of a cross. There was a fire in the corner in a wire cage, presumably to warm the guards, light the space effectively, and heat the tools for use on prisoners. There were leg irons mortared into the floor, above which dangled a neck iron which could be lowered, or pulled taught, using a thick rope and pulley. Off this central area there were two wooden doors with small windows cut in. These must lead to the individual cells. There was a heavily barred window at the end of the room, which let in only a slice of light from the day. There was a chair with arm and leg straps set near the fire cage. Her breath caught in her throat as she was led toward it.

"Stop there," she was ordered. These were the first words spoken to her since she was taken from the farm. Guards came up and undressed her to her undergarments. They tore at her dress, not caring that it was being ripped and her virtue exposed.

"Sit," came the next order. She sat in the hard wooden chair while the guards strapped her arms and legs to it, with no regard for whether it was comfortable or not.

She waited for several minutes, four guards watching her. "I want to speak to Mayor Schulz please," she said, breaking the silence.

The guards continued tying her down, unresponsive to her request.

"Tell him it's a message from Ella Wolff, ah, Ella Baumann." She wanted to be sure her name would be recognised when recanted to the mayor. She thought she saw one of the guards flinch momentarily, but when there was no further movement, despaired that it must have been just the dim light playing tricks on her.

Many more minutes passed and still the guards did not move or speak. Eventually, a well-dressed man entered. He was wearing a mahogany-coloured jacket with elaborate stitching; his sleeves were slit, and his white shirt puffed out underneath. He had an even darker cape on, and a tall capotain hat with a deep red feather. His breeches were black, matching his stockings and boots, and he held a case of sorts in one hand. He removed his hat and put it on a low bench located just inside the dungeon area, then came over to study her, putting his face right up next to hers. She could smell his lunch on his breath: sauerkraut and sausage, and a generous helping of beer. He had piercing, steel grey eyes, they were cold and unfeeling. His hair hung in soft waves, shot with some white, as was his beard and trimmed moustache. After what seemed a short eternity, he stood upright and sauntered back to the bench where he had placed his case and fiddled with its knot, lying flat its contents. He pulled out a metal rod and strode over to Ella, holding it so she could inspect it closely. It had a sharp pointed tip that glinted menacingly in the glow of the fire.

"I am Aleksander Hahn." He twirled the metal rod between his fingers directly in front of her. "Do you know why you are here?"

She detected a slight accent in his voice. He was undeniably well educated and potentially grew up in the north. His words were pronounced in full, every syllable sounded out perfectly. There was no rush to his words, which seemed ironic given the pace at which she was dragged from her home, stripped of her decency, and strapped to the chair. He gave the impression that he had all the time in the world, with no better place to be. She did not speak.

"I said, do you know why you are here?" He yelled and slapped her hard across the face, forcing the chair to wobble. Her skin tingled in pain as her eyes filled with tears. He grabbed her chin and leant in close.

She resisted the urge to spit in his face or scream back, struggling to remain calm. Words were failing her, she was not able to bring herself to repeat what she had been accused of. She noticed he had a harelip scar underneath his short moustache; he must have come from a wealthy background for it to have been stitched so neatly. There had been a young boy in their village that had travelled some distance away for similar surgery, but his parents were mere farmers. When he had returned to Detwang, he was left with an unsightly scar that was barely better than it had been originally. It took months before he could speak properly again, and he carried a severe lisp as a result. This man's surgery appeared to be much more successful, the realignment incredibly precise. She knew his operation would have been quite painful with a long recovery, and he would have been teased as a child before it was corrected, and even after, when the scar was fresh. He had obviously undergone considerable speech training to speak so articulately now. No wonder he relished his chosen profession of torture; he would have lived through something similar when young.

He straightened up, his eyes squinting, as he studied her closely. "You do realise," he said slowly as he strolled, "that I have been brought here to make you talk?" He appeared to be practiced in taking his time to extract the necessary information. "So, speak now, or hold your tongue for as long as you can. I am here with you either way until you tell me what I need to hear." He ran his hand up and down the metal rod he was holding, touching its tip gently to his finger. A drop of blood came easily, showing how sharp it was, and what damage it could do.

He froze still as a statue for some time, as if trying to stare her down. She shifted in her chair uncomfortably, not knowing what to say, or how to start. Finally, she settled on, "Herr Hahn, I think there has been some sort of misunderstanding."

"Oh?" He sounded genuinely intrigued. "Please, enlighten me."

"I have been accused of something I am not guilty of. I am not sure how this has happened, but I am not the person you have been told I am. I would very much like it if I could speak with Mayor Schulz, or if you could speak with him on my behalf. He will be able to vouch for me."

"You are Frau Wolff, no?" He paced slowly in front of her, his eyes focused on the metal rod in his hand.

"Yes, I am Ella Wolff, but I am not... I have not done the things I am accused of."

"And what is it you have been accused of?"

She could not bring herself to say it. "The guards read the charges to me at the farm, Herr Hahn, and to be honest, they were so ridiculous that I have forgotten many of them." She tried to sound at ease but worried she may have sounded a bit too self-righteous for a man like this.

"Uh-huh." Aleksander addressed the guards standing around the room. "Do any of you here have that list of charges?"

"I do, Herr Hahn," came a voice from the far side of the room. The guard marched over to Aleksander and handed him a piece of paper.

He strode rapidly toward the fire, where it was brighter, to study the list for himself. "Tsk, tsk, tsk. You have been blamed for many things." He read silently, shaking his head. "And you say you are not guilty of any of this?" He considered the accusations a moment longer. "Let's see, where shall we begin?" He paced back over to her, the paper still in his hand. "Making a pact with the devil," he announced. "Tell me about this. When did He first come to you?"

"I have not made a pact with the devil," she replied quickly.

"But the other things on that list, they all come from that pact." He strolled past where she was sitting to stare out of the small, barred window. "You have been charged with controlling the weather. Only a witch can do that."

She scoffed, certain of who had been the troublemaker now. She remembered that day on the steps of the town hall where Conrad had mocked her about speaking with the clouds, when all she was doing was reading their patterns, the same as any farm person could have done if they had happened to be there at the time.

"I am sorry, I did not hear what you said?" Aleksander slid in near to her, eerily close and fast.

She could hear him breathe, since she was holding her own. Her pulse was racing. This man did not seem quite right in the head.

He returned hastily to the bench by the door and put down the metal rod he had been holding. "Poisoning the townspeople with a potion that would lead them toward the devil's ways," he again spoke slowly, measured. He nodded his head, pursing his lips. "That I have seen before." He focused on each of the guards. "Did you happen to bring some of those potions back from the farm? It will serve as useful evidence in this trial." They obviously had not, as none of them replied. "Well? Answer me, fools, or has your silence done that for you?" he boomed.

She jumped at how suddenly he raised his voice, and so loudly. She had not met a person who could change demeanour so rapidly. Her breathing quickened.

"You." He marched angrily over to the guard closest to him at that point. "Go now, and fetch some poison from her cottage, before those enslaved to the devil's ways have a chance to destroy it." The guard skittered off quickly at the command.

He stalked back over to Ella. "Did you intend for your poison to kill a child? Or was that just a misunderstanding too?"

Her eyes grew wide. *What could he mean?* "I have not killed a child," she managed.

"Did you treat the child Harvey Engel?"

"Oh." She thought of the pale child, too small for his age, the dark hollows under his eyes. "I saw Harvey, he was not a normal boy. I do not know what was wrong with him, but I know he was not very well. I did not kill Harvey. Has he passed?"

"Of course he has, Ella, but you knew this." He meandered directly in front of her, so that she was forced to look up at his face lest she be staring at his belt buckle. "Did you not realise a child cannot handle much of the devil's poison?" He clasped her chin in his hand, turning her face from left to right as he inspected her closely. "Tell me, where are your marks from Satan?"

She had no idea what he was talking about.

He moved frantically, studying her skin that he could get to, all over her body. Behind her ears, on her neck, on her forearms. He lifted her underdress and inspected her legs. He tore at her sleeves then pulled her forward in the chair, ripping her clothing down the back. Every now and again, he would let out a remark of, 'aha,' and, 'yes, there, I see another.'

Eventually he finished checking her all over and wandered back to stand in front of her, leaning forward so they were eye to eye. "Let me tell you how this is going to go." He slipped back into his slow, measured ways. "You are going to confess to these things, and the other items listed, and I can have this all over nice and fast. You do not need to suffer, I simply need to know when you first signed the pact with the devil, and how many of your followers have signed it also. Tell me who else you have harmed and fix the curse you have put on this land to bring back the warmth and the crops. I will also need to know how many times you have met with the devil and what else you have done in his name." He sauntered around the dungeon, his hands clasped behind his back, glancing over at her occasionally. "In return, I will ask the Prince-Bishop to offer you a swift ascension to the afterlife and a holy burial, such that your soul can be at peace." He shrugged, as if her life meant nothing to him. "Or, you can try to deny your actions, and fail. I will repeat my visits with you until you admit what you have done." He moved swiftly over to her again, his breath warm on her face. "I will not be so nice next time. Apparently, the devil enables his followers to withstand pain that would otherwise make you talk." He rose slowly, his eyes fixed on her, then stalked over to his case, pulling out various metal rods and implements, holding them up for her to observe. "So, you see, the longer you try to withhold the truth from me, the more we know you are in league with the devil." He returned to his unhurried, deliberate ways again, as if he were possessed of split personalities.

It was this change from his slow and measured ways to the fiery, sly agility that unsettled her the most. How could she appeal to a man with two minds like this, or even know which of his moods she was dealing with at any given moment?

He placed the tools back in the case, tied it up and put his hat on his head. "I have grown weary of this today." He swivelled on his heels, preparing to leave. "I will be back tomorrow with some of your potions and see if you have decided to be more forthcoming." He paused to speak with the guard standing at the entrance of the chamber. "See that she goes without food and sleep. I will be back tomorrow afternoon to question her further."

The guard nodded but remained in place until Aleksander left the room, while one of the other guards followed him out. Eventually, the two remaining guards came over to Ella, undid the ties around her arms and legs, and dragged her into one of the empty cells. They dropped her on the floor like a sack of scraps and slammed the heavy wooden door behind them, leaving her in complete darkness.

She cuddled her legs to her chest. She now wore only her undergarments, torn in several places, in what was a very cold and damp room. She spent the first of the interminably long, dark moments trying to feel her way around. There was absolutely no light, and no fresh air, spare the tiny amounts that managed to seep in through the few hairline cracks in the thick cell door. She screwed her nose up as she recognised the smell of stale urine, noticing the moistened hay beneath her, sparsely spread across the uneven stone floor. The wall was roughly built from large stones but secure. No windows, no way out. She settled in a corner, trying to calm her racing mind. She listened for any signs of movement from outside but heard nothing.

She had no idea how much time had passed when the door abruptly opened and in walked a guard with a lantern. He grinned when he saw her, flashing missing and decaying teeth. She huddled up in the cold, dark corner, more terrified than she had ever been in her entire life. He approached her rapidly and kicked her a few times. "Been told to make sure you're awake, I 'ave." He kicked her again for good measure. "Think that will 'elp keep you up for a bit." He left as quickly as he had entered, some of his stench remaining in the still air.

Tears rolled down her face. How could Conrad have done this to her? Her refusal to give herbs to abort Louise's baby must have been the final insult that tipped him over the edge, but still, why would he want to inflict this much fear and pain onto her? She never asked him to be infatuated with her, she never led him on. Of course, he would have seen it all differently. Her gentle nature, her naïve self – he would have considered she was flirting with him. She could see that now, but little good it did for her here. She tried to console herself and keep her mind from slipping to a darkness far worse than the dungeon. She had no idea of time, the long hours interrupted only when a guard would come in to pound on her, or throw cold water on her, or tease her with a flame to wake her up.

Eventually, the door opened again, and in the frame of the cell door she saw the one silhouette she had been dreading. Aleksander was back, and if it were possible, he appeared to be even more menacing than the first time they had met.

Dressed entirely in black save for his stiff white ruff, Aleksander paced in front of her as she was strapped into the chair once again. Deprived of sleep and bitterly cold, her skin drank in the warmth of the dungeon's small fire.

"I should start by telling you that I can be a patient man." He was over at the bench, playing with his tools.

She raised her head groggily toward him, her body ached. Her stomach growled, her throat was parched. Her toes were numb while the rest of her blood was tingling from the heat of the flames.

"But I am not so patient when someone does not want to talk to me." He retrieved a metal rod, sizing up its tip. "Do you have anything you want to say to me, before I begin?"

She sat there, dazed and confused. "I have not done the things I have been accused of," she managed. "There has been some sort of misunderstanding." The words came out in an exhausted mumble.

"Let's see then, shall we, if these marks of the devil bleed with your innocence, or resist the pain with His sorcery." Aleksander stalked over and prodded her arm in random places with the metal rod, pricking her flesh, making her bleed and cry out in agony. "So, she is capable of feeling here," he remarked, but to whom, she was not sure. The guards in the room did not seem to be taking notes of what was going on. He walked back to his tools, exchanging rods. He marched back over while Ella braced for more torture.

This time, he scoured her skin for moles or marks and prodded them very specifically. There was no pain or blood. It was almost like the tool he was now using was blunt. "Ah," he remarked again. "But she does not bleed or have feeling from the marks put there by the devil." He held the tip of the rod in front of her face. It certainly appeared to be sharp, as pointy as the first rod had felt. He held it between their faces, so that only they could see, as he pressed the tip with his finger, and it receded inside the rod easily. He winked at her slyly so she would be sure of his game. Others present would not have understood how she could not be bleeding from it being prodded onto her skin. "See?" he announced to the room and unmoving guards. "You are all witness that she does not bleed from where the devil has placed his marks." His voice was victorious, this proof a testament to his success. He marched back over to the bench and picked up the first rod again then came back before her, pressing it deeply into each thigh.

She screamed. Blood seeped straight through the linen of her undergarment while tears ran down her face. "Please, I did not do anything wrong. Go see Mayor Schulz, he knows me. He knows I have not done any of the things I have been accused of."

"You fool, the mayor has no say in these proceedings," he barked at her. "You need to know this. Besides, why would he threaten his position to defend a lowly witch?" He clicked his fingers and a guard retrieved something from a box that had been carried in and sat by the entrance to the chamber. A bottle was brought over to Aleksander who exchanged it for the rod he was holding. "I have here one of your potions." He held it in front of her face. "I wonder what poison it holds." He removed the cork and smelt it, its pungent herbaceous aroma wafting out. He blocked her nose and started pouring it down her throat, covering her mouth and nose until she reflexively swallowed.

She tasted it and tried not to show her relief. Marshmallow root, it would not harm her. One of the gentler herbs she could have been forced to drink, it was used mainly for digestive disturbances, but was also good for stomach and general pain. A lot of alcohol was used to make the extract, and thank goodness too, it would hopefully knock the edge off her torment.

"So, we have proof of your potions." He remained in front of her face but released the grip on her mouth. "Tell me, when did you sign the pact with the devil?"

"I have not signed a pact with the devil," she replied, the liquid quenching only a small part of her thirst, the alcohol emboldening her words.

Aleksander signalled to the guard, who gave him back the rod and took the bottle. He pricked her rapidly, in four places, along her left forearm. The pain and blood were immediate. "In what form did he appear?"

She screamed and gritted her teeth, the words escaping in a hiss. "I have not seen the devil nor spoken with him."

Four pricks in her right forearm. "How many times has he appeared before you?"

She howled then grunted, "I have not seen the devil ever."

A slow, deep prick on either shoulder. "How many times have you fornicated with the devil, and in what forms?"

Tears streamed down her face beyond her control. "I have not seen the devil nor fornicated with him."

Aleksander switched the rod for the herbal mixture again, pouring it down her throat, she had no choice but to swallow it. She felt a giddy high from the alcohol reaching her empty stomach, but it was not enough to dull the fresh bites of torture being inflicted. The pricking continued, the questions growing more and more insane, the herbs forced on her intermittently.

"Was anyone else involved in your meetings with the devil?

"Did anyone else sign the pact and take part in your dances?

"How many times have you used your poison on others?

"How do you control the weather?

"Why have you destroyed animals and crops?

"Do you desire to return to the arms of God?"

Eventually Aleksander stopped. She was struggling to remain coherent; from exhaustion, from the alcohol in the tincture, from wanting to vomit at the pain. She was bleeding all over, her underdress torn and streaked with blood. He stood back and grinned, as if admiring his work, his demeanour settling into the calm, controlled movements he had held for much of the previous meeting. He meandered back to the bench, replaced his rod, and reached for something else.

What more could he do to me? Ella was barely managing to sit upright. She had lost her strength some time ago but was tied to the chair around her chest to hold her in position. Her hair hung over her face, making it hard to see what he was doing until he appeared in front of her again, squatting low. He had a piece of paper in one hand and a quill in another.

"This can all be over, Ella. Sign the confession." He put the quill in her hand, holding her fingers in a fist. He placed the paper on the arm of the chair beneath her hand, trying to force the two to meet.

She may not have been able to read, but she knew better than to put her mark on something without having it read out to her. She somehow managed to let the quill slip, so that it put a solid line through the words and tore the page. At this Aleksander stood quickly, growling and slapping her hard enough to rock her and the chair backwards. She landed on the stone floor, knocking her head hard while the back of the chair dug into her shoulder blades. She lay there, floating in and out of consciousness, aware he was saying something to the guards but not sure what it was. Next thing she knew, she was being thrown back in her cell, the door slamming out the warmth and light.

As if the room was not black enough before, her world had just gotten a whole lot darker. She barely managed to slip away for mere moments before she was awoken again by beatings, water being thrown on her, or hot wax being dripped on her legs. She lay in the cell, bleeding, bruised, battered and shaking. She had no idea if it was day or night, her hunger now overridden by thirst. Eventually the door opened again, and she shuddered in desperate fear of what was to come next.

"Ella, don't be afraid." The words, so gently spoken, came from a guard. He peered back over his shoulder apprehensively. "My name is Georg, you do not know me, but my wife came to see you a month or so ago. Here, have some water." He passed her a mug.

She was hesitant to take it, she had no reason to trust anyone in here.

"Ella, please take it, I wish you no harm." He held it out to her. She drank it all in a hurry, spluttering as the cold water soothed her raspy throat. "My wife, she was suffering terribly from her nerves and not sleeping, until she came to you. You helped make her better, she sleeps well now, and our house is so much happier for it. I am so grateful for what you did, I do not believe you are a witch." He checked behind him again, listening for movement before speaking. "I cannot help you much down here, but I will look after you where I can. Try and get some rest, it is my watch now, but not for long. Another guard will be coming on shift in a few hours. I am so sorry Ella, I do not agree with how they are treating you, but I have a family to feed, so must do as I am told when someone is around. The other guards… I am the only one here that is on your side. I will bring you some food if I can. Sleep now, I must go." He left the room as suddenly as he had entered.

She sobbed again, although she had barely any tears or energy remaining. Just as she was about to give up on any hope left in the world, this man had shown her kindness still existed; but even he was unable to stand up against the evil of the accusations, and obviously feared retribution should he speak out in her defence. Her heart ached, her opa had been right: once accused, there was nothing she could do to prove her innocence. She let out a groan of despair as she realised her dear mama must have endured similar treatment, but had held out, unrelenting, even to the very end. She must do the same, certain her mama would be looking down on her now.

"Please give me strength, mama," she muttered into the darkness, as she curled into a ball and rest her cheek against the cold stone floor.

She closed her eyes and tried to get what little sleep she could before the inevitable beatings continued.

The next time Aleksander visited she was forced to drink more herbs, this one not such a lucky choice for her: wormwood. Although it was used to aid digestion, it was extremely bitter, and did not sit well on her empty stomach. She vomited it up each time it was forced upon her, and once on Aleksander, which did not bode well for her. Her thumbs were crushed in screws, making her hands throb. She was teased with hot irons burning her flesh. He pricked her skin on another occasion. The pain of fresh injuries kept her conscious briefly before she sank back into delirium. She often passed out during his visits.

The torture and starvation continued for what felt like an eternity. In her more lucid moments, she tried to count how many times Aleksander had come, on separate occasions, to torment her. Was it six or seven?

The only light in this unending tunnel of abuse were the few visits from Georg. He managed to bring her some stew at one point, and water or wine whenever he could. She got to sleep for a few moments when he was on his own watching her but had no idea how often that was.

She prayed early on through her ordeal but realised God must not have been able to hear her prayers from so low down in this hideous dungeon. She prayed to her mama instead, believing she would hear, and encourage her to be brave. She thought of Mayor Schulz and Katherine, walking in their plush chambers above. Did they know what was happening in the dungeons below? Could they have done anything about it, and did they even care? She pictured Conrad. He would no doubt be delighted to know of the agony she was going through. Cruel man. He and that hideous Louise deserved each other.

Her thoughts drifted to her opa, how he'd tried to protect her all these years, how he'd tried to warn her in those final moments. Her soul burned with humility; she should have listened to him when she had the chance. She imagined her smiling, supportive Tomas. Oh, how she longed to be safe in his arms. She must hold out for their sake, knowing they would be worried for her. She basked in the warm memory of their love as she fell into a deep sleep, if that is what it could be called, as it was more like a loss of consciousness at that point.

Chapter 17

God the Almighty has made our rulers mad; they actually think they can do
- and order their subjects to do - whatever they please.
And the subjects make the mistake of believing that they, in turn, are bound
to obey their rulers in everything. – Martin Luther

Carl was very aware that Ella was in the dungeon below, Katherine had been quite vocal on the matter. "You must remove her from that horrific place," she scolded him. "She deserves to be up here, with us. She saved our daughter with her herbs and medicine. It might be different to what the physician uses, but they worked incredibly well. You know she is not a witch. Witches cause harm, take lives, bring about evil acts. She has done nothing of the sort. You saw her here, you shared a meal with her. You must go and do something."

Carl sighed, exasperated. "I am but one who will be presiding over her case. We must first collect her statement and examine that at court. There are fifteen other councillors that will be forming the decision. I am sure they will act justly once the evidence is in."

"What do you call evidence?" She was striding across their parlour. He had not seen his wife so animated, ever. "Surely you cannot take any statement from a prisoner being tortured or starved seriously? What do you expect her to say under such conditions? Would you have them treat me the same way if someone were to accuse me of being a witch?"

"No one has cause to accuse you, dear." He would have liked to calm her, but her movements were too fast, too furious, and the wine he'd had at lunch had softened his thoughts somewhat, made his thinking fuzzy. Best instead to attempt to placate her until she had finished saying her piece.

"No one has cause to accuse her!" She was shouting now. There was scampering in the hall, the servants no doubt listening in. "What has she done wrong? She has slighted your fool of a nephew, that takes no real skill. She has proven the physician old and wanting, perhaps that is simply the truth and about time. Do you really believe for a minute that she has controlled the weather, the winter just gone? She lives on an orchard. Why would she bring hardship on herself? Honestly, the claims against her are ridiculous. I hear better arguments when I pass our kitchen."

Carl groaned. There would be no composing this woman. When a knock came at the door, he was almost relieved. "Come in," he called. "We will finish this later." He motioned for her to sit, then straightened in surprise when he saw who entered the room. "Ulrich?" He had expected his pesky nephew, so this was a welcome change. Having to appease Conrad after the tirades of his wife would have been too much to bear. "What brings you here? Join me with a drink." He motioned to the servant who had led his visitor in. "Sit, make yourself comfortable."

Ulrich sat at the edge of the nearest chair appearing anything but relaxed. He grasped the drink willingly from the servant. "I was wondering if I might have a word, in private."

"Yes, of course." He spoke directly to the servant, "leave us." He glanced over to Katherine, her gaze was frosty, so he addressed her gently. "Please."

The servant exited quickly but Katherine was slower to move, noticeably still annoyed from their previous discussion. She paused to hear Ulrich's first words. "I believe you are holding Ella Baumann downstairs."

Katherine stopped abruptly and re-entered the room. Carl ran his hand down his face as she repositioned herself in her seat. "I will stay for this conversation, if you do not mind. Ella's well-being is my concern too." She folded her hands in her lap. "It is Wolff now, by the way."

"I'm sorry?" Ulrich's brow furrowed.

"Ella. She is no longer Ella Baumann. She married a nice young man from her village, her neighbour. She is now Ella Wolff."

"Oh." Ulrich gulped down his drink and traced the rim of the empty glass. "Good for her."

Katherine's eyes widened at his choice of words. "Well, not presently." Her sarcasm hung in the air like the smell of sour onions.

Ulrich stared silently at his glass for a few moments.

Carl eventually broke their silence. "You came to see me, Ulrich?"

"Yes," he mumbled. "Yes, I did."

"Well out with it, man." His frustration at this ridiculous nothingness of a conversation was growing. First the ramblings of his wife, now the vacantness of this councillor.

"Carl, do you remember when we were much younger, about nineteen? We were a little, well, reckless in our ways."

He nodded. He would have smiled at the memories had the situation not been so awkward.

"All those years ago, there was a young woman, accused of witchcraft. They pushed her off the bridge. A dunking, to decide if she was a witch or not."

Carl nodded. "Yes, I was there with my father, he was a councilman on the jury. That case was most unsettling for him, he never quite forgot it. But I believe their actions were justified; if the council cannot agree, dunking is used to determine if the accused is innocent or not. If I recall correctly, she was found not guilty." His thoughts drifted, his mind trying to touch on a connection, but the fingers of his recollections were just too short to reach. "What was her name again? I cannot recall…"

"Leyna. Her name was Leyna Baumann."

Katherine gasped and fell back into her chair. "Surely not…"

The hairs on Carl's arms raised, goosebumps covered his flesh. "Of course, Leyna. I remember now. She had a daughter out of wedlock. Accused of making that child with the devil because she would not name the father. She used to heal with herbs too, advertised it quite widely amongst the village, charged for blessings as well." He went quiet, rolling the words on his tongue, realisation seeping in. "Ella was the daughter."

"Yes." Ulrich shuffled in his seat. "I am her father."

Carl sobered instantly. "How can you be sure?"

Katherine sat forward, her eyes boggling. "What?"

"Ella is a picture of the way her mother was, but if you look closely, she has my eyes." He chewed his top lip and rubbed at his temple. "I was only young and engaged to another councilman's daughter, my wife now. Leyna was every bit as beautiful as Ella, and even more strong willed. She was fun and carefree, but she had no dowry, no position. I was caught in an engagement with a choice that would please my family. Then Leyna was named a witch and they imprisoned and trialled her. It all happened so fast, it would not have saved her if I came forward." Words were tumbling out of him, tripping themselves up as he spoke. "She died protecting my good name, and I let her." Tears welled in his eyes, he gulped back a sob. "Now Ella faces a similar trial."

"We must do something," announced Katherine as she stared, wide eyed from one man to the other. "Well, are you totally incapable of taking any sort of decisive action?"

Carl sighed heavily. "What would you have me do? I have already told you, I am but one councilman in a seat of sixteen." Carl had drained his glass and was staring at the bottom as if it held the answer. "Even with Ulrich here, we are but two men in a decision that must come from the majority."

"I know." Ulrich's face was one of anguish. "I have been running through all the scenarios in my mind, trying to figure out what we could do. We know Conrad is a witness."

"Yes, but he no longer sits on council."

"Doctor Voigt is a witness, and he is on council." Ulrich shook his head. "He is a driving force behind the accusations. We will never get him to see reason."

"Ah, so you agree there is a lack of reason here?" Katherine spoke with conviction.

The men nodded, Carl voiced the words they knew to be true, "but it is hopeless. There is nothing we can do to clear her name until the matter is brought before the court."

"There is something we can do." Katherine rose determinedly. Carl hoped she would not start her inane pacing again. "We can stop the use of force to extract a confession, and we can get her some food and a blanket."

The men agreed at once and made necessary arrangements that would see Ella fed and kept safe and warm. Her case was in two days, they would make sure she was made more comfortable during that time.

🌷 🌷 🌷

The horse stopped with a short whinny just outside the orchard. It was a week since Ella had been taken from them, and Ernest and Tomas were both beside themselves with worry. It was ironically fortunate it had not been much of an apple season, as the orchard was barely more than a distraction from the loss of their Ella, than the hard and constant work it normally was at that time of year.

Both Tomas and Ernest had tried to visit her several times, taking it in turns to make the trek into town and see the mayor, or knock on the dungeon door. All had been in vain. They could not get an audience with the mayor, nor see Ella. They would give the guards food for her, bread and stew, they even brought her a blanket and some of her perfume. They gave the guards messages and ask that they be passed on. They had no way of knowing how much of their gifts or words, if any at all, had made it to her.

The rider dismounted, dressed in a brown shirt and breeches that was only a shade lighter than his horse. He had an honest and clean-shaven face. Ernest walked toward him with caution; he was prepared to be friendly if not a little wary.

"Ernest Baumann?" the man asked, his hand outstretched in a sign of faith and friendship. He must have known Ernest would be heedful of any visitors at this time.

"Yes," replied Ernest, shaking his hand firmly.

Tomas ran over to join them.

"I have news of Ella." The man turned toward Tomas. "You must be her husband, Tomas Wolff?"

"Yes, does she live?" Tomas spoke fast, desperation spilling out of him.

"Yes, she does." There was hesitation in his voice. "But not well."

Ernest felt his old anger brewing inside, but of course, he knew she would be getting tortured. This should not be of surprise. "Who are you?"

"I am Georg. I am one of the guards that has been placed to watch your granddaughter. Ella helped my wife a month or so ago, we are most grateful that she did."

Ernest drew in a breath sharp and fast. He glanced to his left and then his right, checking to see who could be watching. "Please, come inside and tell us what you know." He ushered the man into the cottage, welcome now, as he would not have come to tell them any news if he were not trying to help.

Once seated, Georg informed them of the line of questioning, of the things Ella had been accused. He told of the torture, much to the angst of Ernest and Tomas. Ernest was older and knew of the violence inflicted on accused witches, he'd seen the results before first-hand, but a lot of this treatment was new to Tomas' ears. Ernest placed a comforting hand on Tomas' shoulder, as his face was almost green, and ran wet with tears.

"I have been giving her water and sleep where I can. Some stew was delivered, I gave that to her too." It seemed as hard for Georg to tell of what was happening as it was for them to hear it.

"That was from us," offered Tomas. "We brought food many times."

Georg nodded. "I cannot say how much of that was given to her when I was not around. I gave her some of my bread when I could, and my wife made her some stew too."

"Do you know how much longer they intend to hold her?" asked Ernest.

"She is due to appear in court two days from now. I have been told she is not to be touched until her appearance at the trial. A blanket and some food were brought to her at the end of my shift this afternoon."

"Do you think she will be mistreated again?" Tomas sat at the edge of his seat.

"It depends on the guard on watch." Georg crossed his legs, shaking his head slowly. "There is one that treats all prisoners as if they were animals. I cannot say what will happen on his watch. The rest are not too bad, so she will get some respite before the trial. At least the torturer has been told to desist."

"That is good news under the circumstances," Ernest agreed solemnly. "Thank you for coming to tell us. We had no idea if she was still alive, so this is better than nothing. I thank you Georg." Ernest rose to his feet quickly. "Now if you don't mind, I have a few things I need to tend to before Ella's trial." He reached out to shake the man's hand and draw him into standing.

Tomas raised his brows at Ernest ushering out their guest so quickly but followed his lead. "Yes, we thank you Georg, please do what you can to make Ella comfortable." He shook his hand heartily, his appreciation unmistakeable.

They bid their visitor farewell at the door. Ernest flopped back in his seat and buried his head in his hands. "I failed her," he wailed. He let his emotions loose. It was not the normal subdued tears of a grown man, but big, heart wrenching sobs that finally dislodged the hurt and anger he had held back all these years. "I failed them all." He cried for the loss of his aunt. He cried for the loss of his daughter. He cried for what had happened, and for the fear of what would happen, to his dear Ella. His tears flowed from pain both old and new.

Tomas crouched beside him and rested his arm gently on his shoulder. The poor boy, this outburst was no doubt unsettling for him. Ernest felt a surge of gratitude for Tomas' support, even as the raw emotion was purged from his body. Last time this happened he was alone. Ernest put a hand over Tomas', only he could understand at least a part of the agony he was feeling.

Ernest wiped away his tears and sat back, summoning words through his receding sobs to explain his sudden outburst. "I have always tormented myself for that day on the bridge."

"Oh Ernest, no one would judge you for not speaking up. You had to stay silent, so they would not take you as well. They already had a confession from your aunt, they would have deemed you guilty of conspiring with the devil too. Who would have been left to raise Ella?"

Ernest's face crumpled, his tears flowed again. "Now they have my Ella." He acknowledged the man next to him. "Our Ella." His lips quivered. "All of my life I tried to keep her from that town, protect her. Keep her safe." He shook his head slowly. "None of it did any good. I left the town, but I did not go far enough to escape the evil of those people."

"To be fair, Ernest, it is not all of them. It is probably just one or two."

Ernest bashed his fist onto the arm of the chair. "It is enough. Do you not understand? It only takes one or two of these people to start this madness and somehow that whips them all into a frenzy. And once it starts…" He raised his face to the ceiling, trying to hold back more tears, pressing his lips firmly together and breathing deeply. "There is only one way this will end."

The men sat in silence for some time. Ernest pondered all the potential scenarios that could play out, then realised, there was one card he could play this time that he did not have before. "Come with me, there is something I want to show you."

Tomas followed Ernest to the packing shed as he led him over to a crate on the back wall. He lifted the lid and removed various pieces of farming equipment. "My tools. I want you to have them. There is a lot of value here." He kept rummaging until he found a carved box at the bottom, then picked it up and presented it to Tomas. Inside a leather pouch sat a knife, Ernest nodded for him to take it out.

Tomas grasped the knife and rotated it, admiring the sculpted handle, and running the tip of his thumb gently along the blade. It was incredibly sharp, his gentle pressure enough to show it could have sliced his flesh easily if he tried. "It's magnificent, the detail."

"I made that when I was much younger. It was a hobby of mine." Ernest ran his fingers over the carvings in the boar tusk. "The blade comes off." He took the knife carefully from Tomas and unscrewed the handle, then tipped it up into his hand. Two little balls rolled out, painted red and black. Ernest held his palm flat for Tomas to see.

Tomas picked one up and inspected it closely, his eyes widening as he must have noticed it was not a ball, but instead a ladybug, fashioned out of clay, painted red with black dots and a tiny black head. "Ladybugs." Tomas sounded surprised and amused.

Ernest raised the other tiny bug to his eyes, examining it closely, smiling for a moment. "Leyna made these for me, they are meant to be a symbol of good luck. She put them in the knife to keep me safe when hunting." Tomas passed the little bug back and Ernest placed them both carefully inside the boar tusk handle, screwing it tightly closed. His face clouded over again. "She made these just before…" He could not bring himself to finish the sentence. He put the knife back in its pouch, then placed it carefully back into the box. "It seems they always protected me, but were not enough to safe-guard her. Now, I give this to you." He handed it to Tomas. "Do whatever you must to look after Ella. I will never forgive myself for not doing enough for Leyna, but it seems I have a second chance to make things right." At that, he walked away, leaving Tomas standing there with the box in his hands and the tools at his feet.

Ernest had made his decision.

Chapter 18

Superstition, idolatry, and hypocrisy have ample wages,
but truth goes a-begging. – Martin Luther

The next time Ella was dragged from her cell it was not into the chamber, but up the stairs and out into the daylight. She had been granted sleep, food, and a blanket for a short period of time, her wounds already forming into scabs. The guards had dressed her in a linen sack of a dress, her undergarments were too bloodied and torn to be considered clothing anymore. They put shackles around her wrists, but there was not much point – she could not have run if she had tried, she was barely able to stand. It burnt her eyes to be back out in the sunlight, her body ached from the abuse she had received, and she was still frail from the lack of food and water. She was so weak the guards needed to half carry-half drag her to the nearby courthouse, where it was time to stand trial.

She was not able to see very well, her hair was in her way and her eyes too sore to focus. Many of the townspeople jeered and threw food scraps, the sound of voices shouting combined to create a continuous low roar. She thought she could hear some call, 'Ella,' and tried to find a familiar face in the crowd without success. Seeing anyone she knew that was on her side would have been incredibly lifting for her at that moment. It was only as she was being dragged up the courthouse steps that she was held at the doors for nobility to pass, unfortunate enough to see Conrad. He screwed his face up, disregarding her immediately. She stunk, having not had a bath or any way of cleaning herself for as many days as she had been held, and she could see dried blood all over her battered hands and nails. A guard held her back as Mayor Schulz and Katherine were allowed to pass in front. The mayor did not look at her; it appeared Katherine tried not to but could not help her natural curiosity. She gave a passing glance, her eyes filled with sadness. Louise was next, pausing to eye her up and down, an evil smirk gracing her face, her belly already rounding out.

Ella was led down the centre aisle, pews either side of her packed with townspeople. There was less jeering inside. She was led to a compact box at the front, to the left of the pulpit at the centre. Forced to stand for herself, she could not help but sway, the shackles heavy on her hands.

Across from her cramped box sat sixteen men on two rows of seats. The back row was higher than the front, so all could rest their eyes on her and watch her actions closely. The mayor nestled in the centre of the front row, glancing over at her for just a moment before averting his eyes uneasily.

She observed a man standing at the pulpit with his chin raised and smug grin; he must be the Prince-Bishop. He was a tall but stout man, he obviously ate and drank well. He had a short brown moustache and beard and was wearing an elaborately embroidered jacket with tall collar that finished well above his ears. His trim hair was tucked beneath a red four cornered cap that sat high on his forehead. It would have been odd to have a Catholic priest preside over a Lutheran town court except that this case ran against witches, and men of self-importance appeared to care more about keeping the lower classes in their place than the religion of the region. She had certainly met enough of them of late to understand how their words seemed to matter more than sensibility. How much she had learnt about the workings of social order from her brief time in town.

The Prince-Bishop pounded a bible on the pulpit and called the court to order. "Ella Wolff, it is on this day, the second day of the month of August in this sixteen-hundred-and-fifth year that you stand accused of making a pact with the devil, controlling the weather, causing severe cold and devastation to crops and cattle, creating potions to trick others to follow your master, and a poison which led to the death of Harvey Engel. I will start by asking, how do you plead?"

Ella at least had the strength to answer. "Not guilty."

"Do we have a confession?" The Prince-Bishop addressed Aleksander, who was perched in front of a small desk to the right of the two rows of councilmen. It sent shivers up her spine to see her tormenter again.

He faced the Prince-Bishop. "No, we do not."

"Was there an interrogation of the accused?"

"There was, your honour, but she refused to cooperate."

"And she withstood your methods?"

"Yes, she did."

"And for how long was she interrogated?"

"The interrogations were held over seven days. We tried to extract a confession using the prescribed methods, your honour, but the devil enabled her to withstand our line of questioning. No innocent person without His evil inside could have resisted."

"Ah, so that would be evidence of the devil at work in itself." The Prince-Bishop nodded his ascent. There were mumbles around the courtroom. "What other evidence do you hold?"

"We have here some of her potions." He reached to a box at his feet and withdrew a bottle, holding it up for the court room to see. A round of, 'oos,' and, 'aahs,' came from the gathered crowd.

"Bring that to me." The Prince-Bishop beckoned Aleksander to show him the bottle close up. Aleksander uncorked it, parading it in front of the councillors before providing it to the Prince-Bishop to see and smell inside.

The Prince-Bishop screwed up his face at the aroma of the herbal mixture. "Take that evil poison away." He waved at it in disgust. "What other evidence do you hold?"

"We have the written records of two witnesses, your Honour." He held up several pages of what must have been the testimony for the Prince-Bishop and councilmen to see.

"Are these witnesses here today?"

"I believe they are, your honour."

"Then I would like to have them testify in my presence," he grumbled. It was almost as if the result was a foregone conclusion for him, and he just wanted the formality of this trial to be over, recorded for posterity, so he could be elsewhere, presumably drinking.

The first of the witnesses to be called was Doctor Voigt. He marched brazenly from the councilmen's area and took to the stand, appearing haughty with his brass rimmed spectacles, plumed capotain and sage green vest. He did not regard Ella for even a moment, but instead, focused on the sea of people that would soon be listening to his words.

Aleksander rose and patted down his vest as he reached for a sheet of paper from which to read his questions. "State your name."

"Simon Voigt."

"And your profession?"

"I am the town physician."

"Do you recognise the accused?" Aleksander pointed to the box where Ella was struggling to stand.

He pivoted his head disdainfully in her direction. "Yes."

"What is her name?"

"Ella Wolff. She was previously known as Ella Baumann." His voice was cold, statements of fact. He may have been saying her name, but he was not talking about her as if she were a living, breathing person whom his words would condemn to death.

"On what grounds do you stand here as witness to her witchcraft today?"

He raised his arm toward Ella, his bony finger extended, but faced the crowd. "She has been giving townspeople her potions under the guise of them being medicines. She has no medical qualifications and is not even able to read or write, nor take a proper medical history or patient record. She has no way of knowing proper prescriptions or how to prepare and dose curative medicines, so has been deceiving the townspeople and taking their money and goods in return for the devil's poison. She has used these potions to make the people addicted to her magic, calling them back to see her, relying on her and the devil for help to cure their ills. She has turned these good people away from proper medical practices recognised by the town council."

"Have you other evidence to report?"

"Yes, as a matter of fact I do." He spoke now to the Prince-Bishop, tilting his chin down so that he was peering over the top of his spectacles, his eyebrows raised. "She had a young boy, Harvey Engel, on one of her potions until recently. I saw the boy just days before he passed. He was not well, there was poison in his blood put there by the accused. I tried to drain him of this wickedness, but it was too late, he was too far gone. The child died because of what she gave him." Murmurs rose from the crowd.

"Thank you, Doctor Voigt, you may step down."

The Prince-Bishop nodded, taking notes, then gazed up before speaking gruffly. His tolerance of this trial sounded like it was drawing short. "Please call your other witness."

"Conrad Sauer, please come to the stand."

Conrad strutted down the aisle dressed more like a peacock than ever before. He was wearing another of his ridiculous outfits, this one a bright royal blue velvet with equally absurd blue plume sticking out from his capotain. He ascended the stand, a self-satisfied smirk on his face.

"State your name."

"Conrad Sauer."

"And your profession?"

"Until recently I was on the town council, in charge of planning and appointments." His eyes narrowed, his face became bitter. "That was until the witch over there spread lies and deceit, which caused me to be demoted."

"So, you recognise the accused?" Aleksander again pointed to Ella, who was growing wearier by the minute. She was leaning on the back of the box where she was held, no one bothering to make her stand.

"Yes."

"What is her name?"

"Ella Wolff."

"On what grounds do you testify against the accused today?"

"I have seen many acts of her witchcraft." He smirked. "I first became aware of her potions about a year ago. She was peddling them to the villagers and townspeople under the guise of healing them, but she was instead making them addicted to the poison for gulden. Her plan was to lead them to make pacts with the devil, as she had done. She cast a spell on me too. I did not have her potions, but she tried to seduce me." The audience started mumbling, their volume rising as he spoke. "She tricked me into bringing her to town, hoping to lure the mayor and his wife into pacts with the devil."

"Was she successful in this venture?" asked Aleksander, his voice taking on genuine intrigue.

"No, I thwarted her attempt. But while she was in town on that mission of the devil, I saw her conjure up the wind and rain with my own eyes." The courtroom came alive with chatter, the Prince-Bishop appeared transfixed by his performance. Could they not see Conrad was trying to cast a spell of his own?

"Do you have other evidence to submit to the court?"

"After I saw her ability to control the weather, I was wary. I made her leave town, promising to take her to trial if she ever came near me or my uncle again. Shortly after this, however, she flew to me on many a night, making me believe it was at first a dream. She threatened to freeze the town and village, kill the livestock and the young, and make our ground hard and unable to grow much in spring if I would not permit her access to my chambers."

The noise from the audience grew out of control. The Prince-Bishop bashed his bible on the pulpit, calling for order.

"Continue." He motioned to Conrad.

"I refused. We all know how cold the winter was after that." He sniffed and wiped his nose as if he was sorry that his actions may have contributed to the recent winter. It appeared as if he genuinely believed in his own ludicrous testimony.

"You may step down."

Conrad sneered at Ella as he passed, all but prancing back down the aisle to sit next to Louise.

The room was silent while the Prince-Bishop consulted his notes. "This is a lot of evidence you have collected."

Aleksander nodded. "It is an easy case, your honour."

The Prince-Bishop addressed the court. "Is there anyone else here who can testify for or against the accused?"

The townspeople muttered amongst themselves softly while the councilmen across from her discussed the testimonies that had been presented. She was unable to make out their words clearly and gazed out at the sea of faces. She saw a few familiar ones from the town, but knew if they vouched for her, they would suffer her fate. She could not blame them for holding their tongues.

The Prince-Bishop watched and waited as the councilmen were in hotly debated disagreement. Moments passed before he called for a verdict. "How does the council find her?"

Carl rose to his feet and tugged at his vest while he cleared his throat. "We have eight votes of guilty, and eight votes of not guilty," he reported.

"Very well then." The Prince-Bishop's voice was gravelly. "Ella Wolff, you have been tried before the council and the town. A hung vote has been recorded, so we must determine if you are guilty by dunking…"

"It was me." A cry came up from the back of the courtroom, cutting the Prince-Bishop off mid-sentence.

The Prince-Bishop raised his head high, trying to see where the voice had come from. "Show yourself and repeat that," he called.

"It was me. I did all of it." The gathering of people parted like a flock of startled birds, and there stood Ernest.

Ella let out a small but terrified moan.

"I say Herr, stop yelling at me from the back of the courtroom and come to the witness stand if you have something to add to this case." The Prince-Bishop beckoned him forward. The courtroom buzzed like a beehive disturbed, the Prince-Bishop trying hard to regain order. Ernest shuffled toward the front of the courtroom while guards moved to bar the exit.

Ella called on the last of her strength to make herself stand as she watched her beloved opa make his way forward. He appeared older and frailer than she remembered, it felt like months since she had been taken from him. Had he not eaten and slept since she had gone?

"Herr Hahn, please interrogate the witness," the Prince-Bishop commanded.

Aleksander shuffled some papers at his desk but regained his composure quickly. It was the first time Ella had seen him unsure of himself.

"State your name."

"Ernest Baumann."

"And your profession?"

"I am a farmer. I work the apple orchard in Detwang."

"For which counts of the accusations are you providing your admission of guilt?"

"All of them," he responded rapidly.

"Name them, then," said Aleksander slyly, his eyes squinted as he rocked on the balls of his feet.

"I first made a pact with the devil many years ago." Rumblings rippled through the crowd.

The Prince-Bishop nearly broke his bible as he bashed it on the pulpit. "Silence in the courtroom!" he bellowed to the crowd. "If I have one more outburst you will all be evicted while we finish this trial!" A hush settled over the spectators hastily; it seemed no one wanted to miss the rantings of a self-pronounced witch.

"Ella is not able to confess because she had no part in any of it." She watched, shocked, as her opa spoke so confidently, commanding the attention of the crowd and nobles gathered. "I put a spell on her to resist your interrogations. The potions she made were simply boiled cups of tea. I made her believe she was preparing medicine for the villagers, but I was really infusing all of the mixtures, after she had made them, with the devils' own concoction that He brought for me to dispense. I put it in the bottles without Ella knowing, promising her it would make the villagers and townspeople well and healthy.

"It was I that poisoned the potion given to Harvey Engel. It was I that conjured up the bad weather Herr Sauer spoke of. I was not happy that it was taking so long to have my followers grow in numbers, so I froze the town and village over winter to cause a famine and illness, so that you would all need the devil's potion. Then you would turn to me sooner, and I could call on the devil to fool you all."

Aleksander and the Prince-Bishop were mute, their eyes and mouths open wide. Ella watched on from the witness box, tears streaming down her face.

"What about Ella flying to me in my dream?" called Conrad from the audience, standing defiantly, his face drained of colour, as if he was about to lose all in a high stakes game of cards.

The Prince-Bishop moved his gaze from Conrad to Ernest. "Well, what do you have to say to that?"

"I asked the devil to change my form, so that I could fly to Conrad at night, and he would welcome me in." The performance was flawless, he did not miss a beat. "I had changed form before, taking on Ella's shape to seduce him on at least two other occasions. It was I that appeared in that dream, in female form, to tempt him to join in my pact."

The courtroom was silent. The Prince-Bishop's brow furrowed, his lips drew tight as he considered all that had been said.

"Is there anyone who can verify these claims to witchcraft?" The Prince-Bishop called out to the room of people gathered before him. "I need two witnesses, if I am to believe this testimony."

Seconds ticked by but no one spoke. The Prince-Bishop slapped his bible in judgement. "In light of this new testimony, I find both the accused, Ella Wolff, and Ernest Baumann guilty of witchcraft. They shall both be burnt..."

"I will testify to the truth of his statements, and the innocence of the accused." Ulrich rose from his position in the councilmen's pews. "He came to me in a dream, in his male form, and told me all of this would happen. He told me he would name me as being a part of the pact if I did not take the potion."

"I will testify." It was Johann this time, sitting at the front, another of the councilmen standing in judgement of the trial. "I am Harvey's father, the boy who passed. He came to me in a dream also, he threatened to take Harvey sooner if I spoke up against him."

Aleksander and the Prince-Bishop stared at the men, standing within the councilman's pews, who had just claimed witness to the testimony. A man stood in the court, his belly round, his shirt speckled with flour. "He came to me in a dream too," declared Hans. Magda rose beside him, nodding her head and claiming the same. Suddenly, over a dozen men and women in the audience got to their feet, claiming Ernest had come to them in various forms in their dreams too.

Ella watched as Katherine rose next, her mouth open, ready to speak.

The mayor's face paled when he saw his wife stand. He jumped to his feet. "He appeared to me too," he declared boldly. "I saw him change form between the old man that stands before you and that waif of a girl, then back again. It was most definitely not the girl. He has been using her as a decoy all this time. It was him." He raised his arm to identify Ernest at the stand. "He has been fooling us all along. For shame, using your own granddaughter to conceal your pact with the devil." He addressed his fellow councilmen.

"Who will stand beside me in declaring this man guilty, and set the accused woman free?"

Ulrich, Johann and Carl were already on their feet. Another five of the councilmen stood straight away. Slowly, most of the men rose, all but Voigt, and Hugo, Louise's father, who sat there solemnly, their faces to the ground.

The mayor gazed around at his council, where thirteen other men were standing beside him, an almost unanimous decision amongst them. "You have your verdict, Prince-Bishop. The old man is guilty, the young girl goes free. Guards, release her at once and take that man into custody."

There was no way for the Prince-Bishop to control the court now. For the briefest moment Ernest reached over to Ella, pulling her head to his shoulder and whispering in her ear, "please leave, and live, while you can." She was rooted to the spot, bewildered and unable to speak. He mouthed the words, 'I love you,' before he was tackled to the ground in an unnecessary display of power by two surly looking guards.

In the commotion, Tomas managed to pull Ella away from the stand, lifting and carrying her from the box. She wrapped her arms around his neck, letting the last of her strength leave as she put all her trust in the man she loved. She could see Ulrich and Hans hold the crowd back, making their escape from the courtroom hasty.

Friedrich was just outside the town gates waiting with his horse and cart. He had brought a load of villagers to town earlier to watch the trial and offer their support. Tomas came trotting over with Ella in his arms.

"Please help me, there is chaos in town. I'll explain once we are on our way."

Tomas could see Friedrich gaze around warily, it was still quiet here at least. He helped Tomas load Ella on to the back of the cart then leaped quickly into the front seat, flicking the reins to drive the horse into action. "Let the villagers walk back, it is not far," he called over his shoulder to Tomas as they sped toward Detwang.

Tomas stroked Ella's hair, cradling her head in his lap. She was shivering and still wearing the shackles, but he had farm tools that could easily remove those. He just wanted to get home, feed her, give her water, and tend to her wounds.

He kissed her face tenderly and whispered in her ear, "we will leave this place and find somewhere new to live. I will take you away just as soon as you are well enough to travel."

She clutched his hand feebly and closed her eyes, sleep descending on her fast.

Chapter 19

There is no gown or garment that worse becomes a woman
than when she will be wise. – Martin Luther

After they cleaned her up and set splints on her thumbs, Ella slept
solidly, waking only for stew and water. Tomas watched over her tirelessly,
while Julia busied herself with fixing food for their trip, packing clothing
and their essentials.

On the second day, Tomas rubbed her shoulder gently to wake her.
"Ella, my beautiful girl, you have a visitor." He stepped back, so she could
see who was there.

She opened her eyes slowly, the world appeared fuzzy at first. She
blinked a few times.

The man in the doorway had ringlets of black hair, his moustache long
enough to flick up a little at the edges. He had a wide, stiff ruff around his
neck, his suit and breeches were slate grey. He smiled awkwardly.

"Ulrich?"

"May I come in?" The question was redundant; he was already moving
forward. He sat in a chair positioned next to the bed.

She sat up, pulling the sheets around her.

"I suppose you are wondering what I'm doing here." He brushed at the
fabric of his breeches nervously, glancing up and down intermittently. "Ella,
there is no easy way for me to say this." His gaze locked on hers, and
suddenly she knew. It was her eyes she saw staring back at her.

"Papa?" Her breath caught in her throat as tears ran down her cheeks.

He nodded, his jaw quivered.

She reached out to him, and he responded quickly. Their embrace felt completely natural, as if a lifetime had not passed between them. Eventually he sat back down.

"Ella, I want you to know, I loved your mama very much. Life does not often proceed how one might plan it."

She put her finger to her lips. She did not need him to explain the why of the past, she somehow accepted that, but she needed to ask, "why now?"

"I could not let the same injustice happen twice."

She bobbed her head slowly.

He wiggled forward in his chair and reached for her hand. "Ella, my dear, as much as I have just come back into your life, I must warn you of what lies ahead if you should stay, and beg you to leave."

Her face snapped toward his, her mouth open.

"Please hear me out," he said quickly. "Conrad is not going to let this rest. He is in a most unhappy marriage and your opa made a fool of him. Doctor Voigt is humiliated, and the town pastor is a bitter old man. I have already heard them scheming, they will not let this rest. While you walk free, you are making a mockery of the court's decision and their efforts, not to mention the expense, in calling the Prince-Bishop to hold a trial. They will try to make another case, and you will be put through this torment again. I know it sounds ludicrous, and it is, but they will come at you again and again until they have their way. Next time it could be a more vindictive Prince-Bishop, or executioner with even more cruel ways." He strode hastily back toward the door and retrieved a heavy bag. He put it on the bed near her feet, it clinked loudly as it dropped. "There is over five hundred gulden in here. Take it. Make your life good elsewhere."

Ella pivoted her head from him to the bag and back again. She opened her mouth to speak then thought better of it. He was right. She did not leave fast enough when she was warned last time, she was not going to take the risk of staying now.

Tomas bent forward and peeked in the bag. His eyes widened.

"I must go, Ella, I am married and to be here would create a scandal that is not fair to anyone. Please know there is not a day that has gone by where I did not wonder about you. You are beautiful and kind like your mama; she would be proud, your opa raised you well. I know money is no replacement, but I want you to have it, and start afresh, somewhere new." He leant forward to hold her again warmly for a moment, his eyes moist. He stepped back then tipped his head to her and Tomas before leaving.

Tears ran down her face as Tomas rushed to sit at her side, hugging her tightly.

Ella stayed locked in his arms for several minutes, weeping, then slowly steadied her breathing. She sat back, reaching for his hands. "Tomas, do you know why opa confessed?"

"While you were in prison, there was a guard that came to see us," he explained, holding her bandaged hands tenderly in his. "He said his name was Georg, he told us what was happening in the dungeons, what they were doing to you, and the questions they kept asking. He told us how you helped his wife, how he was trying to help you. He said he gave you the stew we brought."

"Yes, I remember there being some stew, but he had to be careful, there was not much he could do. So that's how opa knew what to say to get the Prince-Bishop to listen." She brought her hand to her mouth, then turned to face Tomas, her eyes wide. "Did you get the townspeople to speak up as well?"

"No." He paused to stroke her cheek. "They did that without being asked. You helped a lot of people, beautiful girl, and there were many disgusted by what we knew was happening to you, but we were all so scared. If any one person, on their own, attempted to speak on your behalf, they risked being accused too. I guess once the first few testified, the others knew they could not possibly trial them all."

She let out a quiet whimper as the tears ran down her face.

"I know this must be a lot to deal with right now." Tomas could see her battling with her grief; he rubbed her gently on the arm. "I guess it just got too much for Ernest. He knows he is old, he has already lived more years than most. I do not think he ever got over the pain of losing his daughter, he barely slept while you were gone. I did not know he was going to do what he did at the trial. No one did. The townspeople, Mayor Schulz... I guess they could see what he was doing too. We owe it to them to leave in case this craziness starts up again. You heard your papa, that scoundrel Conrad will not be happy to let this rest."

She nodded in agreement. "What of the orchard?"

"It is well established. The mayor will find other tenants easily. He, and his wife especially, will understand our sudden departure."

She bobbed her head, realisation settling in. She gazed up at him again, her eyes wet with tears, her brow furrowed. "Where will we go?"

Tomas shrugged. "We are good workers. We will go as far as we need to find a village where there is no talk of witchcraft – and no town nearby with the threat of accusations either. I just need you well enough to travel." He rubbed the skin of her forearms gently, she still had so many scabs covering her flesh. "We cannot have you treating others when we get settled."

She sobbed. "It is all I've ever known. Are they to take that away from me too?"

"Yes, my beautiful girl, we cannot risk this happening somewhere else."

She felt the scabs on her face with her fingertips, how could he possibly call her beautiful at this moment? "Are we to leave Julia? Your family? They are my family too."

"We must, for now." He smoothed her hair, tucking the loose strands behind her ears. "We will start a new family, and in time, we will find a way to get word to my family — our family — and they will come visit us, wherever we end up."

"Tomas..." She cried anew. "Do you know what is to happen to opa?"

He dropped his head forward, the words barely a whisper. "He is to be burnt at the stake, three days from now."

She wept loudly for several minutes before calming. She cried for the loss of her opa and papa, for the change to how she must live her life, and how she would need to always hide her special skills. She shed tears at the thought of losing her connection with Julia, the only mother she had ever known. She gazed up at him, her eyes stinging. "Tomas, there is something we must do for Opa."

He cradled her chin and hummed, trying to soothe her. "There is nothing we can do. He is held in the dungeons where you were. We cannot get him out, and there is no way I will let you near that town, they would take you."

"There is something we can do." She sounded stronger, encouraged by an idea that was forming in her mind. "But first I must get better as we will need to leave fast. Did the guards leave any herbs in the packing shed?"

"Yes, most of them are still there. They only took a couple of crates for evidence."

"Good. I need you to get me some cornflower extract, it will help me heal faster. You can find it, it is under the bench in one of the bottles, it will have a tag attached with a picture of the flower drawn on it. You know what cornflowers look like."

Tomas nodded and left to fetch her herbs.

By the next day, she had the strength to walk again. It was slow and painful at first, but it was a sign she was ready to travel. She went to the jar under the cupboard in the kitchen, retrieving their savings and showing Tomas how much was there. It totalled just over one thousand gulden. Most of it had been profits from the farm, the rest being payment for her treatments. They now also had the money from Ulrich which would help them greatly.

Tomas counted it up, relief washing over his face at the sum. "This will be enough to help us start our new life."

"Please take what you need to Friedrich, see if he will sell you his cart and horse. We will need it for our journey."

Tomas knew how much they needed the transport, grateful they had something to offer. Friedrich would probably have given them the cart and horse, but payment was much more appropriate.

It would only be another day before she was well enough to travel, but there was one final thing she wanted to do first. She gave Tomas strict instructions and two linen bags, one inside the other. She told him where to find her opa's pruning gloves; he would need them. He set off early the next morning, while Ella and Julia prepared to do some baking.

It was just after lunch when Ella and Tomas left Detwang. The pastor gave them a blessing, while others brought them gifts for their trip. The farewells were sad, but all wished them well on their way, encouraging them to make good their escape. They headed north with plenty of food, preserves, Ernest's tools and that special knife.

Just after they left, Julia set off toward Rothenburg. She shuddered as she crossed the town square where a tall pyre of wood was being assembled for Ernest's burning, nearly finished. She arrived at the entrance to the dungeons in the early afternoon and knocked loudly on the door.

Eventually it opened, a surly looking guard peered out, eyeing her up and down.

"I have something for the prisoner." She opened her basket and retrieved a large slab of cake, handing it over.

He grinned. He was missing a few teeth and in desperate need of a wash. Little beads of spittle formed at the corners of his mouth. "I'll take that for you love. What 'ave we here?" He inspected the delicacy, smelling it and biting into a corner. "Is it blueberry?" He split it in half and examined it closely. "'Ave to check what else you 'ave in 'ere, Frau."

She fiddled with the handle of the basket as she waited. "What do you think I would have in there? It is just a cake."

The guard smirked and took another bite. "Mmm." Crumbs sat at the corners of his mouth as he chewed, savouring its sweet flavour. "Alright then. Off ya go. I'll make sure 'e gets it." The guard stepped away from the door and closed it firmly in her face.

He walked down the stairs and entered the main area of the dungeon room, taking another bite as he went. He held the other half out to the guard standing at the door to the cells. "Want some cake?"

"Where did you get that from?" asked Georg, taking the slab he'd been offered.

"Some woman brought it for the prisoner." He bit into it again, speaking as he chewed. "It's real tasty. Blueberry, I reckon."

Georg patted his belly. "I think I'll let the prisoner have this, I just ate."

There was so much fruit baked into the cake it had taken on a purple tinge, the berries easy to see as chunks.

The other guard glanced over at him, groggily. "Suit yourself." He took another bite and sat down, leaning heavily on the wall.

Georg entered the cell and crossed the short distance to Ernest. The old man had not needed to go through the routine of interrogation and torture, having confessed publicly already, but he'd had barely anything to eat and drink since being imprisoned. "Ernest, someone just brought you some cake."

Ernest reached out to grab it, biting into it eagerly. He was hungry and started devouring it keenly. By the third mouthful, an old memory of flavour dawned on him, and he realised this cake was not made with blueberries. *Oh Ella, my clever little Ella, thank you.* He eyed the cake closely with the narrow slice of light that made its way in from outside his cell. Nightshade berries, the cake was full of them, the flavour strong. He bit into it generously, it was sweet and juicy, and very, very deadly.

"Enjoy it old man." Georg left the cell, locking the wooden door behind him. He strode back into the main chamber where the other guard supposed to be taking over his shift was already resting dormant against the wall. Georg stepped over and kicked him. "Get up, you lazy scheisse, you are not getting paid to sleep." The guard did not move, did not even rouse. Georg shook his head, calling out as he left the room, "I am going home, you better wake up before the next shift starts."

Ernest finished the cake, every last crumb, and laid down to enjoy a peaceful, final sleep.

He would not be burning at the stake after all.

Authors note

Concerning the female sorcerer... women are more susceptible to those superstitions of Satan; take Eve, for example. They are commonly called "wise women." Let them be killed. – Martin Luther

The inspiration for this book came from the beautiful town of Rothenburg ob der Tauber in Germany, which sits at the centre of witch trials from the surrounding region. Rothenburg today appears almost as if it were caught in a time capsule – its buildings and streets, even that incredible wall and the castle gardens, are much the same now as they were in the 1600s. The town has a most fascinating medieval crime museum, and there are several houses and even the dungeons you can tour, all showing with remarkable detail how it must have been to live in those early days.

The Franconian region, like much of Germany and indeed Europe, was gripped by a terrible history of witch trials which peaked throughout the sixteenth to eighteenth centuries. Rothenburg itself ran very few witch trials, even less led to a conviction, due largely to the sensible approach of the councilmen in that area.

The work in this book is entirely fictional, but there are many elements based on events from that time. For example, the public displays of humiliation were all too common, and far worse than I describe in this book. There actually was a woman who was interrogated based on the dream of her young child, and it was common for women in families to be accused and questioned, as it was believed that older women taught their younger daughters or relatives elements of witchcraft to pass on the trade. The images of torture that Ella endured were based on, and similar to, reports in texts given, although there were many accounts I read when researching this book that described far more severe treatments in other towns. Thumbscrews, starvation and sleep deprivation were common, as was pricking, where the executioner would use a sharp tool to prick and cause bleeding from normal skin, and a blunt tool on moles, (considered marks of the devil), so there would be no pain or injury at those sites. The questions used in Ella's interrogation were based on actual records, albeit the true accounts went on for pages, the list of questions reaching well over fifty and far more ridiculous than I have used here.

I provided quotes from Martin Luther, the founder of Lutheranism and devout witch hunter, at the start of many chapters to give a sense of what they believed from the time. I also used quotes from the bible, as religion featured heavily in the lives of all in this period, in stark contrast to how some people actually treated each other.

The truth of witch trials and the witch craze is far more alarming than I have presented in this book. I was paradoxically horrified but intrigued by how educated people who were usually very religious could possibly envision women, in particular, capable of flying, dancing and cavorting with a devil as real enough events to trial, torture and kill them in such inhumane ways. The museum in Rothenburg answered some of those questions, but I continued reading on their histories, to try to understand how human beings could possibly behave this way to each other. The central elements that led to accusations of witchcraft varied greatly: some resulted from differences in religious preferences, others came from a desire to control women from speaking or acting too freely, while other cases started from rivalry between neighbours, and some arose from people we would call manipulators today, regardless of class, just acting out of spite. Idle gossip about neighbours or disgruntled husbands making claims about their wives could spiral out of control, and the men in positions of power and/or religious guidance acted principally out of fear of the unknown, or to grow their social influence, by finding the accused guilty. I remain baffled by their use of dunking to determine a verdict; how anyone could think innocence by death was a good outcome is still beyond me.

I created Ella as a healer and herbalist because there were people trialled and convicted of witchcraft for far less important reasons than trying to heal others honestly. The truth is, in the insanity that ruled in the region in that time, even if Ernest had spoken up at Ella's final trial, along with the others in the crowd, they would have all likely been sentenced and a mass burning would have occurred, or ongoing trials commenced for those who stood in her favour.

I hope you have found this an entertaining read, as the truth of this time was far darker and more unsettling. I wanted to question how humanity could have so readily killed each other for insane reasons in an era like this, where war, weather, famine and disease already wreaked enough devastation. How we managed to survive as a race, through all this loss, is a wonder.

If you enjoyed this book and ever get the chance to visit the captivating town of Rothenburg ob der Tauber I highly recommend it, and I hope you see a little of the life I have created here within those amazing walls.

Acknowledgements

I would like to thank my husband for his unwavering support and encouragement as I wrote this book. He was also the one that took me to the incredible town of Rothenburg ob der Tauber, which inspired the story in the first place. Thank you for listening to my countless plot twists and character traits as we walked the dog each morning, and put up with my angst as I reworked the many versions of the novel until it became what it is today.

Thank you to my wonderful editor, Carlie Slattery, for your words of wisdom, insight and help. I could not have prepared a novel ready for publishing without you, and relish your ongoing words of inspiration and sage advice in polishing my future novels.

Thank you to my dear friend Hanna, for your spectacular cover art, and helping me with the formatting and publication.

Thank you to my audience and readers, for a book is nothing without someone to enjoy its words. I look forward to bringing you many more stories, and hope you are as keen to read them as I am to create.

Please follow me @belindcarli.author and share your thoughts, and this title, with others.

www.ingramcontent.com/pod-product-compliance
Lightning Source LLC
Chambersburg PA
CBHW022028240626
47154CB00007B/2308